- A NOVEL -

SEEN & UNSEEN

JJ RENEK

Also by JJ RENEK
PAYOFF

NOTE: this novel is free of AI generated or revised content.
No portion was written, edited, or enhanced through the use of AI.

- JJ Ranek

Cover Design – Jaycee DeLorenzo
Publishing Coordinator – Sharon Kizziah-Holmes

Published by

LAKEPOINT PRESS LLC

Paperback ISBN -13: 979-8-9905504-3-8
Hardback ISBN 13: 979-8-9905504-4-5
eBook ISBN 13: 979-8-9905504-5-2

"The practice of medicine is an art, not a trade; a calling, not a business; a calling in which your heart will be exercised equally with your head."

- Sir William Osler, MDCM

"The patient is still at the center, but more as an icon for another entity clothed in binary garments: the 'iPatient'."

- Abraham Verghese, MD, MACP
N Engl J Med 2008;359:2749

CHAPTER | 1

May 2022

Kansas City

Ill persons bear a certain look, and this man undoubtedly fit that image. In fact, sitting in the gray vinyl chair staring at the windowless wall, he appeared quite exhausted. Worn. Even sallow. Dark circles framed his eyes. He blended well into his surroundings, the fluorescent lights doing him no favors.

Dr. Hope Nichols gathered those initial observations just seconds after entering the exam room. She threw him a quick smile which he did not reciprocate, introduced herself, and in three steps found the rolling stool waiting near the taupe built-in desk.

No sooner had she taken her seat and turned to the gentleman, than an uncomfortable sensation shouldered in, threatening to distract her. At once, the four walls felt closer, confining, constricting their interaction. Both she and the patient seemed larger than life. If only they could fling open the door and push back the walls, perhaps somehow that would insure the man's better outcome.

"Hello, Mr. Green, I'm Dr. Nichols. How are you today?"

"Not very good."

Hope paused. His flat tone spoke volumes, much more than other descriptors he could have chosen. She said, "I see you're here about your cough."

He nodded and shifted in his seat.

"How long has this been bothering you?"

"For some time."

"Weeks, or months?"

"Couple of months, I'd say."

Hope glanced at her laptop, and noted the triage nurse had charted, 'cough for two months, complaining of fatigue, poor appetite, no real fevers.' His admitting vital signs were normal, his oxygen saturation ninety-four percent.

"Look, I just want something to make this cough go away," Green explained. "I've had a couple of those computer visits over the past month, and they gave me some antibiotics. Didn't work. Second time they just told me I should be patient, these things take a while to clear up, and wouldn't give me any more cough syrup. I need one of those Z-packs and some cough syrup so I can sleep at night. That always works." He paused, then added, "This has thrown me for a loop."

"I understand. May I ask you a couple of questions so we can plan a better approach for you?"

"Sure, if it doesn't take too long. I need to get to my office. Haven't gotten much done lately."

"Right. So, have you coughed up anything?"

Green shifted in his chair, stared at the ceiling for a moment, then said, "Yeah, some mucous now and then."

"Blood?"

"Couple of times, that's all."

"How much blood?"

"Just some streaks in the crud that came up."

"Chest pain?"

"Not really. Maybe a twinge once in a while." He waved his hand over his left side.

"The nurse charted that you haven't had much appetite recently. Any weight loss?"

"Not that I've noticed. I don't weigh very often, and wouldn't mind losing a few pounds."

"You a smoker?"

"Former. Quit about twenty years ago."

"Other than several virtual visits, have you seen your own doctor for this?"

"No, I haven't seen him in over two years. When I called, they said I was considered a new patient and there was a three-month wait for an appointment. That's why I did the computer thing."

Nichols nodded. She had heard that complaint from patients many times before – can't get into their own doctor due to tight schedules and lack of follow-up on the patient's part. As a result, their urgent care department and other such clinics were where these folks often landed.

"Well, let's figure this out."

"Look, all I want is that Z-pack and cough syrup, and I'll get out of your hair."

Clearly, he was losing patience with her and her history-taking. "We'll move this along. Why don't you have a seat on the table? I need to listen to your heart and lungs while you're here. It may make a difference in what we put you on."

Surprisingly, he set his irritation aside and cooperated with her suggestion. Removing his jacket, he stepped up to the table and sat. And slumped. This was a man who likely felt even worse than he looked. And there was something more going on with him than a simple, annoying bronchitis and a few sleepless nights. He obliged her request and opened his shirt for the exam. She was not surprised at her findings – decreased breath sounds over his left upper lung field with scattered expiratory wheezes, quiet breath sounds otherwise, and an occasional coarse cough. And a knot of matted, nontender lymph nodes above his left clavicle. No rashes; no leg or ankle edema; normal abdomen. She completed her exam and stepped back.

"Thank you. You can button up now." She resumed her seat and gestured for him to take the side chair again. When he was settled, she looked him straight in the eye. "Mr. Green, I'm concerned that your lung exam is not normal. You're a former smoker—"

"—Quit some years ago."

She nodded and continued, "So, we should get a chest x-ray while you're here today and some blood work. It's best we sort this out right now and not wait any longer."

"Can't we just try another antibiotic and cough medicine before we do all that?"

"I need to put you on the right treatment for your condition, and to do that we need additional information. Otherwise, I'm concerned you won't get better."

"Won't get better? What are you saying, Doc? Do you think I have pneumonia?"

"I don't know without looking at a few things, including that chest x-ray. I'll order these tests and we'll get back together and go over the results. Okay?"

"I guess, since I'm already here. Might as well." He leaned back in the chair and rested his head against the wall. "Where do I go?"

"The nurse will come draw your blood, and then she'll send you over to X-ray. It doesn't take long to get the results back." Dr. Nichols rose, smiled, and shook his hand. "I'll see you back here soon."

She turned on her heel and went to the nursing desk to make sure her orders were noticed right away, then made her way back to her small cubicle in the doctors' office. She couldn't dismiss her uneasy feelings about Mr. Green's condition. Her instincts told her he was quite ill; someone who would require more than a quick work-up. And her instincts almost never failed her.

She scanned the list of unread emails. The seventh one caught her eye.

From: Rich Rutledge.

To: Staff, South Metro Medical Associates.

Subject: Telemedicine Expansion

A red exclamation point conveyed priority or urgent status. Meaning, do not ignore or pretend you didn't see this. In a few short words, Dr. Rutledge announced to all staff physicians, extender providers, and the entire nursing staff that they were launching an initiative to expand their use of telemedicine throughout the clinic, effectively immediately. More details would be discussed at the upcoming medical staff meeting the following week. Every provider should plan to attend. End of comments.

One added instruction could not be ignored – 'Please click the 'read' button below to indicate you've seen and read this email. Thank you.'

Hope stared at the cryptic message. The pit in her stomach reminded her she'd had too much coffee and not enough food that morning. Queasiness threatened. She knew this day would come, but had so far avoided using virtual visits. Bottom line, she was opposed to this trend, whipping through patient visits online without the benefit of a physical examination. It went against her grain, and her medical training. She was tempted to skip the 'read' click and move on. She could hear the nurses filling the empty exam rooms and patients were waiting. Actual in-the-flesh people who had presented for care, most of whom likely expected 'the laying on of hands.' She considered for a few moments, then decided it was better to avoid drawing attention to herself ahead of the meeting. Okay fine, she would click and quietly maintain her stance. Would quietly resist, and see what happened.

One of the nurses stuck her head around the door frame. "Dr. Nichols, Mr. Green is back. Room 3."

Hope signaled that she had heard, and closing her emails, opened Mr. Green's chart to review his labs and chest X-ray. The pit in her stomach deepened.

Green sat forward in his chair, leaning over his knees, hands clasped in front of him. It was obvious that he was clearly ready for this visit to end, to receive his requested Z-pack and cough syrup and get out of there. That was not going to happen, however, at least not in the way he envisioned.

Hope placed her laptop on the small desk and turned to the man. "Let's go over your results."

Green straightened in his chair, and faced her. "Good or bad?"

"Concerning."

He frowned but asked no further questions.

Hope said, "I've reviewed your lab. You have a mild anemia, but no changes indicating an acute infection. On your chemistries, you have a couple of slightly low numbers, but your liver function tests are normal. Kidney function is also normal."

"So, what's concerning?"

"The anemia for one thing, and your somewhat low sodium level. And your chest X-ray."

Brows raised, he asked, "Oh? So, it's pneumonia?"

His question deserved more than a yes / no answer. "There is a density in the upper lobe of your left lung which is clearly seen. That requires further investigation."

"What do you mean, a density?"

"An abnormality… we can't say for sure what it is just from an X-ray."

Hope turned her laptop toward Green and showed him the films, pointing out the area of concern. He stared at the screen, but said nothing.

"So, we need to take another look. At this point, I don't believe another round of antibiotics will benefit you. I'd like to order a CT of your chest, discuss this with your doctor, and possibly refer you to a specialist if the scan is abnormal."

Green shook his head and stared at the ceiling. He expelled a sigh and asked, "When will I get that?"

"I'll put in the order right now, and we'll see if they have any openings today."

He squared his shoulders, assumed a determined look and countered with, "Look, I just need to get over to my office and get some work done. How about tomorrow? I'm not as busy on Fridays."

"I'll speak with the radiologist, and we'll arrange for that. In fact, he suggested further imaging. Meanwhile, I'll put you on a medicine to help with the cough. We'll change our plans after your CT." She busied herself with orders and entering the prescriptions in the electronic record.

"I appreciate that. My pharmacy is still the same." When she had transmitted those orders, he stood and said, "I've taken a lot of your time today, so I'll be on my way. Thank you, Doctor."

"You needed some time." Hope followed him through the door and paused in the hall. "We'll contact you with the appointment time. Please return for that study. And I'll call your doctor today." Offering him a smile, she added, "We'll both keep after you."

This time he managed a faint smile in return and said, "I'm sure you will." Turning away, he made his way down the hall toward the waiting room. No doubt registering her concern and digesting the not-so-good news.

Hope watched him go, suspecting any future discussions would not be uplifting.

A perturbing thought intruded. If this man had not come in, had relied only on virtual visits, his true situation would not have been noticed for… God only knows how long. And his outcome may have been set. How many others like him were out there? Truly, a disturbing thought. And one which must be addressed at the upcoming medical staff meeting. Here was a perfect example of the flaw in that model. Telemedicine – not ready for prime time, yet?

CHAPTER | 2

Friday

I f asked, she couldn't say her sleep felt restorative. The stage was set the previous evening when too many household tasks begged for her attention, tasks she had put off that week.

Her six-year-old son Noah had also decided it would be a late evening, refusing to take his bath at the usual time, or to put away his scattered toys and gather his dirty clothes for the laundry. He had a baseball game that Saturday and had to endure several reminders to get his soiled uniform into the laundry room. Come game time, his coach would not be pleased if he showed up wearing last week's dirt and grass stains. Oxyclean to the rescue – her best friend.

Hope finally started the last dryer load as midnight approached and heavy exhaustion claimed her. As she trudged off to bed, a lineup of patients reminded her of the day's dilemmas. And Mr. Green kept pushing to the front of that line. After falling asleep, she was aware of tossing and turning throughout the early morning hours, plagued by dreams of men coughing up volumes of blood, while she stood helpless at their side. At one point she slid out of bed, half-asleep, and went to the bathroom, hoping to flush the vivid dreams and reclaim some sort of normal sleep. That did not happen.

Sluggish, Hope crawled out of bed before her alarm

had a chance to awaken her and made use of a hot shower. Feeling only marginally improved, she prepared for her day, and went to rouse Noah for school. The hours would pass, they would both get through their day, and prepare for a more relaxed weekend. He didn't have to go to his father's, thank goodness, but planned instead to spend Saturday afternoon at a friend's after their game.

Today, though, she had another plan in mind and another discussion which needed to take place. Whether she had the energy for it or not.

Hope found Dr. Chet Murdock alone in the kitchen pouring a fresh cup of coffee. More accurately, she'd followed him when he took a quick break during a lull in the action. Hope knew she could approach him, and he would listen respectfully, whether he held the same opinion or not. It might be too much, she realized, to expect him to agree entirely. The sixty-something former ER physician served as the head of Urgent Care, but obviously was winding down. Historically, he was one who avoided rocking the boat, particularly concerning clinic administrative issues, and that perspective had not changed since she'd come on board in Urgent Care. She knew he enjoyed direct contact with patients, had also avoided virtual visits. He would prefer that technology die from benign neglect, he'd said, rather than by direct assault from him.

Murdock turned when she opened the door and greeted him. "Hi, fresh coffee?"

"It is." He slid away from the coffee maker and propped himself against the countertop. They had barely spoken that morning, both busy from the moment the clinic doors opened.

Hope poured herself a cup, took a sip, squinting over

the rim at her colleague. "I had an interesting case yesterday."

"How so?"

"A sixty-two-year-old man presented with a history of cough for a couple of months. Nothing too unusual about it. Didn't see his own doctor; hadn't been in for a couple of years. Prescribed antibiotics twice with no improvement. In fact, he feels worse now. Has coughed up blood-streaked sputum now and then."

Murdock cocked his head. "So, what are you about to tell me?"

"He arrived wanting a Z-pack and cough syrup, convinced that would finally kick it."

"But you didn't do that."

"No, I didn't. Turns out, his exam, lab, and chest X-ray were abnormal. He's getting a CT scan of his chest as we speak."

"A CT."

"Right. He showed up with a lung mass – left upper lobe – mild anemia, and sodium of 125."

"No chest X-ray before that?"

"No. And matted supraclavicular nodes on the left."

"Where was he seen? Who prescribed the antibiotics?"

"A telemedicine doctor from another clinic. He couldn't get in to his own doctor. It had been too long."

Murdock nodded and frowned, took a sip, and placed his mug on the counter. "I suppose you saw the memo from yesterday."

"Yes, I did. Right in the middle of assessing Mr. Green. And it didn't sit well with me."

"I know you're not a fan, Hope, but it's a sign of the times, and I don't think we can refuse to use them. Administration's going to push it."

Hope sipped and waited to respond. She needed to exercise caution. He might appear sympathetic, but she doubted he would be supportive to the degree she desired.

She sensed he might just throw her under the bus if it came down to cooperating with administration or joining her on a difficult path of resistance. Chet Murdock was tired of practice hassles and wished to exit on a high note, at a time of his own choosing.

"It was concerning to hear that he wasn't seen at all before yesterday for his persistent symptoms. It wasn't even suggested that he get follow up. At least according to what he said."

Dr. Murdock didn't budge, apparently ready to hash this out rather than flee. He reminded her, "But, he hadn't been in regular follow up with his own doctor, either."

"True." Hope went on. "I admit I think telemedicine potentially harms patients. And here's a good example. If someone out there had obliged him, given him the cough syrup and another round of antibiotics, no telling how long he would have waited to finally see someone, Chet. I just can't support administration's position on expanding its use."

Murdock pulled himself up and said, "Those things happen, you know. We can't prevent every bad outcome, Hope."

"I know that."

Ambling toward the kitchen door, he added, "I would suggest we see what Rutledge has to say next week at the meeting, and how much of a problem we're facing. Let's don't cause problems in the meantime." He grasped the knob, held the door open, and asked, "Coming?"

There was no point in hanging out in the kitchen by herself any longer; it was time to get back to work. That was clear.

As they approached their individual cubicles in the doctors' office, he turned and said, "Let me know what his CT shows, will you?"

CHAPTER | 3

Dr. Rich Rutledge was an efficient, organized man. At least that was how he viewed himself. At age fifty, he enjoyed a busy, stable internal medicine practice and his newly-earned position as Chief Medical Officer of the large multispecialty clinic, South Metro Medical Associates. He desired to maintain a firm hold on that position and envisioned expanding his role as the opportunity presented. Being in charge of things, particularly clinical care issues, had its advantages. Decision-making had never posed a problem for him, and he more than enjoyed holding sway over monthly board meetings, often trumping the board president's opinion. In fact, he envisioned one day consolidating those two positions. Consolidating that power. Why waste time with too many cooks spoiling the broth?

Rutledge pulled up his clinic schedule for the day, his Friday half-day, and checked the follow ups he would see that morning. The afternoon would be spent completing charts and a few administrative tasks before heading out. No doubt his wife had orchestrated plans for their weekend - dinner out with friends, a few tasks around their spacious property, and whatever else she could think up. And his sixteen-year-old son could use some of his time, too. Rich had been on call two weekends in a row, covering for a vacationing partner, and now looked forward to relaxing.

He gathered his tablet, donned his lab coat and made his way down the hall to the exam room where his first patient waited. The morning would fly by.

There came a soft knock at his door. Rutledge had sequestered himself in his office that afternoon, away from clinic noise and too much staff chatter. He wanted to get his charts done and review his notes for the upcoming quarterly meeting without distractions. His nurse Darlene knew to leave him alone and not disturb him unless absolutely necessary. They had worked together for over ten years, had established a rhythm which benefited them both, and he trusted her judgment implicitly. But it was not Darlene at the door.

"Yes?"

The door eased open and a beautiful, familiar face appeared. He smiled – her cue to enter. His administrative assistant Kalisha Johnson returned his smile. No further invitation required, she took a guest chair in front of his desk, ready for a discussion of issues which must be addressed before the weekend.

A statuesque beauty, she was blessed with enviable skin, which reminded one of café au lait, and full mane of black hair, which she often tamed into a sophisticated updo. But occasionally she let her hair down for more casual encounters. Her wardrobe never disappointed, and the other scrub clothes-clad women around the clinic had made note of the gal who displayed such a knack for rearranging wardrobe pieces to create unique outfits, always in good taste. She made excellent use of accessories like few others – not missed and often envied by the staff restricted by the clinic's boring apparel policy. And her sensuous body made a good hanger upon which she displayed her ensembles.

Ms. Johnson had arrived only a year ago when the clinic decided that board members, and heads of the clinical divisions, could not possibly manage their immense administrative tasks without someone at their side, bearing a tablet, keeping them on track. Rutledge was delighted with Kalisha when she interviewed and quickly turned down two other capable candidates. The pair immediately established a positive working relationship, sensing each other's needs, often before either spoke. With that, though, came a slight unease which he couldn't deny. Kalisha was obviously a strategic thinker, which he valued, but she also exuded a barely concealed tough, ambitious core. Instinctively, he knew she would not be content to hold this assistant position for long.

"Dr. Rutledge, I thought I'd stop in and make sure everything was set for next week."

"Right. How many of the staff have responded to the email?"

"Eighty-two percent, so far. I expect others will do so by Monday."

"That's a good response rate. Any concerns expressed?"

"One or two grumblings, but no, nothing significant."

"Good. I've reviewed my notes and feel ready. Questions, concerns, resisters, so forth – and I'm sure there'll be some – I'm confident we can manage."

"I'm sure." She paused, then added, "I have the agenda prepared for you to review. I'll send it out Monday morning." Kalisha slid the two-page document across his desk.

Rutledge quickly scanned the pages and smiled. "Excellent work again. Thank you."

"Welcome." Kalisha hesitated then slid forward and said, "Well, if there's nothing else, I'll leave and let you get back to your charts."

She rose and strode to the door. With a look back, and her hand resting on the knob, she turned. It was obvious she wished to express one last thought when the door suddenly opened, and Darlene's face and stout figure pushed in. Kalisha stepped aside, barely avoiding being flattened against the wall by Darlene's intrusion.

"Oh, Ms. Johnson, I am so sorry. I didn't know you were here," Darlene said, glancing at the door and Kalisha. Which was a lie. It was clear Darlene did not regret intruding on their conversation nor imperiling the administrative assistant. "Sorry to interrupt, Dr. Rutledge, but you have a phone call waiting. Your wife, on line four." She cast Kalisha another stern glance.

Kalisha, ever composed, smiled and eased her way around Darlene. "I'll see you Monday, Rich," she reminded him as she stepped into the hall.

"Yes, Monday, Ms. Johnson." He redirected his gaze to his nurse and said, "Thank you Darlene. Will there be anything else?"

"No, Dr. Rutledge. You have a good weekend. And don't forget your wife's call." She threw him a knowing look and sashayed out, pulling the door closed behind her.

Chapter | 4

Tuesday

Late afternoon rolled into early evening as Hope finished her charting, signed off her computer, and bid farewell to her colleagues covering the evening shift in Urgent Care. The few part-time physicians left behind would catch the video replay of the staff meeting at their convenience, but as prescribed, definitely within the next two weeks. Or else. It was time to get upstairs before she missed the buffet dinner. Noah was staying at a friend's, which she had arranged the previous week. She would break away as soon as she could and pick him up.

As she entered the large conference room, she spied Chet Murdock with his dinner in front of him, ready to dig in. One other colleague from their department sat with him. She would park herself there and make a show of division strength, or that was her reasoning. It likely mattered little; neither of them would risk speaking up. She made her way through the buffet line, joined by a nurse practitioner from their unit. They both wound their way through the tables to sit with their associates.

An agenda waited at each seat, and her heart sank when she viewed the order of business. The telemedicine issue was last to be discussed. Noah would be at the neighbor's longer than she had planned. It was a school night. She shot off a quick text message to her neighbor, hoping the delay did not create a conflict for her and her family that evening. 'No worries,' she answered.

After the brief dinner half-hour, the clinic CEO assumed the portable podium equipped with a laptop, checked the mic, asked if everyone could hear him, and shuffled papers he carried along. The gathered group quieted, and he called the meeting to order. Two large projection screens came to life, displaying the same agenda they had received via email and which they had before them. A few additional subheadings, recently added, now appeared on the screen. Additional information, for clarification, no doubt. The CEO gazed at the screen over his reading glasses, as if studying it for the first time. Perhaps he was.

Done with viewing the screens, he introduced and dispatched with multiple small points of business, and the consent agenda, before turning to the board secretary, then treasurer for their reports. That dispensed with, he called upon the head of the business office to present production data for the clinic overall, and the separate divisions, as well. Changes in insurance company policies and procedures were addressed, as was their payment behavior. There were no changes or problems with the Center for Medicare and Medicaid Services – CMS to those gathered – which required discussion. Then it was on to new business. He relinquished the podium to the CMO.

Dr. Rich Rutledge took the stage, fiddled with his laptop, and the agenda disappeared. In its place appeared a congested document bearing the title: **Telehealth – Wave of the Future.** The subtitle informed all that, **The Future is Now!**

Headings and subheadings poured down the first page and onto a second, covering only half of that page. From a distance one could only hope to read any of the detailed outline. Hope glanced at Chet Murdock, who refused eye contact, but it was clear he was not amused nor pleased. A deep furrow creased his brow. She knew they would discuss all of this later. In the meantime, she would practice restraint and listen to Rutledge's content and his spin. It would not help anything to call undue attention to herself or her colleagues by asking challenging questions.

Rutledge began with a historic rehash of how far technology had come. How fabulous it was, reminding all those present how it had insinuated into the administration and practice of medicine. His history lesson not surprisingly produced slumping at several tables. None of that mattered anyway; all knew there was no turning back the clock. Following that windy introduction, Rutledge reviewed the advent of virtual visits, extolled their virtues especially during the pandemic scourge, and enthusiastically preached that the discovered convenience and efficiencies would revolutionize the practice of medicine. How could they have ever foreseen such a shift? That comment and his heightened voice tone awoke the dozing doctors who appeared none too pleased to still be there. Most then stared at the screens as if they could not decipher a newly discovered foreign language. It had been a long day for all, and it was time to wind this down.

Rutledge had obviously bought into the concept and would not be dissuaded, making his determined arguments as if strutting before a jury deciding a hapless defendant's outcome. All of it – first, garnering local market share particularly with the younger crowd, second, allowing for shorter visits, which thirdly, could increase the numbers of patients seen per week and productivity, almost exponentially – seemed an exaggeration at best. It was time to embrace this newest trend with open arms and set aside one's reluctance to get with it, or some such words. Blah, blah, blah.

Hope had tuned him out, despite her best efforts to stay engaged. It amounted to propaganda in her estimation. Overall, he had presented a very one-sided argument for the technology's merits, and ignored altogether any demerits such use had already accumulated. Perhaps bad outcomes were only yet lurking on the horizon.

A hand shot up at a far table, interrupting Rutledge's diatribe.

"If you'll hold your questions for now," Rich advised, "I'll address any concerns here in a minute."

The cardiologist, not accustomed to being dismissed and who had been brave enough to be the first to intervene, looked especially put out. Hope heard a mumble, "So, let's move this along," from another nearby table. Who would be next to challenge the CMO's position? It wasn't going to be her. She sat back, locked eyes with Chet Murdock for a second or two, and decided to enjoy the spirited dynamic about to unfold.

Dr. Rutledge consumed another ten minutes outlining their approach for expanding the use of telemedicine, how it could be used effectively by virtually all specialties, and no doubt sensing an ensuing insurrection, beat it to the finish line with his closing comments. When he paused, several hands shot up. Before he could formally recognize any in the crowd, the irritated cardiologist shot to his feet.

For the first time that evening, Hope noticed a beautiful African American woman, toting a portable microphone, nearly sprint to the doctor's side. He needed no amplification, waving off her and her mic. Distracted then, Hope couldn't help but wonder who she was. But it was not unusual in such large clinics for administrative personnel to come and go without the professional staff ever making their acquaintance. She refocused on the cardiologist, who commanded the floor.

"Now look here, Rutledge, this concerns many of us. Being an excellent internist, it's hard for me to believe you can so thoroughly discount the merits of the physical exam. There is simply no way we can recognize subtle changes in our patients' conditions, seeing only their head and neck, if that much, over a computer screen. Maybe neck veins bulging to their ears, but at that point we're in deep trouble." He gestured at his cardiology colleagues for emphasis. "The heart failure clinic, for one, will make only extremely limited use of this technology, if at all, and watch our outcomes very closely. This initiative needs to be examined, not expanded."

A few scattered claps erupted. Having said his peace, he resumed his seat. Murmuring ensued, and Rutledge, lacking a gavel, tapped his pen on the podium over which he leaned. The judge calling the courtroom to order. "Who else?" he asked.

Several other doctors asked either specific operational questions, or voiced their concerns, also rising to their feet for emphasis. No physician assistants nor advance practice nurses spoke up. It would be up to the doctors to carry this torch. Hope knew for a fact that several of the nurse practitioners who worked in Urgent Care felt forced to use virtual visits, but had also expressed discomfort with the limited nature of such assessments. Hope's thoughts wandered back to Mr. Green, just five days prior. She had just received his CT results that day, which were depressing at best. Rushing through her day, she had not called him yet, and dreaded doing so. Tomorrow she would address that issue – not bother him late at night – and make the necessary referrals.

She forced herself back into the present, checked her watch, and listened to the final two questions posed. Rutledge fielded those inquiries smoothly, as if he'd practiced for any and all objections.

She'd heard enough, and she had had enough. It was time to depart and fetch her son Noah. She could mull all of this over later; it would still be there. And her mind wouldn't let it go.

As Hope left the room, along with the majority of attendees, she noted Chet Murdock standing in the hall greeting other doctors as they passed by. He caught her eye, cocked his head for her to join him. When she reached his side, he asked, "Have those CT results yet?"

CHAPTER | 5

Wednesday

Hope stared at the screen, digesting every detail of the CT report. It was time to call Mr. Green, deliver the bad news, and contact the pulmonary division for a new patient evaluation. She knew they would work him in quickly, if he would agree to go. And that might present a challenge. She would make a call to his primary care doctor to make sure he received the results. While processing those thoughts, she felt a presence at her side.

"Dr. Nichols, could I bother you to come see a patient?"

Hope swiveled and asked, "Sure, what's the problem?"

"I'd like you to take a look at a lesion she has."

Hope minimized Green's report; she would get back to it right away.

Off she went down the hall with Susan, the nurse practitioner, who informed her of the patient's age and overall condition, her primary care doctor's name, and so forth. As they reached the exam room door, the APRN also told her that the patient had been seen twice through telemedicine visits for several other complaints.

Hope stopped in her tracks, and asked, "May I see that?" gesturing to Susan's tablet. Without comment, she handed it over. Hope noted the young woman's name, glanced at the virtual visit dates, handed it back and they entered the room.

"Hi, Brooke, I'm Dr. Nichols. How're you today?"

"Okay, I guess."

"Susan asked me to take a look at a nodule you have."

"Yeah, on the back of my knee."

"When did you first notice this?"

"I can't remember, but it's been there a while, I think."

"Give me just a minute while I look at a few things on your chart."

Hope directed her attention then to the two recent virtual visits entered. One for conjunctivitis a month ago, and a second for low back pain, just two weeks prior – those symptoms attributed to acute strain in a fit-appearing twenty-six-year-old, who had reported no unusual exertion. Or none that she admitted to. She turned back to Brooke.

"So, you consulted your primary care via the computer a month ago for eye symptoms and those cleared up, right?"

"Yes."

"Then just two weeks ago you also had another virtual visit for low back pain. Has that improved?"

"Not really."

"Do you know what caused the back pain?"

"No. I hadn't changed my exercise routine or done anything different. It just started bothering me."

From the medical record, Hope reminded her, "They suggested alternating cool and heat packs, stretching, walking rather than running, and Motrin. Has any of that helped?"

Brooke admitted, "Not much, but I didn't take the Motrin regularly."

"And then you noticed the nodule on your knee. Was it there during your second visit?"

"On the back of my knee? Yeah, it was. But I was not

going to stand up and stick my rear and leg at the screen to show them, you know? That's just weird."

"I understand." Hope got to her feet and asked, "Okay, may I take a look at the nodule and examine your back?"

"Sure, that's what I came for."

Hope and Susan proceeded to move through the focused exam. The nurse practitioner stood table-side and looked on. The well-defined lesion on the posterior aspect of the woman's knee was flesh-colored, raised, firm, well-circumscribed. The patient being fair-skinned and blond, the nodule held a pink cast. There was no surrounding erythema, rash, nor satellite lesions. It was nontender. But, her low back was not.

With palpation and percussion, Hope elicited a response to pain from the patient over her lower lumbar and sacral vertebrae. Her skin appeared normal. During the exam, Brooke denied any urinary symptoms and exhibited no tenderness over her kidneys. She had no history of kidney stones or other abnormalities. And though she expressed surprise at Hope's next question, she denied any possibility of pregnancy, stating firmly that she never missed a pill. When Brooke easily reclined without hesitating, Hope performed straight leg raise maneuvers which were negative. There was slight tenderness, however, when she flexed both lower extremities.

Hope assisted the young woman to a sitting position and then settled on the handy rolling stool. "Let's talk about a few things."

The patient stared at her and did not respond.

"I agree that nodule on the back of your knee needs addressing. It is concerning, and I'd like to schedule you to have a biopsy with Dermatology."

"You mean cut it off?"

"They use several techniques for situations like this, but yes, they will likely remove the whole thing at one time, send it to the lab, and find out what it is. If it's a problem, they may go back and remove more surrounding tissue to make sure they got it all."

"Do I get any anesthesia?"

"Local should do it. It will be an office procedure. Usually when we call from Urgent Care, they work people in fairly quickly. Now, to your back. I'd like to get some spine films of your lower back today, make sure those are normal, then we can map out a treatment plan for relief. Sound okay?"

"Well, I have to get to work by noon at the gym. I'm a personal trainer and have clients coming in this afternoon."

So, the patient works out regularly, coaches others in the same, and should not develop back pain out of the blue. Unless she is withholding important information about new or unusual exertions, or an injury. "Radiology can shoot the films, and if you have to leave before the results return, I can call you any time later today."

"All right. Where do I go?"

"The nurse will send you over to Radiology; it's right down the hall. But, before you leave I'd like her to get you an appointment with Dermatology so you'll know right away when they can see you. With your work schedule, that will help your planning." She finished her statement with a smile. "Oh, and one more thing… we should check a quick urine specimen for infection, just in case. We don't want to miss such a simple thing given your symptoms. And since we're X-raying you, we always check for pregnancy in women your age. Radiology will insist."

"Okay, I guess. But, I know I'm not pregnant. I broke up with my boyfriend two months ago, and am not seeing anyone else, yet."

"Just a matter of routine in Urgent Care. We'll also have the other urine results before you leave today, after your X-rays. So, just return here and we'll get back together."

Brooke nodded and stepped down from the exam table.

"Have a seat and I'll let the nurse know our plan. See you in a while."

Hope and Susan left the exam room and walked in silence to the doctors' office. Once out of general earshot, the practitioner asked, "So, your thoughts?"

Hope turned to her. "That lesion's concerning for melanoma."

"Really?"

"Yeah, an amelanotic melanoma. It has to come off and be proven otherwise. And I'm not convinced her back symptoms are unrelated. Hopefully, a separate issue. We'll have to see."

"Hey, thanks, Hope, for seeing her."

"No problem." Not concealing her sarcastic tone, she said, "I'm certainly glad she came in and didn't go with another virtual visit, trying to 'stick her leg up to the screen.' Derm needs to view that thing directly, and deal with it."

"Right."

The nurse practitioner turned to her laptop and the next patient, and Hope returned to her desk. She'd had enough of telemedicine – two compromised patients within one week – and still needed to call Mr. Green. At least they had both had sense enough to come in.

CHAPTER | 6

Thursday

Hope waited outside the office door, having asked for a few minutes toward the end of the day to discuss an important concern. The chief of Family Medicine, Dr. Rachel Baumann, sat behind the closed door, finishing dictations. Her nurse cast a glance at Hope and shrugged, clearly communicating she had nothing to do with the delay. Hope fiddled with her cell, checking emails she'd ignored that afternoon. She could wait.

The fifty-something Dr. Baumann had joined the clinic straight out of residency some twenty-five years before and was firmly established with a stable patient base. She had worked her way up the pecking order to the department head position, but did not demonstrate ambition or desire to move on up the ladder to, say, Rich Rutledge's situation. Although she was the quiet, determined type so, who knew? She might be steadily chipping away at his base all the while. Hope had known her since she joined South Metro five years ago and trusted and respected the woman, but felt the relational distance a power position often creates.

Suddenly, Rachel's door flew open. Hope finished reading an email message and looked up.

"Come on in," Dr. Baumann said.

On her feet, then, Hope wasted no further time in the hall. Both were busy, both needed to leave as soon as they could and take care of other matters. In Hope's case, fetch a child. School had dismissed an hour ago. Thankfully, the school offered an after-school program which Noah enjoyed when Hope worked until late afternoon.

"What's on your mind, Hope?"

"To get right to the point, the telemedicine issue is a concern."

"Oh?"

Hope knew that the majority of family practitioners had welcomed and embraced use of the technology, as had their extenders. She wasn't sure of Rachel's position, but wasn't afraid to confront it. Patient care and possible harm came before the biases of individual staff physicians, including her own.

Hope answered, "Yes. It so happens that coincidentally with the announcement and our discussion Tuesday evening at the medical staff meeting, I've seen two patients in Urgent Care with problems missed through virtual visits. Serious problems."

"Specifics?"

"A man with a lung mass, and a young woman just yesterday with a lesion on the back of her knee suspicious for melanoma."

Rachel frowned but didn't say anything for a few minutes. She then asked, "Patients of the clinic?"

"One, yes, the other, no. And in all fairness the sixty-two-year-old man with the lung mass is a former smoker, but he quit twenty years ago. Both had virtual visits twice before presenting to us. As a matter of fact, the man should have been seen sooner with that history rather than just prescribed antibiotics and cough medicine. That's what he finally came in for, because during a second virtual visit someone turned down his request for a cough syrup refill."

Rachel nodded understanding. "So, what's your

position?"

"I think, in view of these examples and other doctors' concerns, we should push for a suspension of telemedicine for now, until we can dig into data and look at patient outcomes. We should proceed with caution, and exercise a little skepticism about embracing the technology without reservation."

"And you want this division to spearhead such a movement?"

"Basically, yes. I think we can exert considerable pressure which administration might take seriously, given Family Medicine and those of us in Urgent Care see large volumes of patients. Perhaps we are positioned to accumulate numbers faster than several of the other departments. It's obvious Cardiology is not gung-ho about this, either."

"True. They made that clear the other evening." Baumann studied the ceiling, then spun her chair to directly face Hope, and took the time to collect her thoughts. She met Hope's gaze and said, "Look, Hope, I share your concern. I've waited to use it myself, but have found it beneficial for patients in some cases. It saves them considerable time, and several have said they wouldn't have come in if that option had not been available. So, it helps, but I don't think it's applicable across the board. I agree with you on that."

"So, you believe we can at least slow down the full-scale adoption of the technology for now?"

"I'm not saying that... today. But, overall, without compiling convincing numbers showing potential harm, I don't think we can persuade the whole clinic to suspend implementation."

"So, if we can accumulate numbers, you'd be willing—"

"I'm not exactly saying that, Hope. My instincts tell me you should just let it go."

"I don't think I can."

Hope dropped in at Urgent Care to ditch her lab coat, pick up her bag, and bid the evening crew a good shift. Two nurse practitioners labored at their computers, finishing data entry and dictations. Susan looked up as Hope entered.

"I didn't know you were still here."

"Just had an errand upstairs. I'm on my way out now."

"I saw that our patient from yesterday is scheduled with Derm early next week. I'll be curious to see what her biopsy shows."

"Me, too. Let me know. I'm not sure I'll receive a copy of their note since you saw the patient and did the dictation."

"Oh, I put your name on the note also."

"Okay, that reminds me... I'll cosign your notes tomorrow first thing when I get here."

"Sounds good. Thanks."

Hope gathered her things and made her way out of the doctors' room to the coat closet where she deposited her lab coat, and grabbed a sweater she'd left there. As she headed down the hall toward the exit, she heard a woman call her name. She turned and saw Susan approaching.

"I don't mean to hold you up, but if you have a few minutes I wondered what you thought of the medical staff meeting the other night. I didn't want to put you on the spot in front of everybody."

Hope searched her face, and detecting a look of sincere concern, said, "I've had lots of thoughts but can't go into all that right now." She glanced up and down the hallway. Gesturing to an adjacent vacant office, she added, "Why don't we step in here?" It was unlikely anyone would decide to make use of the space so late in the day. She closed the door and glanced at the window, glad for the natural light the miniblinds admitted. She wouldn't have to turn on the overhead light, which could be viewed under the door by passersby in the hall. Those who might get curious and check out who occupied the seldom-used office. She turned to Susan.

"It's no secret I'm not a fan of virtual visits. And I'm sure you heard the comments and arguments presented the other evening. It's clear Dr. Rutledge is bullish on expanding telehealth use, and probably won't tolerate too much resistance."

"Do you think we should stop seeing patients that way?"

"Honestly, I do. But I can't make you do something you're not comfortable with, either way."

"I agree with you, but I don't want Dr. Murdock to get upset."

"He's not totally in the admin camp, either."

"So, what do you advise we do?"

"My advice – cut down on the number of tele-visits you do, and make sure you tell patients to come in or see their primary if you have any concerns they may have a serious condition. Or, one that requires a physical exam. Or, if they've already been seen that way for a complaint which has not resolved. And chart that you told them so." Hope paused, then added, "You can always ask one of us to see anyone you're concerned about."

"That sounds reasonable, but we all feel constrained to follow the clinic policy. Particularly after the meeting the other night. I know several of us worry about consequences."

"There should never be reprisals for delivering good patient care, period."

"I know, but just the same... will you provide us some protection?"

That was a big question. Hope gazed at Susan and let a

few moments pass. What was she about to get into? How could she provide these practitioners any kind of 'protection'? She herself might go down screaming, and what, drag them with her?

"I'm not sure how that would work, but I'll give it a good bit of thought and we can talk again. I certainly don't want to jeopardize your position, or anyone else's. It's a tough dilemma. And by the way, it is not a firm policy yet."

"That's true."

"But I'm afraid it's coming, whether we like it or not." Hope turned toward the door; the conversation was over for the time being. She needed to pick up Noah and get home.

In the hall, Susan faced her. "Thanks, Dr. Nichols, I'm glad I work with you. I feel like I can always trust your judgment."

Not so fast there, Sue. "Thank you," Hope said with a smile, and proceeded down the hall to the exit, now burdened with not only her own resistance but that of others. She wasn't at all sure she could protect anyone.

Twenty minutes later she had shelved her clinic thoughts, at least temporarily, and turned her attention toward her son and their evening together. She had nothing in the refrigerator for a meal, much less a healthy meal, and decided they would stop at MacDonald's on the way home. Noah would approve of that choice. Hopefully, he didn't drag home a load of homework to complete before tomorrow. She had to prepare him to spend the weekend at his father's, who would also likely feed him fast food and might ignore his homework.

Then another thought intruded. Mark, her ex, was an attorney, a litigator to boot. Maybe he would like to weigh in on her situation, give her some friendly advice. It seemed he was always up for some kind of vigorous argument. But admittedly, they were on good terms, most of the time, although he never shied away from giving her a piece of his mind, whether she sought it or not. She'd mull it over and decide by the end of the weekend, when she fetched Noah, whether or not she cared to seek his opinion.

Could be an interesting discussion.

CHAPTER | 7

Friday

Mark was waiting when she drove up. He came up out of a porch chair and gave Noah an enthusiastic wave. Their six-year-old could hardly contain himself before jumping out of the car. Hope knew he loved time with his daddy, and so far hers and Mark's joint custody arrangement had worked well. They kept any passing irritation with each other under control in front of the child. At least they made a concerted effort, most of the time.

Competing schedules and egos had taken their toll early on in their marriage, especially after Noah arrived. It became clear Mark wished for a stay-at-home wife, particularly a trophy wife dedicated to hearth and home, socializing, and his career. Despite Hope's best efforts to stay flexible, such as working variable hours in Urgent Care, it didn't satisfy his need for attention. Admittedly, his career as a litigator was very demanding, more so than she had anticipated when they met and shared their dreams and expectations.

She had discounted his egotistical ways at that stage, considering him to be confident and assured. But, soon she realized he cared more for his situation than anyone else's, including hers. He expressed pride in her accomplishments during medical school and residency, but obviously expected it would not interfere with his life whatsoever, after that. It was her problem alone to keep medicine from intruding and under control. Unfortunately, on occasion when she arrived at his place, she still wondered if she had tried hard enough, been flexible enough. Gone were her feelings of love, true, but at times regret made her wish they could have worked it out.

Noah streaked across the small front lawn of Mark's townhome and ran into his father's arms. The two spun around, and dizzy, sprawled on the new spring grass. While they recovered, Hope fetched Noah's overnight bag from the back seat and met them on the porch steps. It was nearly dinner time, and she knew Mark had plans to take him somewhere fun.

"Did he have a good week?" Mark asked.

"Yes. We got his homework done last night, so he's in good shape for next week. He has a game tomorrow; his uniform's in the bag."

"Good. Are you coming?"

"I might, but I have quite a bit to get done from this week. I'll see you, for sure, Sunday around six?"

"Right."

"Give me a hug," she said to Noah who obliged her and then raced into the house. She descended two steps and turned back to Mark. She said, "There is something I'd like your opinion on, later."

That caught his attention. "Anything serious?"

"Yeah, but it'll keep."

"Concerning Noah?"

"Oh, no. More of a professional question."

He frowned, and said, "Okay. Say when. See you Sunday." He shut the door, obviously not enthused to entertain her clinic concerns, whether then or later.

Maybe it wasn't a good idea to ask his advice anyway. Too much involvement, too much opinion from him – not always a good thing. She returned to her car and drove away, hoping Noah had a good weekend. She suspected she would not.

Saturday

Truthfully, she didn't. Conflicted thoughts pestered her throughout the forty-eight hours.

Saturday morning arrived, and Hope awoke determined to gain some sort of control over her dilemma. A sick housekeeper the previous Wednesday provided her an opportunity to tackle various household tasks begging for attention. Mindlessly cleaning two bathrooms kept her hands busy and her thoughts free to analyze her situation. Finished with that and the kitchen clean up, she ran the vacuum with more-than-expected gusto while her thoughts churned. By the time the housework was under control, she felt energized enough to tackle a few outside jobs.

She attacked several ratty-looking beds, pulling weeds and tilling soil. The emerging perennials would have to survive with little attention from her. It would be weeks before she worked them again. All that done, and finally tired from the exertion, she paused and decided to grab lunch on her back deck and rest a bit.

She'd already decided to skip Noah's game. Let Mark cover that obligation. He'd attended only one of his son's games that season, and she could be working for all anyone knew. No one there would think her absence odd.

She had needed some quiet time alone to sort things out. Her conclusion – it was, after all, probably better she had not confided in Mark last night.

CHAPTER | 8

Sunday

Sunday evening arrived and a refreshed Hope drove across town to Mark's. Though her thoughts and concerns over telemedicine issues never left her, she had come to several conclusions since Friday. She was not giving up her resistance, nor her initiative to work with other like-minded colleagues, and there were a few hanging around. She could not assure any extender she could protect their job; they would have to be willing to risk consequences if they wished to resist. But she would not fade on any of them who chose her route. It was time to turn her attention to Noah, and prepare for the last two weeks of his school year. Then there was a well-deserved vacation planned for the two of them – a well-protected surprise for Noah.

As she rounded the corner, she saw Mark's BMW in the driveway. Obviously, they were home. She mounted his front steps and rang the bell three times before she heard footsteps in the hall. Noah jerked open the front door and yelled, "Hi, Mommy!"

He retreated to the interior as fast as he had come, leaving her standing on the porch, waiting for her ex to invite her in. She never presumed to enter and make herself at home. In the background she heard the music of a familiar Harry Potter movie, one which Noah had watched multiple times. Finally, Mark rounded the corner and gestured recognition. And behind him, a young woman sauntered across the hall to the kitchen, without looking one way or another. Undoubtedly, she was well-aware his ex-wife was at the door and just couldn't help but show herself. Hope had not seen her before and wondered if she was the newest one in Mark's full quiver. It grated on her that he would invite such a creature over when he was tending his own son. *Couldn't he wait to entertain these women?* There was plenty of time for any of them to drop by or stay over without infringing on his custodial time. But Hope plastered on a smile as if nothing could phase her that evening.

"Come on, Noah, bring your bag," he instructed.

While their son scampered around and gathered last minute left-behinds, Mark made his way to the door and eyed Hope. "Looks like you got some rest." After a moment, he said, "By the way, you missed a good game yesterday. Noah got three hits."

Hope smiled, said, "Great! Glad you enjoyed it."

Mark cast a glance over his shoulder then asked, "Ready with your question?"

"Is this a good time?"

"No problem."

"All right, will you step outside so we can discuss on the porch? Noah can run around in the yard for a few minutes."

Mark stepped back and yelled at his companion. "Brandi, will you take Noah to the backyard for a few minutes?"

Brandi, huh? Hope heard an indistinct response in the background, and a door shut at the back of the house. Mark stepped onto the broad front porch and gestured to a pair of chairs. The early May evening was perfect for sitting and lounging, maybe having a drink on the porch, but this conversation would not be relaxing. And there would be no invitation for a friendly drink. All she sought was an objective, nonmedical opinion and he was experienced and at hand.

"So, what's on your mind?"

"I have a situation, or we have a situation at the clinic I'd like to run past you. It may bear legal implications if problems develop."

"Legal implications... like contract issues, or patient care?"

"Patient care problems."

"Well, dearie, you know I don't do malpractice."

"Not malpractice as you might think. But still things could go south if someone suffers harm."

"Okay, Hope, what is it?"

"Recently, our administration has initiated a push for all of us to use telehealth visits. Not just occasionally, but wholeheartedly, a good bit of the time. I'm not enthusiastic and see potential patient harm if conditions go undiagnosed or a diagnosis is delayed."

"So, you don't know yet if someone has suffered harm?" Not waiting for her response he added, "I'm aware it's gaining momentum. I've heard that a lot of younger people like it."

"Actually, coincidentally, I have seen two patients within the last ten days who've suffered a delay in diagnosis by using the visits twice before coming in. And, thank goodness, they decided to present. They both had serious conditions which needed a hands-on evaluation."

"So, what's your question for me?"

"In your opinion would malpractice lawyers advise against going that route, utilizing telemedicine to the fullest extent we could?"

He didn't hesitate before answering. "Yes. But, on the other side of the fence, many malpractice lawyers will view this as a potential big boost to their practices." He added a sly smile for emphasis.

She knew exactly what he meant, and was certain the clinic's administration had not given that angle nearly enough thought.

"So, how resistant are you, Hope? Are you out there campaigning to quash the initiative?"

"I admit, I'm reluctant. I still believe in an in-person doctor/patient interaction. And I believe the physical exam has merit, and can change the diagnosis or alter outcome in many conditions. Virtual visits actually may waste patients' money and delay getting to the bottom of things."

"So, what's the problem if you resist? There must be others who feel the same way."

"There are. A number of the older docs are still not convinced. But, fact is, if they get discouraged enough they'll just hang it up and retire. Then the clinic can hire younger, more eager-to-please doctors in their place, or increase the extender numbers and pressure them to cooperate."

"Has your position been threatened?"

"No, not yet."

"Well, look, bottom line, I think you should cover your ass and keep your job. You can't afford to get fired right now, right? If you did, where would you go? How would that affect Noah? You can't just run off anywhere you please, not with our custody arrangement. Keep that in mind."

He stood from his chair, indicating he'd said all he was going to at that point. Though objective, he was obviously far from feeling empathy or sympathy. He never had regarding the nuances of medical practice. Their divorce settlement had provided no alimony, and most assuredly, he didn't want her unemployed, dragging him back into court to get some sort of support. And she didn't want to become dependent or tangle with him in court, either. What a potential nightmare!

She rose, as he stepped toward his front door.

Turning to her, he said, "I really can't advise you any further. But be clear about this, do not do anything which compromises our arrangement or endangers our son."

Yes, sir, I hear you clearly, sir. "Likewise, Mark. Will you send him out here so we can be on our way, and you can get back to your friend?"

He threw her a smirk. "I'll send him out."

As Hope waited on his porch, she heard him open the back door and yell for his latest friend to bring Noah inside. She couldn't help but wonder whether the young woman was ready and willing to play mommy to a six-year-old. But not to worry, she reminded herself, Brandi's days with Mark Baldwin were likely numbered.

Chapter | 9

Monday

It was only nine a.m., and Hope had already seen five people who presented when the doors opened at eight. Mondays were always busy and this one would be no different.

Next up was a sixteen-year-old girl who presented with abdominal pain. The triage nurse recorded that her symptoms had begun about a week ago, had waned, then worsened again just yesterday. The girl rated her pain as eleven out of ten, and said she couldn't stand up straight without feeling sick. No fever or chills, no pain or blood with urination. She denied nausea or vomiting, except the aforementioned queasiness with standing. She denied any chance of pregnancy, the nurse charted, and apparently was surprised at being asked that question. Though very irregular, her last menstrual period was three weeks ago. On no meds, she had a stated allergy to penicillin.

Hope finished reading the history so far, rose and made her way to the exam room where the young woman and her father waited.

"Hello, I'm Dr. Nichols," she announced as she entered.

The father stood, offered his hand, and smiled. "I'm Spencer Reeves, and this is my daughter Madison. We're glad you could see us today."

"Please, have a seat," Hope said as she took the rolling stool, parked her laptop, and turned to the girl. "Hi, Madison, how are you today?"

"Not very good."

The young woman sat on the exam table, slumped over, both arms clutching her midsection. She was a tall, pretty brunette with clear skin and large blue eyes. Hope noted a strong resemblance between the her and her father. Madison maintained eye contact, not common for most teenagers, and obviously didn't mind speaking for herself. Also, rather uncommon for teenagers accompanied by a parent.

"Would you feel better lying down?" Hope asked.

"Probly."

After Madison reclined, Hope confirmed the history already entered in the electronic chart, and said, "I need to ask you a few personal questions to make sure I have the story straight. Is that okay?"

"I guess."

"Would you like your father to stay?" To which her father responded with a look of surprise. Suspecting he'd not taken his daughter to many checkups, Hope clarified, "Sometimes, girls prefer to discuss certain things with a woman."

Mr. Reeves nodded and offered, "I can leave, Madison, if you want."

"No, Dad, you can stay. I don't have anything to hide."

"All right, then," he affirmed.

Hope turned to the young woman. "So, Madison, when did this start, exactly?"

That launched a fairly thorough discussion of her symptom onset, degree of pain, relationship to her menstrual cycle, and so forth. To her credit, Madison didn't flinch or shy away from discussing such topics and objectively denied the possibility of pregnancy, or the use of birth control of any sort.

Dad sat quietly, hands loosely clasped in his lap, having assumed a neutral expression. It struck Hope that he bore the appearance of a man very accustomed to such discussions, or possibly even interrogations. He did not move, watched first his daughter, then Hope. Rather than off-putting, the whole dynamic struck Hope as oddly reassuring. She completed her history-taking and asked Madison's permission to perform an exam. The girl readily agreed; Mr. Reeves also gave his consent.

That completed, and Hope suspicions raised that Madison bore the signs of a pelvic rather than abdominal or GI condition, she helped her patient to a side-lying position and resumed her rolling stool. They needed to set a plan in motion and get about diagnosing this young woman.

"It appears from your exam that your problem is likely more of a pelvic issue than a gut problem." Madison nodded understanding. Her father leaned forward. "I'd like to order a sonogram today and see what that shows. In the meantime, I'll ask the nurse to draw two tubes of blood and help you get a urine sample to check for infection. And as a matter of routine we always check for pregnancy in young women of child-bearing age, which you are, before we get any X-ray procedures, including a sonogram. Are you up for that?"

Spencer Reeves nodded his understanding, and said, "We are."

"Okay, but I know I'm not pregnant."

"I understand."

"Can I get something for pain?" Madison asked.

"When you return and we know what's going on, we can talk about pain medicine and other techniques which may help. Okay? Can you hang in there a little longer?"

"I think so."

Hope stood. "Let's get on it, then."

Madison gave her a faint smile. Mr. Reeves rose as

Hope left the room, and thanked her for her time and explanation.

As Hope wound her way through the hall to the nurses' desk, she couldn't dismiss curious thoughts about Mr. Reeves. There was just something about his demeanor and interaction with his daughter which she hadn't seen before, or not frequently. It was obvious he wasn't a doctor, didn't display the usual attitude of a lawyer in this setting, and likely wasn't ex-military. But she was convinced this man had seen some things, had confronted serious situations in the past. His was a practiced calmness. And where was the mother? Maybe there was some clue in the demographic section of the chart.

An hour and a half later, they reconvened in another exam room for the verdict, and a plan of attack. Hope had reviewed all the lab and the preliminary sono report from the radiologist. And she knew a bit more about Mr. Reeves and his business.

She began. "I believe we have found the answer to your problem, Madison."

"Really?"

"Yes, so let's go over it."

Hope proceeded to report all normal labs: chemistries revealed no abnormalities – liver function, kidney function, electrolytes, etcetera – a normal complete blood count showing no signs of infection or blood loss, urine specimen without signs of infection or blood, and definitely no evidence of pregnancy, just as Madison had insisted. But, the sono revealed a ruptured ovarian cyst on the left, which would explain her pain and focal tenderness she displayed on exam. Hope finished with, "And, in fact, you have numerous follicles and cysts on each ovary, which may cause you pain from time to time. And which may explain your infrequent periods."

Madison flinched and frowned.

Spencer Reeves turned to Hope. "Cysts? Is that

serious?"

"In most cases, not. And it's not that uncommon."

"Do they cause any other problems?"

"They can be part of an endocrine condition known as polycystic ovarian syndrome, which in some patients can lead to other problems or limit fertility. There's variability between patients – which signs and symptoms they'll have."

"So, is it treatable?"

"Yes. But first, I would recommend a few additional lab tests to nail down the diagnosis. If she does have PCOS, then birth control pills are one option to help regulate her cycles and reduce the development of the cysts. And there may be other recommendations we make."

Spencer looked at Madison and said, "I think we should have her run the other tests, Madi, and check for that. Let's get this taken care of."

"Don't you think Mom will want to know first?"

"I'll explain it to her. And if she has questions, Dr. Nichols can go over it with her." He turned again to Hope. "Her mother is out of town on business this week. She'll want to know, of course, what's going on. Could I call you if she has concerns?"

"Sure." Hope retrieved her card from her lab coat pocket and extended it to him. "Have her call any time."

They finished by discussing use of Tylenol and Ibuprofen for pain, heat packs applied to the abdomen for additional relief, and refraining from soccer practice or games for a few weeks if still symptomatic. Otherwise, Madison could return to such activities after a few days of relief. Hope also suggested other simple comfort measures Madison could try. She expressed agreement and appeared anxious to be on her way, after also accepting an offered shot of Toradol for temporary relief.

As Hope rose to leave the room, she agreed to keep an eye out for the additional lab results, after which she would call Mr. Reeves, and suggested they follow up with their primary care doctor or pediatrician.

Spencer Reeves stood and responded, "You've been so thorough and kind. Thank you." He took her hand in a firm handshake. "We appreciate your time, which was more than Madison got out of a telemedicine visit a week ago."

Hope stopped in her tracks. "Really? And where was that?"

"At another clinic. Her mother arranged for the appointment with Madison. They told her she had an irritated bowel and needed relief for her constipation."

"I wasn't constipated, Dad," Madison said with a roll of the eyes. "They didn't listen."

"I know, Madi. I'm just glad we came in today, aren't you?"

"Yeah, for sure."

"Well, we'll let you go, but thanks again, Doctor. I'm sure we'll hear from you soon."

"You can bet on that. Take care."

Hope left the exam room, let out a long sigh, and headed for the doctors' office. She had had about enough of this telemedicine issue.

Now, what to do about it?

CHAPTER | 10

Spencer listened as the phone rang, and rang, and rang. Why didn't Jacqueline pick up? Without a doubt she could see his face on her screen. He had decided to call her that evening, even though it was late when he finally arrived home from the office. In California for the week, his wife wouldn't be as bothered by the hour. He might bother her, but tough, she needed to know the outcome of Madison's urgent care visit that day.

The Toradol shot had worked wonders. Madison felt well enough – though she had missed the whole day of school – to finish her already-assigned homework and gab on the phone with several friends about her experience. She gushed to the girls about the wonderful Dr. Nichols who'd seen her, such that she thought she just might consider a career in medicine. What the great woman doctor did was definitely cool. Spencer hadn't had to eavesdrop to overhear his daughter's side of the conversation, and chuckled to himself about the double benefit of having gone in to be seen.

At the fifth ring, Jacqueline Taylor picked up. "Hi, late day?"

"You could say. How's the west coast?"

"Oh, you know, the usual. So, just checking in or is

something going on?"

You would think a married couple might anticipate nightly phone calls with each other when on the road for business. Not to keep track, but just to touch base, make sure the other felt cared for, and convey important information on occasion. But he knew Jacqueline didn't expect that, perhaps even found it a bit annoying. Spencer was, however, used to staying on top of things, and wanted the conversation each day.

That day their daughter's physical condition warranted such interest, and he intended to inform her mother of the new diagnosis – and the former incorrect one – and the plan of action going forward. She should welcome the update.

"Well, both. We made a visit to the doctor today."

"Who's we?"

"Madi and I."

"Oh, which doctor?" *Not, what's wrong / is Madison okay / or, what happened to either of you?*

"A very nice, thorough urgent care doctor at South Metro Medical Associates."

"We don't go there."

"Well, *we* did. And Madi has a condition you need to know about."

"What are you saying, Spence?"

"She had more abdominal pain again yesterday after you left. It got worse overnight, so I decided to have someone take a look at her. Her pediatrician's office said they didn't have any openings, and recommended the other clinic. We went in early this morning, she was evaluated, and they arrived at a diagnosis which makes a lot of sense."

"So, don't keep me in suspense. What is it?"

"She has a ruptured ovarian cyst on the left. In fact, a number of other cysts on each ovary. And they're looking at some additional lab work to see if the diagnosis can be confirmed. Polycystic ovarian syndrome, they said." With a confident tone he read that to his wife from the back of

Hope's business card.

"Really?"

"Yeah, really."

"How did they find that out?"

"Lab work and a sonogram of her abdomen and pelvis."

"Did she feel comfortable talking about all that in front of you? They did check her for pregnancy when they ran tests, didn't they?"

"Yes, Jacque, they did. And Madi bore up under their questioning and scrutiny very well. She's a real trooper. I'd say, she's tired of you suspecting she's going to get pregnant any minute. And by the way, this condition can interfere with fertility. So, birth control pills may be the treatment they recommend, anyway."

"So, you don't know this for sure, yet?"

"It's the working diagnosis, the doctor told me. An additional test or two and we should know."

"Did he have to do a pelvic exam on her?"

"It wasn't a he, Jacque. She saw a woman doctor this time. And no, she didn't do that today. You know, it's probably best it wasn't her pediatrician. I'm not sure he would have thought of this. Issues like this may be out of his league."

Silence extended between them. After a few moments, Jacque said, "Don't be snide, Spence. Her doctor has been very good."

"But, maybe it's time she change to an adult or family medicine doctor who covers all the territory."

"True, maybe it is time." She paused, then asked, "Young or old?"

"What?"

"Was the woman doctor young or older?"

"I don't know… younger than some, I guess."

"Spence, you're good at nailing people's age. Was she too young to be considered competent?"

"Okay, I'd say she was about thirty-five or so, and appeared very competent. You know, age doesn't always confer competency. Your tech world is all about youth, right?"

"Okay, all right, you win. So, how's Madi doing tonight?"

"Much better. They gave her a shot of pain medicine, and it worked wonders. She finished—"

"—they didn't give her narcotics, did they?"

"No, no. Toradol, an anti-inflammatory. Then recommended Motrin or Tylenol and heat packs for pain if it still bothers her. But, she's practically bouncing off the walls, extolling the virtues of the great woman doctor to all her friends."

"Sounds like Madi, our little cheerleader."

"At any rate, speaking of competence, that virtual visit you arranged last week completely missed the boat."

Jacqueline didn't answer for a few moments, perhaps not expecting the side-swipe, but finally retorted with, "Spence, telehealth is where it's at now. We can't impugn it just based on Madison's situation. It has many applications, and there are more to come."

"I'm sure you're busy right now dreaming up advances – maybe even AI providers – which will treat all kinds of serious disorders. Eliminate doctors once and for all. Who needs hands on, right?"

"You're being obnoxious…"

"Really? I would call it being concerned for our health care, as our daughter's example shows. So, in the future, she and I are not going to sit in front of a computer screen and pretend a provider on the other side can see everything important about us and make a correct diagnosis on the spot. No, for me and mine, I want to go eyeball to eyeball with the person diagnosing and treating me, and know I trust them. And no robots, please."

"Please, we're not spawning robots yet. You're too

much, Spence. And just because you're so used to staring down a perpetrator or a witness doesn't mean all disciplines require that you even sit in the same room with someone."

"It helps... person to person... in the flesh..."

"Okay. So, she's doing better. Can she go back to school tomorrow and resume soccer practice?"

"Plans to. If the pain stays under control. Dr. Nichols said to reduce her physical activity like her soccer for a couple of days, then try back."

"So, does this Dr. Nichols have a number where I can reach her if I have questions?"

"She does. And she proposed that very thing, gave me her card. You want her number?"

"Yes, I do."

After he had relayed the phone number to his wife, he reiterated the clinic's name, and which shifts Hope said she would work that week.

"She sounds like a smart woman."

"I would say she is."

"Sounds like you're very impressed."

"I won't deny that."

"Have a good night, Spence."

"You, too, Jacque."

CHAPTER | 11

Tuesday

Rich Rutledge forced himself to get up earlier than usual that morning, and get with it. He wanted to go over clinic business before seeing patients at nine and before Darlene would arrive around eight. There had been little or no time the day before, Monday being a Monday, to meet with Kalisha about the previous week's medical staff meeting and receive her other observations. She had agreed to arrive around seven-thirty so they could enjoy a quiet period before the clinical office came to life.

Moments after he'd sat down, she appeared in his doorway, quite well put together for the hour. Always stunning, she appeared particularly so that morning.

"Coffee?"

"That would be great."

Knowing her way around his office, she served herself from a carafe arranged on a large tray with all manner of additives, which was situated on a sideboard under his large window. The position he had attained afforded him a spacious corner office, more than the other internists enjoyed, another perk he wished to preserve. Steaming fresh coffee in hand, she assumed a chair to the side of his desk, made room for her coffee on his desktop, and opened her tablet.

"Your weekend went well?" she asked.

"Very." He gazed at her for more than a moment, wondering just what she had engaged in, and with whom. There wasn't a man who wouldn't notice her, and no doubt many had thought they could capture her time and attention. Most likely struck down before making any headway. Her exotic looks and dismissive behavior created allure he wouldn't deny.

"So, okay, your observations from last week's meeting."

"Right. I believe you presented a strong argument, a strong position, for the expansion of telemedicine. You hit all the points we'd developed, very persuasively I thought. Your enthusiasm came through."

"Thank you." His ego didn't need her padding, but he appreciated her recognizing his efforts and verbalizing as much.

"I am concerned, however, that there are those who clearly resist the concept. The cardiology division for one... they don't appear ready to adopt the technology at all."

"I would agree. And to be frank, I understand their perspective from a purely clinical standpoint."

"But, that can't stand in your way."

"Agreed. We'll have to ease them along, bring them around. Think we can do that?"

"There are ways."

"What new ideas have you developed?"

Kalisha paused, pouted her full lips, and tapped away at her tablet before answering. If she sat there all day striking that pose, he would not object. She matched his gaze, then, and suggested, "Why don't we ignore those resisting for now, such as the cardiologist who spoke up? We'll work on the others who are straddling the fence. Gain more acceptance overall, and let that bring pressure, let that evolve organically. In that way, you can spread the responsibility for making this happen. Delegate some of the push to others. You won't remain a sole target for the stragglers."

"I like your thinking." *And other things you offer.*

She nodded and smiled. "And I have another idea which may help our strategizing."

"Yes?"

"I have been wandering around, visiting several divisions, even before last week's meeting. I plan to do more of that. Drop in unexpectedly, inquire about their needs, observe their patterns and conversations if I can stay close enough to overhear. Find out who in the various divisions is resistant. We can analyze those observations and know better where to spend our time and energy."

"You mean spy on my colleagues?"

"I don't care for that term, but yes, basically gather information or 'intelligence.' It will become quite useful, I'm sure."

Rich smiled at his assistant. She was very capable of developing all kinds of strategies and carrying them out effectively. "So, what are your impressions so far?"

"Family Medicine as a whole is coming around. They're more comfortable than say, the medicine subspecialties, but I've only been to a couple of those divisions. Urgent Care, however, is not jumping on board, which surprised me. They are the ideal department to wholeheartedly embrace the technology. I felt a tension there when I visited, particularly from several of the doctors. The nurse practitioners kept their distance; I had trouble engaging them."

Rutledge pulled up the Urgent Care division home page and reviewed the doctors and extenders listed. Chet Murdock and Hope Nichols were regulars, four others worked part-time variable shifts, and three extenders rounded out the clinical team. He angled his monitor so Kalisha could view their pictures with him.

"Who did you observe?"

"Hope Nichols, for one. When I was there she stayed busy, didn't hang around to chat. Chet Murdock definitely didn't engage. I was fairly invisible to him."

"That might work in your favor as you move around."

"True. And the extenders just left, ran off to exam rooms, without returning to the providers' room between patients."

"Where do they do virtual visits, if they, in fact, do them?"

"In their chart room, unless it's too busy and noisy. Then they go to a vacant office in the back hall."

"I think I know where that is. You know, maybe if they had a nice, new station dedicated to virtual visits they would become more enthusiastic."

"Perhaps."

"Did you talk with any of the nurses while there?"

"Only to say 'Hi,' let them know I was there, just passing through. They didn't pay much attention. But, I think I can cultivate those relationships fairly easily, if I take some time."

He angled his screen back, and said, "Sounds like a good idea. They could become real allies, I would think. And here in Internal Medicine, what do you see?"

"I need to spend more time here but, other than you, I'd say about a third of the doctors and extenders are positive or somewhat positive about using the visits. Mostly for follow ups with uncomplicated patients. There is definitely more work to do here in your department."

"I like what I'm hearing so far. And I encourage you to keep it up. It'll be surprising what you might overhear the more they get used to you coming around, every now and then, of course. I would certainly rotate my visits, if I were you. Otherwise, they may suspect you're scoping them out."

"Of course. My plan exactly."

"Great, well—"

Without announcement, the door opened wide, and Darlene stood there, surveying Rich's office and the occupants. He straightened in his chair and directed his attention away from Kalisha. *Why did this woman seem to always know when Kalisha's present?* A competent nurse can be a pain, and in the way sometimes.

"Yes, Darlene, good morning."

She cast a suspicious look at Kalisha, and replied, "Good morning, Dr. Rutledge. You look busy already. Is there anything I can get you or Ms. Johnson?"

"No, I think we're fine. Just about to finish up."

"Right. And your first two patients have checked in. I'll be rooming them in a few minutes. Have you looked over your schedule for the day?"

"I'm about to do that."

Kalisha powered off her tablet, sipped her cold coffee, and moved around as if she intended to leave shortly.

"Well, you'll see that we have two additional work-ins late morning. Should keep us hopping. Not a lot of time for anything else today."

"No doubt."

Darlene turned on her heel and retreated to her desk just five yards from his door, which she left standing wide open. Her message: It was time to get started with patients. He silently motioned with one hand for Kalisha to close the door. She read his mind and body language before he finished gesturing, eased the door closed, and turned.

Assuming a low tone, he said, "I would like you to carry on with your observations, and we'll need to meet more frequently to tweak our plan."

"I agree."

"How about Thursday evening at the Wine Cave on the Plaza, say around seven?"

"I can make that happen."

"Excellent. See you then… if not before." He finished with a wink.

CHAPTER | 12

Wednesday

It surprised Hope when she saw the message. The pathology report was back on the young woman with the leg lesion from just a week ago. Usually, such tissue diagnoses took longer to return.

As she suspected, it was an amelanotic melanoma. The specimen displayed adequate, clean margins; they would not have to go back and take a wider excision and remove additional surrounding tissue. The dermatologist was referring her to oncology for follow up and further staging, particularly considering her persistent back pain. It was disheartening to read that, and hopefully, the young woman would not ignore the referral, nor any further testing recommended.

Melanoma was not a good actor. Being such a healthy, fit young person, it worried Hope that she might be shocked and frightened enough to run away from the process which lay ahead. She would call Brooke herself later and assess her response to all this. She whipped off a quick email to Susan, the nurse practitioner, to make sure she also saw the results.

She had yet to hear from the pulmonary division regarding Mr. Green's situation. No doubt it would take longer to receive his path report, and for the necessary staging to be completed. He had a long haul ahead of him, and a lot of doctors would join him on his path. She would stay out of the way for now, and touch base with him the following week, if she had not heard anything by then. He was a busy man, now busier than ever.

She gathered her laptop and headed to the next exam room.

An hour later, and after addressing the needs of five patients with minor complaints, she made her way to the nurses' station to see how things were going at their end of the suite. How were they doing? How many more people were checked in and waiting? One RN rose and joined her on the other side of the long desk. It was obvious she had something on her mind, and apparently thought Hope could provide the answer. She beckoned for the two of them to take a stroll down the long hall toward a procedure room. Curious, and able to spare a few minutes, Hope followed.

They entered the procedure room, and the nurse closed the door. She pretended to check the stocked cabinet, then turned to Hope. "Have you noticed that woman who's come around recently?"

"Not sure that I have. Who?"

"Well, that's my question… Who is she?"

"I'm not sure who you're referring to."

"Tall, beautiful, black woman. Younger, exotic looking, always dressed to a 'T.' She strolls through, carrying her tablet, chats a bit, then leaves. Says she's Kalisha Johnson."

Hope searched her memory bank and asked, "Does she ask anything?"

"No. Just chats us up, then says she must be on her way, and leaves."

Suddenly, Hope remembered a person matching that description carting the mic around for Dr. Rutledge at the recent staff meeting. *Could it be?* "Did she say she's with administration?"

"She hasn't said that directly, but it's obvious she's not a nurse or doctor. We know everyone else around here, except for some of the administrators. And she's not a unit manager."

"You're sure? Maybe they hired a new one."

"I don't think so. We usually get a memo about that."

"So, she doesn't do anything or ask any particular questions?"

"Sometimes she just stands there watching, says a few words, then leaves. It's kind of weird."

"The other nurses agree?"

"Some ignore her; others don't like it at all. They feel watched."

"How often does she come by?"

"I've only seen her twice, but I'm not sure if she's dropped by on my day off."

"Sounds interesting." After a pause, Hope said, "You know, I have an idea... why don't we try to sneak a picture or video when she comes around again. Think you all can pull that off without her noticing? I have a hunch I know where she's from."

"We can try. It'll be easier to get audio of a conversation; a video may be more challenging. I'll talk with several of the others, see what they think."

Hope smiled. "Sounds like a plan. And let's stay in touch about this. In the meantime, if she returns and asks more questions, or says something more, let me know. If I'm here, I'd like to make her acquaintance."

The nurse quit fiddling with boxes of 4 x 4 gauze pads she held and threw her a skeptical look. She observed, "Things are changing around here, Dr. Nichols. Changing."

"It's very intriguing, don't you think?"

The RN shrugged, said, "Glad you think so. I'm not so sure intriguing is good."

Well, she wouldn't totally disagree with that.

Finished, they left the room and parted ways in the

hall, each returning to their respective duties. Hope retrieved her laptop and made her way to the next exam room, her mind full of various theories about the mystery woman. But there was clearly one viable answer. The woman was a 'spy,' sent by Admin – probably Dr. Rich Rutledge himself – to scope them out. Probably other divisions, as well. What a thought! Likely, it was all about telemedicine. And they might just have some fun with this.

Hope stood at the closed door, her mood improved, and prepared to meet the next stranger waiting within. She glanced at the medical record she'd pulled up. At the top, under the patient's name, she read:

Attending physician: Richard Rutledge, MD.

Chief complaint: Not better since e-visit last week.

CHAPTER | 13

Thursday

The Thursday evening crowd, anxious for the weekend to get underway, had already jammed into the popular wine bar. Young professionals in need of socialization at the end of their fast-paced business week.

Rich Rutledge, undaunted, arrived early and secured a small corner booth in a secondary room, away from the madding crowd. He wasn't worried they would be recognized by anyone. He carried his tablet, and he knew she would bring hers as well. They could feign meeting for business reasons if they had to. The story he gave his wife – he had a called board meeting, which might last several hours. Important clinic business. Hopefully, she believed him and wouldn't check with another doctor's spouse... or, God forbid, Darlene. He had informed the hostess of his expected guest and, in the meantime, busied himself with his cell phone.

Shortly, Kalisha appeared and strode to his table, obviously comfortable with the attention she garnered. He stood, they shook hands for show, and she settled into the booth, maintaining a respectable distance. He put aside his cell, as did she. A waiter swooped down on them before either had a chance to survey the extensive wine menu. Rich waved him off, stating they would take a few minutes to make their selections. The young man bowed away.

Kalisha took only a moment with the drink menu.

"Ready to order?" Rich asked.

"Yes, and I think I'll have a small plate as well. That'll suffice as my supper."

Rutledge signaled their waiter, who promptly returned, prepared with his tablet to assist.

"This will be separate tickets," Kalisha informed him. "I'll have the house pinot and the ceviche plate."

He turned to Rutledge, who voiced his selections.

The young waiter signaled his approval and sped away to submit their requests.

"You don't have to pay for your food," Rich said.

"Best not to leave a paper trail, right?"

"It's cash night. No trail," he informed her.

She nodded, smiled, and positioned her tablet in front of her. "So, what do we need to discuss this evening?"

"We can pick up where we left off the other morning. What have you observed since then?"

He watched as Kalisha surveyed her tablet, then met his gaze. "I paid Urgent Care another visit Tuesday."

"And...?"

"Just stopped in, chatted with a couple of the nurses, and watched their activity."

"Do the nurses engage?"

"Some do, others, not so much. They don't have time to stand around chatting. Most stay on the move."

"And the doctors?"

"Same. They are in and out of the providers' office, in and out of exam rooms. Come to the nurses' desk to clarify orders sometimes."

"Using the back hall office for virtual visits?" he asked.

"I didn't see that happening, either the doctors or extenders. It was somewhat difficult from my vantage point to view that office door clearly, but no one came and went while I was there. It's possible they assign or volunteer one staff provider to take it each day, and I just couldn't see that. I need to spend more time there to further assess."

Interrupting their conversation, the waiter returned with their wine. Close behind the server arrived with their plates. Making sure they had no further needs, he quickly retreated and left them to enjoy their food and drink.

"Sounds like you do. They are the ideal unit to use the technology, and we must monitor their cooperation. The providers there could serve as a real asset for our promotion to the wider clinic staff. Are the nurses in favor?"

"Can't tell yet."

"How long have we been working on our initiative?"

"You know perfectly well... since I came on board a year ago."

"And how have we marked our progress? Let's review."

"Multiple ways. Assessing the various software packages and choosing one with sufficient capacity, and approval from CMS and the insurance carriers was our first step. That took considerable time to plow through. Secondly, bringing the board of directors along in their thinking. We've made a significant impact there, I believe. And most recently, addressing the entire medical staff last week was a major milestone, given the scattered resistance within the divisions. Back to the board, getting their approval to address the larger group took time and effort to arrange."

Rich nodded his agreement, and said, "And don't forget, finding you, and the relationship we've developed since I hired you. That was the first major step, and the most important one, I believe." He extended his hand toward hers, rested it inches from her long, slender fingers and waited. She grazed his hand with her manicured nails, which brought on a welcome chill and building pressure he couldn't deny. What a fantastic woman!

She threw him a sensuous smile, and withdrew her hand.

"I would turn the same question to you. How do you think we've marked our progress?"

Rich grew serious and paused before answering. "I am pleased with our software package and the technology upgrade we've purchased and launched. And the cooperative lines of communication we've established with our agency partners. That's crucial. One individual, in particular, at HHS is very supportive of this clinic's position, and I see the incentive structure he's proposed nearing implementation."

Kalisha responded with a broad smile. "Are you referring to the bonuses we've discussed?"

"Definitely. Having the feds on our side has particular benefits, which I believe we'll realize in the very near future. But, we do have to show over seventy percent adaptation on the providers' part. So, we must keep an eye on what they're doing, and identify resistant pockets where more pressure is needed. That's where you come in."

Their waiter materialized, suspended their conversation, and inquired of additional needs. There being none, he presented both with their bills and left. Rich snatched hers away before she could pick it up.

"Right." Kalisha's eyes darted away for only a second, but her behavior was not lost on Rich.

He chose to ignore her seeming distraction and continued, "Achieving our goals and beyond can position you for interesting advancements, either in our organization here in Kansas City, or perhaps elsewhere. I have ways of making that happen."

"I'm well aware of the opportunities I could enjoy, and the financial benefits of bringing this around." She again glanced beyond him.

He turned slightly and attempted to see who or what might have caught her attention, but saw only scattered men and women at various tables. No one seemed to pay them any mind. "Something interesting over there?"

"Oh, no. Sorry. My mind wandered for a moment and my eyes with it. Back to your point, I know what I have to do, and how to do it."

"You're a real asset." He smiled, and asked, "Done? We need to get out of here, so we can finish our evening." He loaded the check holder with sufficient cash to cover their tab and please the solicitous waiter.

"Absolutely."

They prepared to leave and, scooting from the small booth, wove their way through the throng. None of the younger crowd paid them any attention.

When they reached the main bar area near the entrance, Rich noticed a lone man, likely in his mid-forties, nursing a drink. The man threw a look their way, his gaze lingering a bit too long on Kalisha. Concerned by the man's interest, he ushered Kalisha past the hostess and exited. When Rich glanced back, the man paid them no attention, staring only at the mirror above the bar and the rows and rows of up-lit glass shelves, all crowded with unique liquor bottles. He quickly dismissed his uneasiness – guilt, maybe? – and attributed the man's interest to Kalisha's magnetism. It never failed. Someone always took notice.

Outside, he reminded her, "We don't have much time. I'll have to leave by nine or so."

Hope gripped the suitcase handles and called Noah to come fetch the smaller one. No answer. She bundled the cases into her bedroom, and returned to the hall, preparing to summon him again, when he jumped around the corner in his sock feet, nearly colliding with his mother.

"Hey, watch out, young man," she admonished with a smile. "No injuries before tomorrow."

"Where're we going?" he implored.

School had dismissed for the school year just that afternoon, and she had kept her secret for as long as she could. Noah was bouncing off the walls and needed a purpose to direct his attention and energy. "I think you'll be pleased when I tell you."

"Can I take my Bey Blades?"

"I don't think you'll need them."

"Mom…" he whined.

"Okay, here it is. We're going to Disney World!"

Noah stood stunned for a moment, then jumped straight into the air, and bounced around her room, yelling and whooping for added effect.

"Okay, calm down. Here's your suitcase. Why don't you go get started on your clothes first, while I load the washer? Then we'll see how much room you have for toys." She handed her son his smaller suitcase and sent him leaping his way to his room. "And you can take a backpack, too."

From in the hall, Noah yelled "Yippee," "Wow," "Yea!" and other assorted kid expletives, then asked, "Is Dad going, too?"

"No, not this time. It's just us, but he knows we're going." There was no question she'd had to inform her ex-husband of her plans to take their son out of state for vacation. Had to get his permission, if not blessing. Thankfully, he had lodged no objection this time, and kept her secret, probably relieved he could spend unfettered time with Brandi, or whoever.

That didn't seem to dampen Noah's enthusiasm. Still vocalizing, he tore off to start packing. Hope welcomed the time they would spend away, too. Away from clinic conundrums and telemedicine and snoopy administrators. A whole week of fun in Florida – yes! It had been a while, and she was due. But the next thirty-six hours could be a real challenge until they boarded that eight-a.m. flight to

Orlando.

She stuffed a large load of tee shirts and shorts in the washer, slammed the door closed, and hit the appropriate settings. Time to get on with it.

———————

Kalisha slid out of bed, fetched her silk robe which she had flung on the floor, and padded into the ensuite bathroom. Rich had departed fifteen minutes before, left her lounging in bed, wondering if she had made the right choice.

They had sped to her place, bordering the Plaza, and barely made it inside before he propelled her to bed. With urgency, they wound around each other, tumbling and twisting in her sheets, until sated, they fell still. And thirty minutes later, they had enthusiastically engaged in round two. The man had incredible staying power, and she couldn't deny enjoying their trysts. He repeatedly let her know she was exceptional in bed, no others like her existed, and he couldn't get enough.

She realized he would eventually have to get over her, go back home, and quit cheating on his wife, who no doubt was another exceptional woman. One who had put up with his arrogant ways for years. Kalisha had other objectives, but he was admittedly an attractive distraction in the meantime. She had known what she was undertaking from the get-go. Part of the process, part of the plan. Now, it was time to move this along, ensuring it turned out in her favor. He would have to fend for himself then.

Kalisha picked up her cell and hit redial.

CHAPTER | 14

Saturday

Orlando

The captain's announcement suddenly broke in, informing all aboard of their initial approach to the Orlando airport. Noah alerted, ignored his little tablet, and looked around. She and Mark had traveled with him numerous times before, and without fail he always expressed interest in how the plane operated and what the crew must actually do. One day, he announced, he would be a pilot and fly them anywhere they wished. With the expected jolt, the plane settled onto the runway, and their Disney adventure was underway.

They retrieved their bags at baggage claim, breezed through the car rental line, and easily found the sedan they would drive for the week. At last, on their way to the resort and relaxation, she felt herself letting go of the previous weeks' toil and trouble. It was good to get away. Noah rode with his face glued to the side window, remarking on the flat landscape and palm trees as they whizzed by. This was his first trip to Florida.

Twenty minutes later, they checked in and found their room at the Grand Floridian. Hope had reserved a two-bedroom suite, a real splurge, though she knew they would spend little time lounging about indoors. Admittedly, she wanted to treat herself. Full of energy, Noah sped through the rooms, checking everything out – particularly thrilled with the TV in his room which was not permitted at home – and pronounced all of it 'super.' The balcony spanning their suite was a hit, too. From there he surveyed that end of the resort and informed her of all he could see. Wow!

So far, so good.

She corralled him to help unpack and get settled in. There was still plenty of time to check out the pool and plan how to spend the rest of that day and the next, she advised. Within minutes, though, he had thrown all his belongings in his bedroom drawers, donned his swimsuit and tee-shirt and stood at her door ready to go. Forgotten were his Bey Blades, and off they went.

By late afternoon, Hope was lagging. When Noah dragged himself from the pool, she convinced him they were both spent and in need of an early supper, and rest. She informed him Florida was one hour ahead of their usual time at home, and bedtime would seem to come earlier that night. He expressed skepticism at her reasoning, told her not to trick him like that, and gladly accepted his towel. Despite his initial resistance, his tired eyes told a different story. The in-bedroom TV would likely go to waste that night. He then turned his attention to where he could get corn dogs and fries for dinner.

They headed back to their room to change and secure a table at one of the family-friendly restaurants on site. Maybe Goofy and Pluto would drop by their table? She could only hope.

CHAPTER | 15

Tuesday

S unday and Monday flew by at the Magic Kingdom, consumed with standing in long lines for all manner of rides, flying or otherwise, which put her inner ears to the test. Unphased, Noah recovered quickly after each, and tore off to the next venue. By Monday afternoon he had gained courage enough to try one of the moderate roller coasters, declaring that with practice he'd be ready for 'the big one' – Expedition Everest at Animal Kingdom – the next day or maybe the next, next day. After a couple of turns on the Slinky Dog Dash and Big Thunder Mountain Railroad, she hoped he'd lost some of his spunk and interest in pushing the limit. No such luck. He insisted they would tackle it the following day.

Hot, tired, and hungry, they welcomed the swift monorail ride back to the hotel and supper. Hope decided to steer him toward the resort activities the 'next day,' even if it meant she would have to lounge by the pool all day. She needed a rest. A spa appointment sounded good, but who to trust with Noah? A resort sitter? She'd have to think about that.

Tuesday morning arrived, and Noah spoke up before she had a chance. Over breakfast, he informed her he was still tired and wished to hang around the hotel that day. Exploring each of the pools sounded just fine to him, and then maybe he'd be ready for the 'big one' the next day.

With only three more 'next days' left before journeying home, Animal Kingdom sounded great, but Hope didn't plan to push riding the behemoth Everest coaster if she could avoid it. She hurt in places she'd forgotten about long ago, and needed soothing, not more hurtling here and there.

He donned his dinosaur trunks and matching shirt, she her new bikini and sarong, and off they went. She had nabbed a large, straw sun hat in one of the resort shops, and prepared to combat the sun, if she could. They arrived at the Beach Pool, not too busy that morning, slathered on sunscreen and dove in. It was good to have pure play time with her son – unfortunately, a rarity anymore – work the roller coaster kinks out, and relax. Soon, Noah was freely cavorting, pretending to be a porpoise such as those he'd spied at the resort's various water features.

After a poolside lunch, Hope settled onto a lounge chair with a paperback romance novel she'd found at the same resort shop. Give her a good mystery any day, but this time, not so much. She preferred to take a mental rest, too, and read something she could pick up or put down at will. It would be easier to keep an eye on her son than if she became engrossed in an intricate plot. That was, at least, how she rationalized her reading selection. Noah splashed nearby and made ample use of the various slides dumping kids of all ages into the water. She would read a bit more of her book, then join him, take a dip later.

She felt his eyes scrape over her, as an unwelcome chill crept up her spine. His hot gaze threatened to melt her steel core of resistance. How could she hold out?

How could she keep reading this stuff? She had only

made it through half of chapter three when, over the top of the paperback, she noticed not Noah, but a man's hairy legs restricting her view. How annoying, and he was partially obstructing the sun. She'd not ordered an umbrella drink, so who…?

Hope noted the page number, closed the book, and attempted to look up, but the brim of her hat all but blocked her view. She curled the edge upward, surprised at the tall, slender man in swim trunks standing before her.

He removed his shades and spoke before she had a chance to utter a word. "Fancy meeting you here."

She sat speechless, allowing a few moments to lapse, frantically searching her memory bank. He looked so familiar, but often seeing someone out of context, and in distinctly different attire, can jumble name recollection. She hated it when that happened.

He clarified. "Spencer Reeves. You saw my daughter Madison in Urgent Care."

Of course! "Oh, my gosh. I'm sorry I didn't recognize you right off. *And not in such nice trunks.* My lapse."

"No need to apologize. You certainly wouldn't expect to see me here. May I?" He gestured to Noah's adjacent lounge chair.

"Of course." Hope reached over, and dragged the beach towel out of the way. Spencer parked on the chair and gazed at her.

"So, is Madison here, also?" she asked.

He turned toward the pool and squinted. "Somewhere over there with a friend."

"An end-of-school trip with her friends?" *And where is your wife?*

"Right."

"How many parents does it take to ride herd on such a group?"

"Several. Another couple brought along their younger two kids. Their daughter and Madi are very close. And the two of them each dragged along another friend. It's quite a group." He paused, and apparently thought it necessary to explain, "Madi's mother couldn't make it, a business trip came up at the last minute."

Madi's mother… not 'my wife'…

"Sounds like she's very busy. I recall you said she was also away last week on business."

"Yeah. She's an executive with a tech company. Involves a lot of travel, often to the west coast. But a problem developed in Washington, and she had to go. Madi was pretty disappointed, but seems to have gotten over it. So, you're here alone?"

"Oh, no. My son Noah is out there frolicking. Can't get enough of the water. This is the second pool we've been to today. We're scouting all of them."

That invoked a chuckle, then another look as his eyes drifted to her hands. "And Noah's father?"

How easily you pry. "My ex-husband stayed home."

He paused, then said, "I didn't mean to—"

"—No problem."

He took a few moments to survey the pool, then turned back to her. "I bet you're enjoying the time off. Seemed like the Urgent Care department was fast paced, always busy."

"Most of the time, yeah. We don't loll-a-gaggle too much. So, how's Madison doing?"

"Great. You cured her."

"Oh, I doubt that. Her other lab hadn't returned before I left Thursday night. I'm sure it's back by now. I'll check when I get home."

"It's not that important, is it? She's so much better, maybe it doesn't matter."

"I'm glad to hear that, but I'd like to tie up the loose ends, and at least you'll know. And it may make some difference in how she's managed. Your wife called and I explained all that to her, also."

"Good. She asked for your number, but I didn't hear whether she'd called you."

"Yes. We had a good conversation. She made it clear that Madison would see her own pediatrician in follow up."

"I'm thinking she should change to an adult doctor, someone like you. I bet her middle-aged, male pediatrician won't care to manage her problem."

"Perhaps not."

"Can patients come back to you in Urgent Care... for regular visits?"

"No, we don't have that type of practice. But there are plenty of other good family medicine and internal medicine doctors who are accepting new patients. If you're interested, I can recommend someone."

With a fleeting frown, he nodded understanding.

Noah popped out of the water and ran toward his mother. Hope handed him his towel, and after he'd wiped his face, she introduced him to Spencer Reeves as a man she knew from the clinic. Noah squinted, cast a skeptical eye on Reeves, who smiled at the child, addressed him as 'young man,' and shook his hand.

Apparently surprised by the gesture, Noah sat on the end of Hope's chair, and looking serious, asked, "Are you a doctor?"

"No, I'm not."

Hope noticed Reeves didn't volunteer any further information, such as owning some sort of security business.

Noah wasn't done with his questions, either. "Do you have kids here?"

Spencer, apparently surprised at the six-year-old's frankness, answered, "Well, yes, I do. I have a girl who's here with some of her friends."

"How old is she?" Noah asked.

Spencer smiled. "Sixteen."

Noah nodded knowingly, and observed. "So, she's a teenager? That's old."

Spencer couldn't suppress a laugh, and clarified, "I'd say she thinks she's older than that, Noah."

That puzzled the kid for only a moment, then he concluded, "Well, too old to play with me."

"You're probably right about that."

Noah ignored Spencer then, and implored his mother about getting a snack. She agreed, and prepared to follow him to the snack bar a short walk around the pool.

As they stood, Spencer turned to Hope. "Where are you two staying... here?"

"Yes. We're right here."

He nodded. As he backed away, he said, "Well, maybe we'll see you around."

"Yes, maybe we will."

CHAPTER | 16

Thursday

The morning dawned cool and hazy, but by eleven a.m., the sun blazed. Hope sought shade and relief. Standing in long lines for rides had worn thin. Considering all options as they waited, she decided to cajole her son into an air-conditioned venue after lunch. There were plenty of interesting shows and performances to choose from. Surely, she would find something which would intrigue him, at least temporarily. Otherwise, she wasn't sure she would make it through the afternoon to Noah's satisfaction. Theme parks are so exhausting.

They still hadn't tackled the giant roller coaster, either, which was just as well. Noah hadn't pressed that morning, and she hadn't mentioned it. She doubted she could willingly strap herself in and undertake such a ride. As she and Noah made their way through the growing crowd and approached the next ride he'd chosen, an individual stepped into their path – a man in shorts, polo shirt, and billed hat, his eyes concealed by wrap-around shades.

No, really... again?

Hope stopped in her tracks, grabbing Noah's arm to prevent him from running into the ride line, and waited. In such an expansive resort, offering multiple venues to visit, how would this happen more than once? *Is he keeping track of us?* She pushed her paranoid thoughts aside, and smiled.

He greeted her. "Seems we have the same thoughts."

I don't know about that. "Seems so. Or, these are the most popular rides."

"That, too." He removed his shades, turned to Noah, "Keeping your mother in tow, my man?"

Noah squinted and cocked his head, "Huh?"

"Keeping your mother busy?"

"Yeah." Noah ignored Spencer Reeves then, and pulled Hope's hand. "Come on, Mom…"

"I won't keep you. You're in for a treat on that ride. Enjoy!"

"Oh, I'm sure we will. Where are you off to now?" she asked, wondering if they were destined to repeatedly run into each other.

"The Haunted Mansion." Before she could turn away, Spencer said, "Hey, would you all be up for a bite later on? There are some great cafés right around here."

Hope lowered her sunglasses, met his gaze. "Sure, why not? We could use a break soon… right, Noah?"

Her son cast a disparaging look at Reeves, and whined, "Mom… come on. There's more people. We'll miss the ride."

Reeves suggested, "Why don't we meet right here after you've had your ride?"

"Okay. We'll be here," Hope agreed.

Noah had broken free and secured them a place in line, lest they miss out on It's a Small World.

By the time they finished the ride, met up with Spencer and Madison, and made their way to a nearby café, the lunch crowd had thinned. They succeeded in nabbing a table at the edge of the sidewalk café and settled in, very much ready to relax and eat.

Noah, anxious to order his burger and fries and get on with it, seemed impatient with the adult chatter. Initially, Madison also appeared a bit ill at ease lunching with her doctor, but as soon as conversation unfolded, she relaxed and engaged. She explained that her absent friends – thoroughly exhausted by the Magic Kingdom and swimming for two days – had opted to sleep in that morning. Soon, she was chattering away about all they had done and what the upcoming summer had in store. She looked forward to finally getting her driver's license in July, hoped to find a summer job, and was ready to roll.

Despite his approving smile, Hope sensed Spencer was not looking forward to the associated parental challenges that teenage driving brought with it. And, no, there would not be a brand-new vehicle sitting in the driveway on her birthday. He made that clear.

Noah on the other hand, kept an eye on Spencer. Discussing driving held no interest for him, and he had little to say to the teenager until she mentioned Harry Potter movies, which immediately riveted his attention. After that, the two carried on as if they were long-lost friends, discussing this movie versus that, which character did what, who possessed the more important role, and so on. What was meant initially as a 'bite to eat' morphed into a two-hour lunch.

"So, what's left on your agenda for the week?" Spencer asked.

"I think we've covered most of what we wanted to see and do…. multiple times. I'd like to get Noah over to Animal Kingdom at least once before we leave." She added, "And I'd like to fit in a spa visit, but I doubt he'll go for that."

"And, when do you leave?"

"Saturday afternoon we fly home."

"So do we. Which airline?"

"American."

Spencer smiled. "5670?"

"How did you know?"

"It's the best time and connection."

"Right."

Spencer seemed lost in thought for a moment then looked at Madison and Noah, engaged in their Harry Potter discussion, and said, "Well, the two of them seem to get along. How about if she and her friends watch him so you can do that? I'll keep an eye on all of them."

Hope, surprised by his offer, waited to respond. Was he suggesting he'd babysit? She hardly knew this man; did not have a clue about his background. Her instincts told her he was to be trusted, but she'd never left Noah with a perfect stranger... well, he seemed not a stranger any longer and she had interacted with him and his daughter rather personally and he'd trusted her with Madison and... "Why not? That sounds great. It'll have to be tomorrow, though, if I can get an appointment."

"You check, and let me know." He took out a card, wrote his cell number on the back and handed it to her. "It would be fun to let him run us around."

She checked the number – 202, a D.C. area code – and glanced at the front of the card.

Select Security Solutions
Consultants for all business and private security needs
Experienced | Discrete | Available 24/7

Finished, she looked up and met his eyes.

He smiled and clarified, "That's right. I'm your SSS guy."

"So, I see. How intriguing. I'll call for that spa appointment and let you know." *And meanwhile, I may check into a few more things, as well.* "Ready, Noah?"

CHAPTER | 17

Saturday

They were cruising smoothly along at 30,000 feet, and all was well. The Reeves and assorted other friends occupied seats toward the back of the cabin. They had exchanged greetings and chatted at the gate before boarding, but she did not intend to venture to the back of the plane and continue the conversation during their trip. The flight was packed.

They could not go on like this. She knew she must leave or become mired down in his mess. Still the scent of his pure maleness when he stood close, when his muscular arm encircled her tiny waist, very nearly melted her core. She had never felt like this. She, a woman who prided herself on staying in control...

Oh, for God's sake. Who brags about a tiny waist anymore? Next, I'll be dreaming of bare, hairy legs standing in front of me. She stared out the tiny window. *Well, that did happen...*

Hope put aside her novel and gazed at her son. Noah in the window seat had dozed off, tired of his tablet and games. Leaning against the small pillow, his long eyelashes gracing his cheeks, his mouth in a full pout, his tousled chestnut hair – a characteristic he shared with his father – he looked so innocent resting against the wall of the cabin.

It had been a full week. They both needed to get home and rest. Despite the luxurious accommodations, she was anxious for her own bed and time tomorrow to lounge around. Next week, summer would officially launch.

Noah would head off to Summer Season, an eight-week all-day program he loved. To say he was excited was an understatement. It would be his second summer there, an opportunity to re-acquaint with kids from other schools, including his own. Their activities centered around the outdoors and nature, with all variety of field trips and plenty of time to burn off excess energy. Reading skills, and a few crafts, filled the hot hours of the day. And a token rest time. Electronic devices of all sorts were frowned upon, requiring parents to check them at the door each morning or take them home. No exceptions. That policy and the whole structure pleased Hope.

Hope's timeout for the spa appointment had been worth it. One can't beat a thorough massage, a facial, and a sauna, although after all that, one typically wishes to lie down right there and take a restorative nap. No such luck. She hadn't booked a slumber room, and had to wind her way back to the hotel whether ready or not. There she found Noah having a blast with Spencer and the girls, watching movies and enjoying whatever snacks they desired. It didn't look like he had missed her for a moment. It also looked like Spencer got a kick out of having a little six-year-old boy around for a change.

She stayed and chatted for a short while, then insisted Noah return with her to their room and prepare for their next-day departure. Despite his protests that packing would only take a few minutes, she put her foot down, and he acquiesced. That evening, she did not wish to dine with the Reeves, delightful as they were, but wanted to be alone with her son before their return home. Truthfully, she hoped to curb her swirling thoughts concerning the man who had entered her life less than two weeks before. The spa visit had allowed her sufficient time to entertain all sorts of notions regarding him – his background, his wife, his daughter, his intentions, and so forth. Had she had too much romance novel? Probably, and she wished to shut off that part of her brain.

But, before much longer they would descend onto the runway in Kansas City, and the vacation mentality would dribble away. Time to re-orient to reality – home, the clinic, Noah's summer program, Mark... the Magic Kingdom didn't exist in her reality.

———————

Hope opened the back door, disengaged the beeping security alarm, and dropped her suitcase right there in the laundry room. Noah trudged in behind her. She heard the hum of the air conditioner in the background. It was good to be home.

"Can we get a pizza, huh, Mom?"

"You know what? That sounds good. Let's do that. Why don't you take your backpack to your room, and we'll call in our order."

Off Noah scampered.

The suitcases could wait until tomorrow. Maybe they would just unpack them right there in the laundry room. Their clothes needed to be dumped in the washer, anyway. How much easier would that be?

Before Noah returned from his room, Hope went to the kitchen land line and called Mark. The obligatory check-in call after being gone with their son. Five rings, and no answer. She left a 'we're home' message and hung up, wondering how long it would take before she received a return call. Not that he was burdened at all about their return. She doubted that. Likely, he was busy with Brandi and wasn't concerned one bit, or he would have objected to them going in the first place. She knew he just wanted to keep track of her comings and goings, especially when Noah was involved. Likewise, she expected that of him.

"Mom, I want pepperoni," Noah yelled as he jumped down the stairs. "And extra cheese!"

"You got it, kiddo."

CHAPTER | 18

Monday

Kansas City

The first day back from a week-long vacation, and a Monday, was a double whammy. Hope stared at the rows of e-mails cluttering her inbox and turned away. Dozens waiting for her attention. She would deal with as many as she could that day, and the next, and the next until they were tamed. But more important was the line of patients waiting to be seen, for all manner of conditions, some due to excess celebrating over the Memorial Day weekend and the start of summer.

It never failed that the warm weather brought in numerous individuals with spider bites. Brown recluse spiders flourished in the area, and with the advent of Spring people rummaged through their garages and many suffered bites. Some big, most smaller. Tending to those wounds effectively, no matter the size, was essential in an urgent care practice.

After seeing no less than three people with such a condition, and a number of others suffering 'summer colds,' Hope returned to the doctors' office and dropped into her chair. Soon, Susan joined her, and they struck up their first conversation of the morning.

"Welcome back," Susan said, her voice tone reflecting a frown, though a smile decorated her face.

Surprised, Hope answered, "Thanks." She waited a moment, then asked, "How's it been?"

"Typical." The nurse practitioner paused, then added, "If you mean, how's the clinical work gone."

Hope swiveled her chair and turned toward the extender, who busied herself tapping away at her computer. "That's a loaded statement."

Susan finished her data entry and swiveled her own chair to engage with Hope. "True."

"So, what's happened?"

"Heather's gone. Kaput."

"What?"

"Yeah, just last Thursday. Here one minute seeing patients, gone the next. She disappeared right after lunch. Like she was raptured. They didn't even wait until the end of her shift. She left patients in exam rooms, one getting an IV, one waiting on X-ray results, just like that."

"What on earth?"

"I thought about texting you, but decided I wouldn't ruin the last few days of your vacation. What could you do from there?"

"Did she give a reason as she ran off?"

"They didn't allow her to engage in any conversation. Stood there while she cleaned out the few things she had here, escorted her to the back door, and took her ID card. She didn't run off."

"Figure of speech." Exasperated, Hope asked, "Okay, what's this all about?"

"From what I've heard – and one of the nurses called her – it was about her refusing to use virtual visits."

Hope's stomach flipped. She stared at Susan. Her protection plan hadn't amounted to much. But, in all fairness, she had not guaranteed them cover. She had made that clear almost three weeks ago when she and Susan spoke, when she had thought she had time to flesh out her strategy. Time to consider an appropriate approach for the department. But now, with this new development, she had better work out the nitty-gritty fast before anyone else got snatched.

Obviously, they had waited until she was off the unit, out of town, and in no way could impact this outcome. But, wait, did they actually know she was opposed to expanding virtual visits? Why would they care about her? No doubt, she wasn't their prime concern. She had only discussed her concerns with two colleagues, Chet Murdock and Rachel Baumann, other than the two nurse practitioners. Exactly. Would either of them take that information and 'tell on her'? It was a question she must now consider.

Her mind wandered momentarily to the conversation she and the RN had shared prior to her vacation. The nurse's concern about a 'spy in our midst.' So, it seemed it wasn't just paranoid fears; it was real. And was this first dismissal a not-so-veiled threat?

Susan's voice ran in the background as Hope attempted to corral wild thoughts. "Pardon? You were saying?"

"I said, I think it's pretty clear what we have to do from now on, whether we like it or not. And you can't protect us, Dr. Nichols. Not unless you're willing to be expelled along with the rest of us."

Hope didn't answer. What could she say? Offer some weak promise of protection? Tell them it wouldn't happen again? One question sprung to mind. "So, what did Dr. Murdock say when all this was happening?"

"He was off that day, too. But when he came back the next day and found out, he was upset, but then told the rest of us to just let it go. Don't rock the boat, or it may go badly for us."

Hope only answered with a nod. So, as she already realized, Murdock was just biding his time. Whether he reported to any of the higher ups or not, he would only serve as a weak ally, at best. Protecting his position as long as he could was his priority. That was clear and, to be fair, understandable.

She spun her chair, viewed the growing patient list on her screen, and said, "Well, enough discussion for now. We have to attend to these people's needs." Not waiting for Susan's response, she stood, disconnected her laptop from the power cord, and left the doctors' room. She had said enough, perhaps too much.

God forbid... were there listening devices planted everywhere?

'Short of breath, need inhaler refill.'

Hope read the next patient's chief complaint. A common concern which they frequently addressed. She noted the patient was a seventeen-year-old male with a history of asthma. She entered the room.

After greeting the young man, it was obvious he was foreign. She turned to the middle-aged woman with him, who immediately explained that young Sven was a Norwegian foreign exchange student who had resided with her family for that academic year. He had used an inhaler occasionally for such symptoms and just needed a refill. Sven took over the history and said his shortness of breath with exertion had worsened again. He added that recently headaches bothered him, too. Of interest, he was an elite soccer player and planned to remain in the U.S. through the summer, training for his college soccer career, and perhaps beyond. He would attend the University of Texas come fall and had big plans.

Hope asked a few other questions for clarification, then took a few moments to affirm what she had noted earlier. His blood pressure, as recorded on the chart, was too high for such a slender, fit-appearing young man – 160 / 90 was not what you would expect in such an individual. Asked about his personal history for hypertension and his family history for the same, he denied knowing anything about that; he'd never been told he had a problem. She took his blood pressure herself with the manual cuff, checked both arms, and confirmed it was elevated. She needed to perform another assessment, explained that to the pair, and excused herself from the room.

On her way through the hall, she met up with a staff nurse, requested a different blood pressure cuff, and returned to the exam room. In the meantime, Hope had asked the young man to remove his jeans, and prepare for the exam. She assessed Sven's femoral pulses, both diminished relative to his upper extremity pulses. Shortly, the nurse appeared bearing a large leg cuff. It was not a common practice in urgent care to assess leg blood pressures, and few of the nursing staff had ever performed the maneuver. Hope knew how, and it was the thing to do in this situation.

As she had suspected, his leg blood pressures were notably lower than his arm pressures – a distinct abnormality. This young man needed further work-up, not a simple refill of his inhaler. Of course, he could suffer from both asthma and the condition she suspected he'd had since birth. If true, how had it gone undiagnosed for so many years, especially at his level of elite athletic performance?

"This is not a normal situation you have."

The exchange mother frowned. "All he needs today is the inhaler."

"No, ma'am, I'm afraid it's not. We need to get a chest X-ray today, then possibly refer him to a specialist for more evaluation."

"What kind of specialist?"

"A cardiologist, at least."

"Oh." Staring at Hope, the woman fell silent. This was

obviously not what she had expected of the visit.

The young man's eyes widened. "Ja?"

Hope asked him, "Have you had a chest X-ray in the past, whether here or at home?"

"I do not remember."

"Have you seen an asthma doctor or a lung specialist in the past?"

"No. I have been only to our general doctor at home."

"Since you were a child?"

"Ja."

She nodded understanding and suggested, "Let's start with the chest X-ray. It's simple, won't take long. We'll meet again after that, and map out what you need."

"His parents, of course, are in Norway, if there's anything serious," the woman said.

"We'll cross that bridge when we get to it. Let's start with the simple."

She took her leave and informed the nurses of her orders. Thank goodness he had come in. An inhaler refill would have been a very simple request to accommodate through a telemedicine portal.

And the missed diagnosis could have proved fatal.

CHAPTER | 19

It didn't take long to confirm her suspicions. Young Sven's chest X-ray findings were consistent with a coarctation of the thoracic aorta, a congenital narrowing of the large main artery exiting the heart. His extended from below the arch of the aorta, which appeared abnormally dilated, six centimeters inferior, or downward, involving the descending aorta traveling through his chest. This condition did not just develop recently. Hope was well aware that congenital abnormalities such as this one could go undetected for years, but the fact that he was an elite athlete engaged in fast-paced soccer competition and had gone undiagnosed up to that time was astonishing. He definitely required further work up.

After delivering the startling news to Sven and his exchange mother, Hope put in a call to the outspoken cardiologist. She knew he would be very interested in the case, take the situation seriously, and likely work the young man in without delay. She also knew this young man was facing a major cardiothoracic procedure in the near future.

Would his parents demand he come home, or trust the American doctors to render care and fix their son? Likely the latter. After all, his Norwegian doctor had not assessed this child accurately, had not noticed blood pressures that high? Not that she was passing judgment on their healthcare system. Well, maybe a little.

After they recovered from the unexpected news, the pair both agreed to go directly upstairs to the cardiology suite to be seen that day. The cardiologist was fascinated and agreed no further delay was warranted. They would perform an ECG and echocardiogram right away, and plan further assessments from there. Send him on up!

Hope returned to her computer station. She would dictate his note later, which would take longer than most. She sat down, her heart pounding, her own body finally reacting to the near miss she had just confronted, realizing then how hungry she was after her long morning, which had morphed into early afternoon. It was nearly two o'clock.

After inhaling a small microwave meal and collecting herself, she returned to the doctors' office, determined to tell Chet Murdock about the case when he returned to work on Tuesday. Whether he agreed or not, it was time to pay a visit to the chief medical officer Dr. Rich Rutledge and outline her concerns. She didn't care anymore whether she annoyed senior staff physicians and those in administrative positions of power. Already within the month she had seen three or four individuals who were misdiagnosed or whose diagnoses would have been missed with a virtual visit. The potential consequences were too serious to ignore.

With no one else hanging around, she picked up the phone and dialed the number. A melodious voice answered, and discussed with her various scheduling challenges Dr. Rutledge faced. But as luck would have it, the day after tomorrow, Wednesday, he just happened to have a small opening late afternoon. Would that work? Yes, that would. Thank you very much. They set the date.

She had no sooner hung up – relieved to know when she would face her opponent – than she heard a voice nearby ask a nurse if Dr. Nichols was back from vacation.

Hope swiveled her chair, surprised to see who had come to pay a call.

"Hello, Dr. Nichols?" Extending her hand and a big smile, the woman said, "I'm Kalisha Johnson, Dr. Rutledge's administrative assistant. I thought I'd drop by and introduce myself. Is this a good time?"

CHAPTER | 20

Wednesday

Hope waited outside Dr. Rutledge's fourth floor office in the Internal Medicine wing. His nurse Darlene had parked her in a comfortable armchair where she could keep an eye on her. He was done seeing patients for the day, freeing Darlene to sit at her nursing station and return calls, enter messages into the electronic record, and monitor the unit's goin's on. Hope speculated his nurse was very good at her various duties, including keeping track of people and things. In her free moments, Hope focused her attention on her phone and scanned through messages and various emails she had ignored all day. How quickly they pile up. She required no further preparation for this meeting, knowing exactly what she was going to say. She had honed her pitch and, in one or two sentences each, knew how to grab his attention with the four illustrative cases she had amassed.

For his part, Dr. Chet Murdock had expressed notable interest in the young Norwegian's case, fascinated with his history and presentation, and her clinical acumen. He had not, however, exactly put his blessing on this meeting, but had agreed she probably should bring these situations to Dr. Rutledge's attention. What could it hurt? he had posed. Well, maybe a lot if she became a target of the CMO's annoyance, or if her colleague Chet was throwing her under the bus. Her stomach let loose a cloud of fluttering butterflies. She took a swig of water from the handy bottle Darlene had offered, hoping to wash them away. There was no reason to be nervous, was there?

Within moments, Rutledge's door swung open. He stood in the opening, a smile plastered on his face. "Come in, Dr. Nichols, come in."

She stood, gripped the water bottle, pocketed her cell, and forced her own smile. It would accomplish nothing to start with a frown. "Thanks."

No sooner had she entered than she realized they were not alone. No, this would be a threesome. Sitting opposite Dr. Rutledge's desk, and also smiling, was the ever-present Kalisha Johnson, administrative assistant extraordinaire. Before taking a seat, Hope extended her hand, greeting the other woman, then took the remaining chair in front of Rutledge's desk. Perching on his high-back leather desk chair, he quickly minimized the screen he'd been viewing and turned to the two ladies.

"Dr. Nichols requested this meeting today," he began, as if Kalisha had no clue Hope was coming in.

She nodded understanding, and said, "Yes. Dr. Nichols and I met just yesterday. We had a very pleasant conversation." To Hope, she added, "I was very impressed with how busy Urgent Care is, and how efficiently you operate there. I appreciate you making time in your crowded day."

"You're welcome. I enjoyed our brief chat." In fact, it had been just that. A few words here and there, circling around important issues and each other, but never conveying their true thoughts. Feeling each other out: *Just who is this woman I may have to tangle with?*

No way was she going to bring up the fired nurse practitioner. Very bad idea. That topic was to be avoided.

"So, Dr. Nichols, why don't you start with your

concerns?" he suggested.

"All right." Hope, dividing her attention between Rutledge and Kalisha, said, "Over the past three weeks I have personally seen four patients in Urgent Care with serious conditions. Three of them had had virtual visits before presenting to our division in person. Their diagnoses had either been missed or could not have been accurately assessed using computer screens."

She paused and took note. Rutledge maintained an impassive expression. Kalisha displayed a concerned frown, her head cocked as if to invite – *Tell me more.*

"What types of cases?" Rutledge asked.

"A lung mass in a man with a persistent cough. A young woman with an amelanotic melanoma on the back of her knee. A teenage girl with a ruptured ovarian cyst and PCOS, and a young Norwegian exchange student this past Monday with a thoracic coarctation who requested an inhaler for worsening dyspnea."

Dropping his bland expression and appearing startled, he asked, "You see that type of thing in Urgent Care?"

"Matter of fact, we do, although I admit several of the cases surprised even us. Particularly the young Norwegian elite soccer player."

"I thought most of what you saw were coughs and colds."

"That, too," Hope answered. She went on, "I attended our quarterly meeting two weeks ago—"

"—Good turnout, I thought."

Kalisha smiled her approval.

"Yes. And interesting." Hope continued, "My question is... how are you and the board addressing the medical staff's concern over expanding virtual visits? The cases I just spoke of could not, and should not, have been handled adequately or safely via a computer screen. Several of them had already wasted time and paid good money using virtual visits, and were not better off for it. I believe it's a safety issue. Perhaps a liability issue, as well."

That last comment, especially the term *liability*, drew a knitted brow from Rutledge and a sour expression from Kalisha.

"Well, I believe, Dr. Nichols, that we should not generalize a few cases to the vast majority of patients who report good experiences with those visits. The few do not reflect the whole. I'm sure you understand that."

"Of course."

"Further, this is a technology which isn't new, has gone through sufficient development and vetting to be considered safe. It's an efficient way to conduct many visits, has increased productivity for most clinics using it, and brings in younger patients who frankly won't make time for in-person appointments. If we don't use it, we risk missing out on an entire segment of the population."

"I understand those concepts very well. But, it minimizes or eliminates the in-person interactions with patients and the opportunity for an examination, even a focused exam, which may reveal other serious conditions the patient doesn't even realize they have. Every condition can't wait for a scheduled annual exam." A good internist couldn't deny she had a point.

He frowned and shifted in his chair.

Hope went on, "As I listened to the discussion the other night, I got the impression not everyone was jumping on board with telehealth expansion. And I agree with them."

"What exactly do you suggest?"

"That we suspend the use of the technology until we can gather more data regarding usage and the number of cases such as I just mentioned, which would have been inappropriate for virtual visits. Get our own numbers nailed down. Also, review again the data from across the country regarding good and bad outcomes. I think we need a realistic perspective on how and when to use it." She paused.

Kalisha furiously tapped her tablet. Rich steepled his fingers, squinted at Hope over his reading glasses, and rocked his chair. Both said nothing.

You could have cut through the tension with a dull spatula.

Finally, he spoke. "And what do you think is an appropriate period of suspension?"

"I would say that's yet to be determined, based on what we find."

He sprung forward, leaned his arms on his desk, and gave her a direct look. "That won't work."

A deafening silence descended. During the tense interval, Darlene eased open the door, shot Rutledge a look, and suffered the consequences. "Not now, Darlene," he snapped. She needed no further chastisement and eased the door closed.

"I believe it could, and we could expedite that process if we formed a dedicated team—"

Obviously more than annoyed, he interrupted, "We don't need any damn team messing around. The technology is in place, we have come online with it, and will not set it aside until further notice. It's no good thinking otherwise."

Kalisha sat mute, had done so throughout the discussion, and not once had Rich looked at her nor asked her opinion. That was probably a good thing. Hope didn't think she could tolerate an administrative assistant weighing in on clinical matters.

Hope said, "I am sorry to hear that, and I believe others will be, as well."

"So, have you rallied others to join forces with you? Is that why you made this appointment?" His voice held an edge.

"No—"

"—Look, Dr. Nichols, this is the deal. Telemedicine is here to stay, and we will put it to good use. We are not turning back. And I would suggest that you stop resisting and get in line. If that is unacceptable to you, then there is always another option. You may resign. Or you may be relieved of your duties."

"Despite doing the right thing for patients—"

"Despite your good care of patients, yes. We aren't neglecting patients, and I resent you suggesting so. You've strayed too close to the line, Hope. Don't bring that charge, or there may be serious consequences." He rested back in his chair, his speech complete.

Hope divided a look between Rutledge and Kalisha, who didn't restrain her smirk. She stood. "You've made your position clear, Rich." A few steps took her to the door. Gripping the handle, she added, "Thank you for your time."

There came no answer from behind her. With that, she left, pulled the door closed, and walked past Darlene. The woman glanced up, gave her a sympathetic look, and heaved a sigh. Hope knew she had put up with him and his arrogance for a long time... *how can she stand it?*

Suddenly, a wave of exhaustion washed over her. She must make it down from the fourth floor to the ground level, despite her wobbly knees, where she'd gather her things and hurry to pick up her son. Away from the clinic, in the safety of home, she could think.... later, after settling Noah for the night.

CHAPTER | 21

Thursday

Thankfully, Noah behaved that evening, entertaining himself with reading and a bit of TV. She didn't think she could handle any rambunctiousness from her six-year-old. Perhaps he had sensed she needed peace and quiet? Whatever the reason, she was relieved.

Otherwise, the night brought her no peace. Tossing and turning, despite trying to distract herself prior to bed, had completely disrupted her sleep. It seemed she had not slept at all, drifting in and out, not dreaming of anything. She arose in the morning, still wired, dreading going to work and the long day ahead. Clearly, she had backed herself into a corner.

After dropping Noah off at Summer Season, and wishing him a great day, she took her usual route to the clinic, maneuvering along on autopilot. When she pulled into a parking space, she realized she could not recount a single traffic detail during her drive. She prided herself on being observant, aware of her surroundings. Well, almost always. This situation had morphed into a definite problem. More than a problem, it had taken over her thinking, and she could not deny it.

As she stepped from her car and locked the door, her thoughts pestered her. She had thoroughly analyzed her position, admittedly overanalyzed it. If she resigned over this issue, that action would invoke her restrictive covenant. A contractual, legal constraint on where she could practice, no matter that she worked urgent care and could not take a cabal of patients with her. Which made no sense no matter how you looked at it. Hers was an arbitrary fifty-mile radius prohibiting her from joining another clinic or free-standing urgent care practice. If she did, she would owe South Metro twenty-five thousand dollars and twenty percent of her productivity for the next two years. Onerous, to say the least. Obviously, it amounted to a significant financial hit. And a significant distance restriction.

She also knew that the state's highest court had already weighed in on just such a case, and held that the contract remained valid; that clause could not be rescinded. Her own situation did not differ from the index case… except the practice type. Urgent Care. She doubted any court would grant leniency on that particularity. And besides, litigation to test the waters would be a very expensive venture, one she must avoid.

She entered the back hall of the clinic, removed a fresh lab coat bearing her embroidered name, and proceeded to her computer station. No one else was there, apparently all busy seeing patients. As she sat down, another unwelcome thought intruded, again. There was the issue of Mark and their custody arrangement. He had already made his position clear. 'Don't do anything to screw up your job situation.' She needed to get her priorities straight. Ignoring or minimizing certain aspects of this and plowing ahead could lead to a very bad outcome.

Maybe it was time to acquiesce, do the best she could in the circumstances, wait and watch.

She pulled up the list of patients checked in, noted all of them were covered, and decided to review her fresh emails. She heard a rustle behind her, then a voice said, "Good morning, Dr. Nichols, have a few minutes?"

Kalisha Johnson had come to call.

"A few." *Forget emails.* Hope stood, laptop in hand, signaling to the woman that this would not be a long talk. "And good morning to you. What's on your mind, Ms. Johnson?"

"I want to follow up our meeting with Dr. Rutledge yesterday."

Our meeting? We are not a team. Hope didn't answer, waited for Kalisha to articulate the specifics of the follow up to which she referred.

"Your impressions, any further thoughts you have?"

"Oh, I've had thoughts, most of which I expressed at the time. But right now, I need to shelve all that and go see patients. Is there something more you've considered since then?"

Kalisha struck a casual pose and smiled. "I thought Dr. Rutledge, bless his heart, sounded a bit gruff. He is so impassioned about telehealth, he has a hard time restraining himself or listening to other opinions."

Hope said, "Discussing other perspectives, experiences, and opinions usually leads to a better conclusion, I believe."

"Of course, you make a good point. I'm sure you're well aware he is tasked with leading the medical staff with innovations and addressing productivity issues, particularly ensuring the third-party payers cooperate as they have contracted to do."

"Of course."

"Within the last six months, the federal agencies – HHS and CMS – have approved the expanded use of telehealth and have agreed to pay well for those services. The diagnostic codes now cover it, and those codes have been loaded into systems across the country."

"I'm well aware."

"Everyone is coming on board, and patients are certainly enthusiastic."

So if everyone says jump off the cliff… "I'm aware."

"So, we would like you to keep an open mind, increase your use of virtual visits, especially here in Urgent Care, and give us your opinion on its effectiveness. We value your input."

Uh, huh. "I believe I gave you my opinion based on seeing patients who required much more than a virtual visit. And I suspect there are many more out there who are being missed. Diagnoses, that is."

Her cell vibrated in her lab coat pocket. Hope took a moment to check – hopefully not an issue with Noah. She saw the 202-area code of a number she recalled: Spencer Reeves'. Choosing not to answer at that moment, she would wait for his voice message.

Kalisha watched her, and asked, "A call from home?"

"No. A patient's father."

Showing surprise, Kalisha said, "So, you receive cell phone calls from patients' families?"

"Sometimes, yes." Hope pocketed her cell and walked to the door of the doctors' office. "Now, if you'll excuse me, I have to get busy."

She had not turned into the hall before Kalisha added, "You might want to reconsider your position. You're a good doctor. I would hate for it to go badly for you."

CHAPTER | 22

What does he want? The question would not leave her. Nor did Kalisha's words of warning.

She labored to contain her thoughts and attend to her patients' needs as the morning wore on. She succeeded most of the time, but between patients, she couldn't keep her mind from wandering. It was no good. Kalisha's comments could wait until later, but she'd have to take a break and return Reeves' call. Maybe Madison had developed a problem.

Hope ducked into the back hall where she would not be overheard. At least not the entirety of the conversation, if someone happened to walk by. She dialed his number.

"Hi, Dr. Nichols," he answered.

"Hello. I saw that you called but couldn't pick up right then. Is everything all right?"

"Oh, yeah, we're fine."

"Good. I thought maybe Madison had developed symptoms again."

"No, she's good, but she would like a referral to a woman doctor for further care."

"I can do that." Hope paused, waited.

"So, if you can take a break, I would like to bring some lunch by. If you not too busy…"

She took only a moment. "I should be able to do that."

"How about Subway? Any choice?"

"Turkey and all the fixin's sounds good. And don't forget the chips. I'll have drinks."

"Will do. Be there in about an hour."

"I'll be here."

"See you then."

As the time grew near, she texted Spencer with instructions. He was to let her know by text when he had arrived, and she would come to the secured back entrance to admit him. Better than him trying to explain to the front desk clerks why he was there, carrying a bag of food only for Dr. Nichols. He certainly didn't resemble a drug rep bringing in lunch for everyone. It was no use parading him past the receptionists – the gatekeepers – who often remembered individuals who had recently been seen. Their facial recognition skills were impressive.

She had just finished a dictation when her phone vibrated signaling his arrival. After admitting him to the back hall, she gestured for him to follow. The small, vacant office in the hall seemed the best place to meet and lunch with him, in the same room just three weeks before where Susan had alerted her to the extenders' fears of reprisals. It was a given, she couldn't very well park him in the doctors' office where he might hear privileged information and her colleagues would wonder, or in the kitchen where a parade of staff could scrutinize him and eavesdrop.

They pulled chairs up to the desk, and spread their lunch bags over the surface. She had brought two bottles of water with her, and began with, "So, this is a surprise."

"I hope a nice one."

"Lunch is always a welcome treat. Many times we go without."

"That's not surprising." He swallowed a bite, and said, "Things going well since your vacation?"

"Fairly so."

"Your son, if I may say, is a charming young man."

She smiled. "But he's still a little boy in my book."

Spencer smiled in return.

"So, how's Madison since getting back home? She seemed to not be bothered at all while you were in Orlando." Hope paused then added, "I did receive her additional lab results this week."

"Great. No more pain right now. But as you said, it will probably come and go. Were they normal?"

"The hormone levels we got support the diagnosis of PCOS. I think we can treat her effectively."

"As I said, we would appreciate your referral."

"Family Medicine or Ob-Gyn?"

He stared at her for a moment. "Family Medicine would be great. Cover all the bases. Actually, I don't know which her mother would prefer; I'll ask."

"Is she traveling again this week?"

"A few days, but she returned last night. I'll talk with her and get back to you."

"That's fine."

He waited a few moments, then observed, "You seem a little off today. Tired?"

This man is too observant. "You could say. I didn't sleep well last night at all."

"May I ask why?"

She examined his face and saw no humor, no smirk, detected no guile. *But you will pry, whether I say yes or no.* "You may. I tossed and turned, and I'll tell you why."

"Shoot."

"You mentioned it yourself several weeks ago when you were here with Madison, and I believe we may be on the same page about this. It's the telemedicine thing here at the clinic."

"And elsewhere."

"And elsewhere, yes. I confess I'm opposed to

expanding its use. Honestly, to its use at all. That's not a popular position, and I've been told to get in line or else."

"By whom?"

"The powers that be here at the clinic. Well, at least a few key individuals in decision-making positions."

"What about your associates here in Urgent Care?"

"The head of our department is plus/minus about using it. He doesn't want to rock the boat, not at this point in his career. Others have tried it, but also have to see patients who present – that keeps us plenty busy – and don't often volunteer to man the computer for a day of virtual visits. At least from what I've observed."

He nodded, and she went on. "In fact, one upsetting issue is that while I was gone, one of the nurse practitioners who followed my lead got fired. Suddenly, one day, kaput, gone. Of course, I found out when I returned on Monday." She paused, focused on eating her sandwich and chips, and watched his response.

Spencer nodded, ate his own food, and seemed deep in thought. "Just the one?"

"Yeah, so far. The other advanced practice nurse expressed some fear when she told me about it. Apparently, I hadn't adequately thought through my offer to give them cover before I left town. They're scared, don't want to be sacrificial lambs and lose their jobs, and I don't blame them. They've been hushed.

"And on top of that, after seeing another patient with a very serious condition, and who might have been harmed by a virtual visit, I made an appointment with our Chief Medical Officer to discuss the situation. He dismissed my concerns, especially the patient cases I mentioned, and basically threatened me with termination if I resisted any longer. His message was clear."

"Has he done anything else?"

"Not yet, that I know of." She chewed a bite, swallowed, and clarified, "Well, he sent in his spy this morning."

"Spy?"

"His administrative assistant, who trails him around, comes in and out and talks with the nurses while she's observing us work. The nurses have complained to me about the situation. They're very uncomfortable with her visits."

"Him who?"

"Dr. Rich Rutledge is the CMO. He's held the position for about a year now, and loves it. That's obvious."

"So, what did this administrative assistant do this morning?"

This feels like an interrogation. "Greeted me, chatted me up, expressed concern about my meeting Wednesday with Rutledge, and asked me to reconsider my position and cooperate. I said I had been clear, and she followed that with a threat."

"How so?"

"She said I was a good doctor, and she would hate to, quote, see it go badly for me, unquote."

"Hum."

Hope resumed eating. She had done too much talking already, and her lunch break would end too soon. She didn't want to go hungry the rest of the afternoon. "I need to finish up and get back out there."

"Right." He rearranged his sandwich, seemed very deliberate when he asked his next question. "Would you like me to check around a bit?"

She stared at him. "Check around? What do you mean?"

"Nothing too intrusive. I have some connections."

Connections? Hope said nothing right away. At once, a burst of excitement whirred within her, and a deep visceral pull nagged her center. *Who is this man, anyway?*

"I have to get back to work."

CHAPTER | 23

Friday

Yes, he had connections... at home and from his previous life. Spencer Reeves couldn't contain his excitement, being back in the active snooping business. He knew exactly who he would call, before he and Jacqueline had their little chat. It was clear Hope Nichols had a problem, one which likely ran deeper and had developed more side channels than she could imagine. It smelled.

It was a slow Friday at **Select Security Systems**. One associate out of the six he employed busied herself in her private office, and said she'd be gone within the half-hour. All others were out and about, working the clients and cases their group had accumulated. They'd be occupied elsewhere all day, all weekend. And their middle-aged receptionist Phyllis usually took Friday afternoons off, which was fair. The sturdy, dependable woman put in twelve-hour days during the week without complaining, and often fielded his calls when he was out of town. He relied heavily on her, and she deserved a break most weeks. He'd be alone after that.

He dialed a familiar number, got the curt voice greeting he expected, and left only a, 'call me when you can,' message. That done, Spencer turned his attention to the few pieces of untended paper lying on his desk, and the glut of emails he needed to prune. It wouldn't be long before he heard back.

Thirty minutes later, the call came.

"Hey, thanks for calling back. This line good?"

"As always. What's up?"

Jacob Nelson never wasted time on small talk, always got right down to business. He didn't want to know your personal problems, what your family was doing, or where you'd been recently – unless it pertained to your reason for calling. This time some of what Spencer was going to tell him had seeped into those arenas.

"I have a question."

Jake didn't respond, his usual way of signaling you to go on.

"I've met an individual recently with a problem."

"Who doesn't have problems?"

"Just listen. A doctor who saw my daughter at her urgent care clinic. I ran into her several times after that at W-D-W where we both vacationed."

Jake jumped in. "How convenient. This a head or a heart matter?"

"Hold on. Steady there." Spencer took a sip of cold coffee and went on, "This week, I saw her again at the clinic – *not going to admit I invited myself and took her lunch* – and became aware of a situation which seems out of whack. It has to do with high tech, telehealth, and a threat she's received."

"Go on."

"Seems she's resistant to the use of telemedicine for all the right clinical reasons, which puts her in opposition to the higher-ups there who are hell-bent on expanding its use. They've basically told her to get on board or things might go south."

"So, you're seeing a lady doctor, now?"

"No, Jacob, I'm not seeing a lady doctor. I'm married,

remember."

"Seeing, as in 'going to' for medical care."

"No, I'm not doing that either."

"So, what might go badly, and why are you telling me all this?"

"I'd like us to check into what's going on behind this initiative. Is there something driving these administrators to insist that everyone use telemedicine, and to threaten their colleagues if they don't comply? She said not all the docs have embraced the technology, so their administration might have a hard time herding cats, so to speak."

"Us?"

"You and me, and maybe Skipper G, if we need him."

"By 'something driving these individuals,' do you mean kickbacks, fraud, that sort of thing?"

"That and maybe other incentives."

Jake didn't answer right away. Spencer knew to wait; the man was thinking, considering the task, and would give him a measured opinion. Spencer fiddled with papers while his buddy contemplated. What would he do if his friend and former colleague at the Bureau said no? Go it alone, without the resources Jake could supply?

Finally, Jake spoke up. "From what you've said, it sounds like it may extend beyond the four walls."

"That's exactly what concerns me."

"Okay, Spence, I'll agree to this… if you give me some names, I'll dig around, see what if any connections there are, general stuff, and get back to you. If we see troublesome ties, then we'll have to decide if there's anything we can or want to do."

"Sounds fair."

"Now, get me as many names as you can."

"Got it. I have one for starters."

Spencer relayed Rich Rutledge's name and after a few other pleasantries, Jake hung up.

Spencer leaned back in his chair. *Now, how am I going*

to squeeze names out of Hope Nichols without revealing what I'm up to?

Second question: How was he going to squeeze his wife for information about her tech company and their role in telehealth development? They were in it up to their necks, had been for five years. But did it go beyond mere software creation?

It looked like he might be sleeping with the devil. An asset or a liability?

The hum of the garage door rising caught his attention. He stepped to the kitchen window and watched Jacqueline's car pull into the garage. She was home and the weekend spread before them. When to have their little chat had occupied his thoughts all afternoon. And he'd arrived home early to get prepared. He would offer her a drink... yes, maybe that would help. It was Friday, after all – TGIF.

Spencer entered their large walk-in pantry and pretended to shelve things. She'd think nothing of him having run to the store for a few last-minute items. He could emerge, acting surprised and pleased at her homecoming. She had endured more travel than usual the past three weeks. Regrettably, they had barely crossed paths. As a result, there had been little physical contact between the two of them, even when she had been around, but he couldn't say he'd missed it.

He heard her step into the kitchen, her heels clicking on the hardwoods, her large shoulder bag hitting the countertop, and a cabinet door shutting. Maybe she was ready to hit the bottle? Wearing a smile, he stepped out of the pantry closet. "Hi, Hon. You're home a little early."

Jacqueline checked her oversized wristwatch and said, "Not really, for a Friday." She stepped to him, gave him a peck on the cheek, and turned around. "Your day go well?"

"Can't complain. A little slow right now."

"Oh?"

"Well, I mean everyone is busy with established clients, and Fridays are Fridays around there."

He knew that bugged her if his security business slowed, or if he even used the term 'slow.' Lack of productivity and/or new clients spelled a dollar downturn for them which grated on her no end. She hadn't been altogether thrilled when he'd left the Bureau and started his private security business, and had argued she carried all the financial weight in their household. Admittedly, as a senior executive in a tech company she did make great money, which had afforded him the freedom to step away. He was well aware of the disparity between them.

"Do you still give that woman the day off?"

"That woman. Do you mean Phyll?"

She threw him a look. "Of course, I'm referring to Phyllis. Does she still take Fridays off?"

"From time to time. Jacque, the woman puts in twelve-hour days all week, and covers the phone remotely. And she keeps coming back for more. She earns her days off. End of comment."

Jacqueline gave up the fight and pivoted. "So, how's Madi? Is she here?"

"No, she off at a friend's. They're having a swimming party this evening."

"Which friend? Are the parents going to be home?"

"Brin's, and yes, they're home tonight. I checked."

As she dug through her enormous leather bag, she added, "And no cruising around, I hope."

So, you've suddenly turned into the helicopter Mom? "I didn't check on plans for cruising."

She looked up, apparently thought better of asking him to get on that, and said, "So plans for the weekend?"

"How about cocktails for starters?"

A small smile appeared. "Sure, why not? I want to go

change first, and I'll have my usual if you're tending bar."

"Nothing would make me happier."

Fifteen minutes later, drinks in hand, they settled onto cushy patio chairs on their large deck. Northeast facing, they were shaded from the late afternoon summer sun. A breeze helped cool the air.

Spencer stared at the wooded ravine behind their home, which added distance and privacy between them and the neighboring lots, and which lent a natural, even rugged, flare to their property. That feature appealed to him when they bought the place five years before. With the trees leafed out, he could see nothing of the neighbors' doings, nor them his. In fact, that had sold him on the property. And a bonus – Jacqueline loved the house. Although now she treated it as a convenient stopover between trips. The bonus about that – she was not sitting at home dreaming up remodeling projects ad nauseum. He counted that in the plus column.

He took a sip of whiskey and asked, "So, tell me, how was your week?"

"Hectic."

"What's new? You're always busy."

"More than that. When we get one challenge under control, it seems another pops up."

"Kind of like stomping cockroaches?"

She threw him a sour look. "What?"

"Poor choice of words. Sorry."

"You're forgiven."

"So, I thought you were feeling very bullish about how it had gone. That there was intense interest in the technology, and you could see a huge emerging market."

"That's true, but as usually goes, challenges declare themselves after the technology is adopted on a wider scale."

"The trip to D.C. last week?"

"That's part of it. Working with HHS and CMS can be a pain. The bureaucrats can't do a damn thing without asking five other people, numerous departments, or whole agencies for permission. Or maybe even Congress. No one, and I mean no one, thinks for themselves. It's a requirement for getting, and holding, their jobs, I guess."

"Hum…" He sipped and listened. *Best to just let her roll once she starts talking.*

"The other part has to do with glitches within the program itself. How it stores data, how one retrieves that data, how the billing process is integrated, all that."

"Storing data… does it store the virtual interactions, the videos of patients and doctors during the visits?"

"Sure. How else could they verify the visit and bill properly for it?"

"So, what happens with those videos?" *No wonder Hope Nichols is opposed to this.*

"That's what we're dealing with. There's encryption, but we've got to work out some kinks in the system. It doesn't always function right once installed in various clinics."

"And you were comfortable having Madison see someone that way last month?"

"Yes, I was, at the time."

"And now?"

"We're working out the kinks."

They both fell silent and sipped.

Spencer spoke first. "Speaking of Madi, I can get a referral to an adult doctor for her."

"From that woman doctor you saw?"

"Yeah, we saw. I told her I'd let her know which way we want to go after I spoke with you. Either family medicine or gynecology."

"I'm home all next week. I can give her a call. But, I'm thinking gynecology is probably the best route. I'll see if mine can get her in." She glanced at him, gave him a little smile. "You may not need to call your new friend."

But I need to get names from her, somehow. He ignored her snide comment. "Sounds good. But if you run out of time…"

"I'll make time."

"Hungry?"

"In a bit. Where do you want to go? Maybe we should just get takeout tonight."

"Anywhere you'd like."

CHAPTER | 24

Saturday

The washing machine whirred in the background, completing its last spin cycle. Hope had gotten up early, ready to attack the laundry and make fast work of it. She had a full day ahead, which included prepping Noah to go to his father's the next day.

Since they had returned from vacation, Noah had spent no time at Mark's. He was overdue, and starting the next day, would stay the whole week with his father. Until next Saturday evening. Mark had made it clear weeks before that this would be the only 'opening' he had the rest of the month, or during the next month, for that matter. A big trial in Chicago the following week dominated his schedule; he and his team might be gone for several weeks. He made sure she knew he had scrambled to prepare so he could have his son for the upcoming week, reminding Hope every time they spoke of his intense schedule. She was clear on that.

Noah and a little buddy ran down the hall, through the kitchen, and off to the back deck, toting their Bey Blades. That would keep them entertained for a while. After that, the neighborhood swimming pool beckoned, then errands. Take-out for supper sounded like a real good idea.

Spencer sipped fresh coffee and glanced at his tablet, catching up on email clutter, and surveying for important messages he had received. He knew Jacob would call from his personal cell, not use email, if he had anything to say. His own task for the day, or the weekend, was to get more names out of Hope. There would be an opportunity when Jacque left for errands and long-delayed shopping she had mentioned last night. After that, he wasn't sure what she had in mind for the evening. But it would not include him riding his cell with another woman.

His wife entered the kitchen wearing her usual work-out clothes, obviously ready for an active day. She poured a cup of coffee and regarded him from across the room. "Sleep well?"

"I did. How about you?"

"I just died when I hit the pillow."

"I noticed." He felt her eyes, glanced up, and noted her annoyed look.

She apparently dismissed her irritation and joined him at the table. "Madi's not up?"

"No, sleeping in. Too much swim party last night, I guess."

"Busy with business today?" Jacque asked.

"Just getting rid of a bunch of emails." He set aside his tablet. "Nothing pressing. Are you going for a run?"

"Thought I would, while it's decent outside. Then I'll do the errands. You've already been?"

"Yeah, got mine in early." He sipped, regarded his wife, and said, "When you get back, there are a few things we need to go over."

"Oh? Why not now?"

"It may take a little while, and it'll keep. You need to get your run in; it's not getting any cooler."

She threw him a skeptical look, got up and searched their pantry for a protein bar. "When I finish this, I'll be on my way. You've piqued my interest. Do I need to prepare?"

"No, you can come as you are."

When her cell buzzed, Hope glanced at the screen, surprised at the number she saw. What was Spencer Reeves doing texting her on a Saturday? She slammed the dryer door closed, chose the settings, and hit start.

Still standing in the laundry room, she swiped the screen and saw the brief message. 'Need more names. The admin assist you mentioned, your UC partner, and other higher ups you spoke to.' She stepped into the hall, wanting more time to think, questioning how far she should go with this. Was it wise to give this man names, so he and whoever could dig around, looking into her colleagues? Maybe even her. What about Mark? What about their privacy rights? Was she breaking some law doing this? Hope went to the kitchen, poured a cup of coffee and sat down at her eating bar. Maybe she could use a splash of something stronger.

In the background, Noah and his friend shrieked every time either of them scored big with their Bey Blades. Good. They were occupied and would stay so for at least a while. She had better think fast.

Would she answer, or wait until Monday to respond? She saw that he was already entering another message and waited to read that one. 'Need them today if you can.'

That answered that. She must tell him something. Either, no, I am not giving you more names, or here they are… have at it.

After finishing her coffee and contemplation, she knew what she would do. Kalisha Johnson was up to something, had scoped out her department multiple times, had leveled what amounted to a threat, and really deserved no protection from her. It was a given Rutledge was out to get her, or so it seemed. *Where do these paranoid thoughts come from?* Besides, Spencer already had his name. That was done. Chet Murdock and Rachel Baumann were a different matter, yet both of them had advised her to let it go. Why? Maybe Spencer and 'his connections' could get an answer to that. She hesitated no longer, tapped in the three other names, and hit send. It was done.

She got up and tossed her coffee remains. What had she just unleashed? On second thought, maybe they *should* talk before Monday.

Spencer glanced at his screen again. There was the message from Hope. Three names – two doctors, one administrative assistant. Hope had said nothing previously about the other two physicians. Perhaps scrounging through their backgrounds would produce nothing of interest. On the other hand, one could never predict. He sent a 'call me' text to Jacob, as he heard Jacqueline enter the back door.

He looked up and smiled. "Good run?"

"Yeah." She shed her running shoes, and said, "I'd like to shower and change before we talk. Will that work?"

"No problem." *It will give me time to speak with my co-conspirator.* "Take your time."

Off she went. Within moments he heard the shower. And it wasn't five minutes before his cell buzzed with the return call.

"Hey."

Jake returned the greeting.

"So, I got more names. Two doctors, one administrative assistant who works for Dr. Rutledge."

"Okay. Give 'em to me."

Spencer finished handing over the names, relayed what

Hope had told him of Kalisha Johnson, and pled honest ignorance of the other two. They finished conversing, and Jake promised to call by Sunday evening with anything he'd latched onto in the meantime. Spencer knew his word was good.

From behind him, as he waited on their screened porch, came Madi's voice. "Dr. Hope told you what? She wasn't talking about me, was she?" She entered the porch, flopped down on a lounge chair, her cell and a glass of orange juice in hand.

Spencer pivoted, shocked his daughter had overheard anything. Shocked she was up at all. *Don't teenagers sleep 'til noon?* "You're up earlier than expected."

Madison shrugged. "I'm going shopping with Mom." She checked her screen. "So, what did Dr. Nichols tell you?"

"Nothing of real importance. And it's not about you."

Madison squinted at him over her screen, said, "Whatever," and let it drop.

Thank God, since Jacque was due to emerge any minute. She always took quick, very efficient showers. No lingering and lathering, or lotion slathering.

And emerge she did, decked out in a casual shift, ready to discuss. She turned to her daughter. "Madi, would you excuse us? Why don't you start getting ready? I won't be long."

No, you probably won't. Spencer nodded at his daughter, who took the hint and left.

"Now, what do we need to talk about?" she asked.

"What we didn't finish last night."

Jacqueline said nothing, took a chair, and waited.

Spencer knew this discussion could degenerate; he had to handle her with kid gloves. "We touched on the telemedicine issues over drinks, but let it drop a little too quickly."

"How so? I explained what we at the company are

faced with."

"If mentioning 'kinks' amounts to a full explanation. Which it doesn't."

"What do you want to know, Spence?"

"Over the past several weeks, I've grown concerned about the whole telehealth issue. I have information to support that concern, and think we should discuss details. You've been gone basically the whole time since this came to light, and it's time to spread some facts on the table."

"Is this about Madi's visit?"

"Yes, and no. To be honest, she's one case in which a virtual visit didn't solve her problem, and actually misdiagnosed it. And even though she's better and we have a handle on what she has, I don't think that's a small thing. What about others with more serious conditions?"

"Look, Spence, I'm not going to argue with you about telemedicine. It's a good innovation, helps many people receive health care they might not otherwise, and as far as I know, doesn't warrant trashing. There are no statistics to suggest that large numbers of people have been harmed."

"My point precisely... there are no numbers. Or does the industry have data which they are not releasing?"

Jacqueline sat forward, obviously upset at his suggestion. "Now, just stop it. Are you accusing my company, or me, of deliberately concealing data which shows harm?"

"Stranger things have happened."

"You're out of line, Spence. Way out of line. I would not do that. And I am not involved in some coverup if that's what you're suggesting. Quit thinking like a spook." She flopped back on the chair cushion, and stared at their lush backyard.

"Not exactly the right term." After a beat, he said, "Okay, all right, but maybe someone else at the company is. Maybe you're shielded from it, perhaps because of my former life."

Apparently tired of staring at trees, Jacqueline's gaze swung back to him. "Why do you think your 'former life' in the FBI would be the cause of some coverup? You're no longer there, haven't been for five years, I don't carry your last name – which I'll remind you was for that very reason – and I have not told close colleagues what you used to do. Everything doesn't revolve around your former career with the Bureau, Spence, hard as that is for you to comprehend."

"Don't be dramatic, Jacque. Of course, I don't think everything revolves around my former career. But I am concerned about your involvement in telemedicine development, and the expanding use of it. It will be subject to hacking or theft of patient identification and data, until proven otherwise."

"You're getting way ahead with your assumptions."

"I don't think so. We may lose control if significant protections aren't in place. That's been a problem since the day computers were developed and their use implemented everywhere. You can't deny that."

"No, I won't. And we share your concern, but we're not turning back. We can't." She paused, then added, "There's been huge growth and financial gain in our markets, and we certainly haven't been harmed by that, have we?"

The almighty dollar… justifies everything. He smiled. "We certainly haven't."

It was time to end this. Nothing more could be accomplished with both of them dug in. Next stop, a shouting match which the neighbors across the ravine might hear. He dropped the smile, grew serious and stood. "Money isn't everything, Jacque. A word of caution… I would say, be careful when you're dealing with the feds. They'll protect their own, most of the time, and they certainly won't cover your ass. Quite the contrary, they'll bite it off if it suits their purposes."

Pleased with his speech, he abruptly left the screened

porch, left Jacque sitting there to digest his words and consider her position. His wife had spearheaded the development of the technology necessary for telemedicine to exist. Through that, she had rocketed to a prestigious position in her company, and now, it was clear she seemed to have grown numb to its consequences.

Maybe he could do without her money and prestige, after all.

CHAPTER | 25

Sunday

Noon arrived and it was time to get Noah over to Mark's. He had asked Hope to bring their son earlier than usual that day, so he could get settled in before evening. Mark had said he wanted to get a calm start to his week ahead. The long week ahead. It had surprised her that he volunteered to take Noah one week before a big trial. Was he feeling guilty, perhaps?

Since their divorce, Mark had rarely kept his son for an entire week, often arguing that he maintained long hours at his law firm, which interfered with expanded parental duties. That was true. Never mind her medical practice, variable hours in Urgent Care including evenings, and all sorts of schedule challenges. His was always the determinative career. As Hope pulled into his drive, she again wondered if sweet Brandi would play mommy all week. Could she, Hope, stand that?

Maybe she should hire Spencer Reeves to keep a sharp eye on that situation while she was at it. That might prove productive and very interesting.

———————

Spencer read the text and took a few moments to

consider his response. He wanted to stay in close touch with Hope, but couldn't divulge anything right then. There was nothing to divulge, yet. He composed a cryptic response and hit send. She would have to wait, as impatient as she might be.

While he mindlessly unloaded the dishwasher and nursed his thoughts, Jacque sauntered into the kitchen. She started with, "I don't want to have tension like this between us. It could be a long week."

He set eight dinner plates on the counter and locked eyes with her. "I agree. But to be honest, tension's been building for a while." He turned back to the dishwasher and pulled out the utensil basket, bearing all manner of tableware including sharp knife blades glinting in the downlights. He set that on the counter and waited for her next response.

She glanced at the utensils standing by and filled a glass of water from the refrigerator dispenser. After consuming half of it, she said, "I realize that. And I've considered what you said yesterday. What I don't think you understand is that I cannot just stop the tech world. Can't stop what has already been set in motion some time ago. Even if I tried, I'd fail."

"Okay, I get that. I'm not that dumb, but is it worth it to participate in something which may bring harm, may have already brought harm?"

"I guess we don't see things the same way. I realize sometimes we have to take the bad with the good to achieve our goals. It surprises me a bit that, with your history, you don't see that."

"Of course, I understand that, Jacque. But I'm coming to the conclusion also that business and tech don't blend all that well with medicine. I guess Madi's experience opened my eyes."

Jacqueline ambled from the kitchen, leaving him to his tasks, and said over her shoulder, "I don't suppose this conversation is over, is it?"

He answered, "No, I don't think so, either."

———————————

Madison had sequestered herself in her room, the drone of her voice telling him she was engaged via phone with a friend, and from the sound of it, not a boy. She would be occupied for a considerable time. At least she was actually talking to someone and not immersed in social media. Given his background, he had reluctantly agreed for her to engage on social media, but only in a very limited capacity on one account. No matter how loud she howled, he stood firm, and she finally acquiesced. Madison had no choice, and she knew it.

Jacque had withdrawn to her home office, and busied herself, as always, with emails and generating policy notices and memos for distribution the next day. Getting ready for her week at home would keep her focused for hours. No worries.

Given those circumstances, he could retreat to his quiet place, a room he used for security surveillance activities in his business. Situated in their lower level, adjacent to a large theater room and game room, neither his wife nor his daughter liked to enter his sanctum, both declaring it 'too creepy.' He did not share their opinion, of course, having designed it with his comfort in mind. No use being cramped or out of sorts while spending long hours there. Insulated and upholstered walls, carpeting, and select furnishings created a quiet work atmosphere in which to conduct his business. And all manner of memorabilia from his youth and early years at the Bureau reminded him of the disciplined work he had accomplished before he had decided to change course.

It was time to call Jacob. He readied a yellow legal pad for any particulars he cared to note. After two rings his buddy picked up. They spent little time with greetings and got down to business.

"What did you find?"

"Not enough, but a few things of interest."

"Go on."

"Well, for starters, your doctor friend Hope Nichols has nothing of record, other than her medical school and residency training trail, and her board certifications in Family Medicine and Urgent Care. No malpractice suits yet, no complaints to the state board. Of course, you knew about her divorce…"

"Yeah, she mentioned an ex-husband."

"Well, he's a lawyer, a courtroom brawler of some repute. But, he doesn't take on ne're-do-wells, jerks, those sorts. Mostly, corporate litigation, all that. No record, no complaints to the bar. They've been divorced two years. One son, a six-year-old."

"Who has no record, either?"

Jake retorted, "Don't be a smart ass."

"Go on."

"Okay, this Dr. Rich Rutledge is a fifty-year-old internal medicine doctor. Has a wife, same one he married twenty-five years ago, two kids – a daughter in college and a son in high school, a junior. No one with records. He got promoted to Chief Medical Officer a year ago at the clinic. He's been seen in some political circles with various reps and senators, found a few shots of him in Washington and at your state capital, photo-ops over the past five years."

Spencer's ears perked up. He scribbled 'befriends politicians' under Rutledge's name. Hob-knobbing with politicians often led to 'opportunities' which could lead to other 'opportunities.' That was worth checking out.

Jake pre-empted with, "I'm digging further on that."

"My thought exactly."

"The gal he took on a year ago is something. She seemed to come out of nowhere and apply for his administrative assistant job. Well-credentialed, undergraduate degree from Northwestern and an MBA from Columbia. He apparently took one look and hired her immediately. She's thirty-two, very smart, and a looker, according to sources."

"Married?"

"Widowed."

"Oh?" Spencer added that factoid to his scribblings.

"She lost her husband to a car accident five years ago. Have more work to do there. Question – is she legit, or up to something?"

"Agreed. She's the one Dr. Nichols said was visiting their unit, bothering the nurses, and who told Hope it might go badly for her."

"Yeah, I remember you said that. So, more to do there. Now, to the other two doctors. This Chet Murdock is an older ER doc, in his sixties, who's probably about ready to hang it up. Reportedly, tired of the ER routine and a tad burned out, he took over the Urgent Care department at the clinic six years ago at age fifty-eight. He's considered a nice guy, patients and staff like him, and he doesn't go on any campaigns or rock the boat. No recent suits, but ER docs always accumulate a few along the way, and no complaints to the state board; basically boring."

"And the other woman doctor?"

"Yeah, that's Rachel Baumann, the head of the Family Medicine division. She's boring, too. No suits, no complaints. Has been with the clinic twenty-five years and showing no signs of going anywhere. Stable and dependable. She's worked her way into the department chairperson spot over the years. More power, more clout."

"Maybe no one else wanted it, or it was her turn."

"Could be. We need to look into her, dig a little deeper. See if there's any serious behind-the-scenes alliance with Murdock or Rutledge. Birds of a feather..."

"I hear you. So that's it?"

"For now. Most of it is general stuff, but a few things are worth pursuing."

"Agreed. So, when do you think you'll have more?"

"Not sure. Couple of days probably."

"Make it as soon as you can. I've got my eye on something else."

"Yeah?"

"Yeah. Let's talk tomorrow or Tuesday."

CHAPTER | 26

Monday

R ich Rutledge made his way along the fourth-floor hallway, lost in thought, his eyes focused on the carpeted floor in front of him. His call weekend had gone reasonably well, but the hospitalists had paged him numerous times about patients in his practice, and those of his internal medicine partners, who had been admitted through the ER or who had suffered setbacks. At times, he wondered if it would be just as well if he and his colleagues still rounded on their own patients, whose clinical histories they knew well. But, he had no desire to turn the clock back and take up hospital work again. He could bear up under the occasional phone call even if it came in at two a.m. He glanced up and saw someone he'd been meaning to speak with, Rachel Baumann, striding toward him. Her office was just around the next corner.

He raised a hand in greeting. Coming to the corner, he stopped. She paused, as well.

"Hello, Rich. Haven't seen you since the staff meeting."

"Yes. It's been busy." After a moment, he asked, "Have a minute?"

Rachel checked her wristwatch and cocked her head toward her office. Together, they set out in that direction.

As they passed her nurse's desk, the young woman said, "Your nine o'clock canceled."

"That gives us a few more minutes," Rachel said. Rounding a corner to her office, she added, "Have a seat."

Both settled, Rich leaned back in the chair, affecting a relaxed attitude, and asked, "So, how's it going around here? Virtual visits picking up?"

Rachel gave him a long look. "It's going. I wouldn't say we're setting the world on fire, but gradually getting more comfortable with it."

Rich nodded. "We've got some holdouts in several departments, but I think we'll overcome their hesitancies fairly soon." He waited, hoping she would catch his drift and mention names.

Rachel viewed her computer screen, not hopping onto the topic as fast as he would prefer. *Is she protecting someone?*

Anxious for her to engage, he said, "I know one doc down in Urgent Care is not so hep on the idea. I'd say she's hostile." He waited.

Rachel turned her chair and locked eyes with him. "Can you be more specific?"

"Sure. Hope Nichols."

"Oh, Hope." She chuckled. "She's always on some tear."

That was news to him. Or was Rachel just making light of Hope's position, the mother hen protecting her brood, so to speak? *The big, bold internist can't come up here and attack one of our family medicine comrades.* He smiled, trying to signal some degree of congeniality.

"I wouldn't pay her any mind. Let her blow off some steam. She'll come around," Rachel added.

"Well, it would help if she would get over it soon, and get on board."

"I also noticed, Rich, that cardiology isn't gnashing at the bit, either. In fact, they sound like they're still sitting in the station waiting for the next train, or deciding whether to take the trip at all."

"How colorful you are, Rachel. Cardiology can't go anywhere, no matter what they're mad about. The restrictive covenant and all. They'd be fools to try."

"We're all constrained by that, aren't we? Doesn't give any of us many options, does it?"

He smiled again, this time sincerely, as he realized the hold he had over essentially all the clinic physicians. Or that the board had over them. Then another thought intruded – everyone's feet were bound in cement. Even his. *What a terrifying thought!*

He said, "I guess you're right about that." On that note, he rose, ready to confront his day. No need to parry with this colleague any longer.

Rachel turned from him to her computer screen and her patient list for the day. Thirty patients, minus the one cancellation, all coming in to see her. Two already roomed.

Over her shoulder, Rich noticed her full schedule, twice as many patients as he would see, and added, "Looks like you're bursting at the seams."

She said, "Doesn't look like they wanted to stare at me through a computer screen, does it?"

He left without saying another word. Score one for Rachel Baumann. Best to not completely alienate this woman. But he *would* prepare for the inevitable next round.

———————————

Hope began her day checking emails. Was there anything of note which might change the course of her day? News from Spencer Reeves might, but she wouldn't hear about it through these channels, and had to practice patience anyway. Her eyes landed on a message from the pulmonary division. Subject line: Patient Report.

Mr. Green's consultation report had arrived, and it was

not encouraging. Squamous cell carcinoma of the lung, the biopsy report declared, metastatic to several regional lymph nodes. His workup was completed. She read the full reports and the oncology consultation note as well. Given his age and overall condition, they would start with radiation, with immunotherapy likely to follow. He had agreed. And so it would go. Thank God, someone had not given him the requested cough syrup and another round of antibiotics and waited. He'd have the same diagnosis, but hopefully his coming in had bought him some time and might make some difference in treatment options.

She would not see Mr. Green again, and silently said goodbye coupled with a little prayer that things would work out for the man. The lack of ongoing interaction with some of her patients did bother her from time to time, but that couldn't be helped. She had to hand them over to others when their clinical situation warranted, or send them back to their own physicians for management. Hers was not to hang onto them.

Finished with Green's reports, she rose, gathered her laptop, and left the doctors' room. Another man waited down the hall, bothered by no response to treatment for cold feet.

Hope arrived at his door, answered a question from a nurse as she cruised by, and checked the electronic record again. Attending physician: Dr. Rutledge. That gave her pause. She wished she could go find Chet Murdock and hand off this man to him. She had just given up Rutledge's name to someone 'with connections.' Wasn't that betrayal? Now, here she was seeing his patient. Was the sudden warmth she felt guilt, or anxiety, welling up? Either way, it was distinctly uncomfortable. And she might have to tell Rich he had missed something.

She opened the door to a fifty-seven-year-old man sitting in one side chair, a similar age woman in the other. Man and wife. Hope introduced herself and claimed the rolling stool. The room stunk of cigarettes. Clearly, someone had just finished a smoke before entering the clinic. And that very well might be at the heart of the matter.

Hope reviewed the medical record with him. His wife threw in her two-cents worth whenever she could. The back and forth painted a fairly complete picture. It was the right foot, not both. 'Who wrote that in the record?' the wife asked. Then Hope confirmed the smoking history. He had quit five years before, threw them in the trash, just like that. He'd given up a two-pack-a-day habit lasting thirty-two years, plus four more years at one-pack-per-day: sixty-eight-pack-years all the way back to age sixteen. His wife, on the other hand, still smoked, but always went outside, of course. She was concerned about him and their dog, a smart schnauzer who sneezed all the time around smoke. The vet had even encouraged her to quit but, you know, 'her nerves and all' prevented such a commitment.

"Let's take a look at that foot," Hope suggested.

The man took off his shoes and socks, and got up on the exam table. Hope slid his pant legs up to his knee. His right foot was rather pale and cool to the touch compared to the opposite one. He lacked hair on his lower legs, his skin appeared rather waxy in appearance, particularly on the leg in question. Hope palpated his left foot and ankle pulses, impressed but not surprised at the faint pulsations she felt, and in the right leg, nonpalpable pulsations. She asked him to remove his slacks and checked pulses to his groin. He had them, but none strong enough to allay her concerns.

His habit had caught up with him.

During the examination, she asked again how long this had bothered him, and whether Dr. Rutledge had seen him recently for this. 'One month,' answered her first question, and 'no' to having seen Dr. Rutledge. About two weeks before, he'd called in and had been told there were no openings, but he could see someone via the computer. He did and their advice: prop your leg up when it aches, and put a warm pack on it from time to time.

"They couldn't even see his leg," his wife announced. Her voice tone rising, she asked, "How could they see his leg?"

"Of course," Hope agreed.

"And propping it up only made it worse, I'd say."

"Hurt like hell," he added.

"That's right," Hope agreed.

After the gentleman redressed and found his chair again, Hope informed him and his wife in plain terms that he likely had serious vascular disease from his smoking.

"What? It causes that?" his wife asked.

Bluntly, Hope said, "Yes, all the time."

Shocked, the woman kept quiet after that.

Hope outlined an appropriate plan for an immediate workup and ordered a vascular study, as soon as possible – that day, please – in the cardiology suite. Then he would be off to the vascular surgeon, who in turn, would express surprise the patient had just walked in off the street into Urgent Care with such a condition. He or she would then request clearance from pulmonary and cardiology before any surgery. Or, the man might end up in surgery that evening for a 'cold leg.' His calendar had just been turned upside down.

As Hope wished them well, and sent them on their way to the vascular lab, she returned to the doctors' office, questioning how she would inform Rich Rutledge that his patient had failed a virtual visit which should not have occurred in the first place. Admittedly, she actually relished the whole prospect, but how to say it…

First, do no harm?

CHAPTER | 27

Tuesday

"Good morning," Kalisha announced as she slinked into Rutledge's office, relieved Darlene was not 'manning the gate' at her nearby desk. Apparently, the woman was engaged elsewhere in the suite. Rich had let her know he'd finished seeing patients for the morning. They had timed their meeting accordingly.

"It's almost good afternoon," he replied.

She smiled and assumed a chair in front of his desk. "Lunch, maybe?"

"I think a drug rep is about to arrive. We can eat here."

"Sounds good." She tapped on her tablet, and asked, "So, what are the main things we need to discuss today?"

Focused on his computer, he didn't look at her when he said, "I'm not pleased with the telemedicine initiative."

"So, what's new?"

His gaze swung to her, an irritated look she did not appreciate, and said, "Of course, my concerns are not new, but I've picked up on something I don't like at all. There is considerable passive resistance to the idea... I'd call it real passive aggressive behavior."

"So, who are you referring to?" She waited, expecting Hope Nichols name would immediately come up, and was surprised at what he said.

"I had a chat with Dr. Baumann in Family Medicine yesterday. She seemed... well, not excited at all. In fact, a little guarded." He turned back to his computer, and frowning at the screen, said, "I thought we had her on board."

From her vantage point it was hard to see what he was reading. An email from administration? A patient report? Kalisha said, "I haven't spent time in that division, I guess because that was also my impression. They are embracing it, no complaints. Do you want me to pay them a visit, scope it out?"

"No, not right now. Dr. Baumann's a smart woman. She would know immediately what you were doing, and close ranks completely. I said my peace, and we need to let that lie for a while. The bigger problem is in Urgent Care."

Kalisha said nothing.

"Damn."

"What?"

"Speaking of which, one of my patients went to Urgent Care yesterday, and Dr. Nichols saw him. He has a major problem with circulation in his leg, and she had to refer him to a surgeon."

She hated it when he talked down to her. He apparently thought she knew no medical terminology, and didn't need to. Little did he know. "Well, if he has vascular disease, isn't it good she caught it?"

Rich turned away from the computer, locked eyes with her, and said, "Of course, but he had a virtual visit a couple of weeks ago – through our division, but not with me – and was not managed well. That's on us."

What goes around comes around, Rich. Kalisha straightened in her chair, when she heard the door open behind her.

Darlene stuck her head in, paused, then said, "Lunch has arrived."

"Yes, thank you, Darlene."

"Do you want me to bring you a plate, Dr. Rutledge?"

Kalisha maintained her composure, refrained from twisting and turning to acknowledge the woman. *None for me, I suppose.*

"What is it today?" he asked.

"Chinese."

"Okay, we'll be in."

Kalisha felt Darlene's eyes boring through her back as she withdrew. *Yes, I will go in there and partake, whether you like it or not, lady. I'm paid to trail him around, and I won't go hungry in the process.* One of these days she'd say just that, out loud. Disgusted, she wondered how much longer she could stand this. Changing the subject, Kalisha asked, "What else do we need to discuss after we eat?"

Rich Rutledge thought out loud, reminding her of the other issues the clinic's Board of Directors were tasked with besides telemedicine: whether to go forward with the proposed satellite clinic – including another urgent care department – physician recruiting for several of the divisions, and the preliminary clinic budget for the next fiscal year was due soon. The budget must be finalized by September first. He droned on about the new equipment radiology had requested. Better yet, they wanted a new wing to house several latest generation scanners. And Urgent Care needed two more procedure rooms. Pulmonary constantly asked for more room for Respiratory Therapy in their suite, which served the entire clinic, not just their own patients, remember? How could they do their jobs in such a cramped space? And so on.

"That's a lot to cover at once. Which shall I focus on?"

He looked at her. "All of it," he said with a tight smile. "And telehealth. Let's keep up your rounds on the divisions, but avoid Hope Nichols for now when you go downstairs. Why don't you chat with Dr. Murdock when you pass through there? See where he's at. He's usually agreeable."

"I can do that. And when the budget requests come through, I'll organize those folders for you."

"And the status on recruitment." He got up from his desk. "I don't know what I'd do without you, Kalisha. Now, let's go get something to eat, before it's all gone."

————————

At one o'clock Hope pulled into a parking slot in front of the one-story red brick building. Tucked into a wooded area at the perimeter of an office park, the facility was accented by neatly trimmed shrubs and large maples scattered here and there. She noted three other cars in the lot. *Which one is Spencer Reeves'? That big black Navigator? Is there another partner I'm about to meet?* She'd find out soon enough.

It was her only day off for the rest of the week. She would put in long hours through Saturday – while Noah visited his father – before next Sunday and another break rolled around. She had other errands to run that afternoon, and hoped Spencer could relay what he had learned with dispatch. Yesterday's clinic workload had helped her practice patience, though, and hopefully, whatever he told her would justify her having handed over the names. Her guilty feelings were fading, but not fast enough.

Hope entered the sleek, minimalist reception area and was greeted with a friendly smile from Phyllis. Yes, they were expecting her and would she take a seat. She would let Mr. Reeves know of her arrival.

Phyllis disappeared through a substantial door into the interior, which closed and locked with a loud snap, leaving Hope to survey the decor, and the centerpiece – a huge, sparkling aquarium. As she took a seat close to the feature, all the tropical fish appeared to react to her presence, zipping across the tank, in and out of half-submerged grottos, appearing thoroughly excited. Several stationed

141

themselves near the glass to keep an eye on her. She was impressed, and stared at the tank for several moments. She then turned her attention to the magazine collection on a side table. All the journals were business or travel oriented. Slick, glossy publications which bore little sign of overuse. None were out of date. She wished she could say that for the clinic's selections, which often included rumpled year-old Sports Illustrated or Better Homes and Gardens with torn pages. The patients might as well take them home, they were in such bad shape. As she prepared to read about Kauai, Phyllis reappeared and beckoned her to follow through a side door. Forget the fish and Hawaii.

Spencer stood in his doorway anticipating her arrival and gestured for her to enter. With a nod of his head, Phyllis knew what to do, and left to fetch coffee and sparkling water. They seated themselves, both in front of his desk. No position of power nor barrier between them. Phyllis materialized with a small tray equipped with a carafe and all manner of beverage supplies, smiled, and withdrew. Hope felt like a real client.

She opened with, "Your aquarium is fascinating, very well done."

"Thank you. I enjoy fiddling with it. Have since I was young. But I have a maintenance company come in weekly to do the real work."

"It's soothing, relaxing."

"Yes." Pause. "So, how is your day off so far?"

"Going well."

"How's Noah this week? Enjoying his summer activities?"

"Oh, yes. His summer program keeps him busy Monday through Friday, and he loves it. They have recreation, arts, music, field trips, all sorts of things. But this week, he's spending at his father's."

"He doesn't take him to…?"

"Oh, Noah still goes to Summer Season every day. Just

spending the rest of the time with Mark. He has a big case next week in Chicago, and I didn't expect he would want to keep him all week. But he insisted."

His face reflecting surprise, Spencer only nodded in return. Apparently, he had not delved into her ex's schedule for the month…. or maybe he had.

Pleasantries aside, he asked, "Coffee?"

"Sure. Black, please." She received her mug from Spencer, he poured one for himself, and they settled in for the real discussion.

Regrouping he said, "So, I've heard back from one of my contacts and have information for you. It's all pretty basic, some of which you probably already know."

"This is regarding the people whose names I gave you?"

"Yes."

She sipped and waited. *Connections, contacts – who is he referring to?*

He continued, "I spoke with a former associate who has done research for me in the past. He took those names and checked backgrounds, records, that sort of thing. I heard from him again this morning."

"Associate, where?"

"I'll get to that." He paused, sipped coffee, and asked, "So, how long have you known Dr. Rachel Baumann?"

Expecting he would go immediately to Rutledge, Hope was surprised he mentioned Rachel first. "Since I joined the clinic five years ago. She's the head of Family Medicine. Is she a problem?"

"I wouldn't say so."

"Well, okay." She eyed Spencer and continued. "So, I was first recruited for that division, but they needed someone in Urgent Care right away and offered me that position. It suited me, so I took it. I've become better acquainted with her over the past couple of years. She's been there a long time."

"Yes, I know. Are you involved in AAFP activities much?"

Surprised he knew the acronym for the American Academy of Family Practice, she said, "I've been to a few of the meetings. Their headquarters are here in town, you know?" She paused and sipped. "Why do you ask?"

He ignored her second question. "Right. I do know that. And it seems Rachel Baumann has been active in that organization for some time."

"That's not surprising."

"No, it isn't. But that put her in association with national AAFP officers who are politically active. She, in fact, held several of the organization's state offices years ago, back before your time."

She'd take another stab. "So, what are you saying? How does that affect me now?"

"It may not, but the AAFP has taken a strong stand in support of telemedicine, and she may be quietly pushing for expansion inside your clinic."

"So are a number of others." Hope sipped coffee, then asked, "Where is this going?"

"We're digging around to see if she has maintained any political connections and whether she may be compromised by an agenda pushing expansion of telehealth. Are there incentives involved, that sort of thing."

Hope stared at him. *No, not Rachel...* She asked, "Who else?" But she already knew the answer to that.

"Rich Rutledge, of course. You can't be surprised at that."

"No, not at all. So, what did you find?"

"Same thing. A few associations in Washington and Topeka. Through the American College of Physicians, he's attended quite a few national meetings and conferences aimed at lobbying, hob-knobbing with various legislators. Our question – could those associations provide opportunity to participate in any initiatives with kickbacks for pushing the technology?"

"I see what you mean." Hope squirmed in her chair, sipped her cooling coffee.

"One of our key questions is, when the feds, through HHS and CMS, introduced the idea of telehealth, to what extent did they underwrite the development of the technology? It appears that the money flowing forth from the feds to emerging tech companies was substantial. Public/private partnership – that sort of thing. As a result, they – the companies and the feds – had a vested interest in seeing it flourish. Big time. Question is, did they find individuals around the country willing to push this at their clinics for, say, what? Financial incentives?"

Hope sat silent, regarding his wall art, weighing what she now knew, and feared. Had she opened Pandora's box? Scratched the surface of… what? And how did this man find out all these details in such a short time? She turned to him.

"My question – Who is *we*? How did you find all this out, and so fast?"

Spencer got up, rounded the corner of his desk and sat down. He pulled open his center drawer and presented his current business card to her. She'd seen that before, still had the one he had given her in Florida. She looked up, and saw he had presented another business card and a set of credentials, both marked with a familiar-looking insignia – Federal Bureau of Investigation – although she couldn't claim she'd ever seen it before. The credentials were clearly marked 'Retired.'

Flabbergasted, she sat mute. Suddenly, things came into sharp focus. A vivid mental picture of her first encounter with this man intruded. Her question then about his quiet, deliberate demeanor in the exam room, his attentive stare, all of it flashed through her mind. Maybe that's why his young daughter didn't react in his presence;

she, of course, knew.

"I don't know what to say. You've surprised me, and you know that. So, your connections are… at the FBI?"

He nodded.

She chuckled. In a smart tone, she asked, "So, is this being recorded?"

He shook his head.

"So, why am I the only one talking now?"

"You aren't."

"That's better. So, if you're on the outside now – *or is all this a ruse?* – how can you still go inside?"

"We don't lose all our friends. And they sometimes help us with our other work."

She nodded, not sure she wished to remain involved at all. Maybe her protest should end right now. Get off the bandwagon, accept telemedicine and whatever comes next, and move on. "Considering all that, what do you suggest I, or we, do from here?"

"We gather more information."

"Until the cows come home."

"Or until we have enough to stop what someone is doing, or they do something stupid and stop themselves." He paused, then said, "Don't change anything for now. If they engage you in discussion, engage. Don't give them any reason to think you've been instructed to act different. And watch what they're doing."

"You mean Dr. Rutledge and Rachel Baumann? I don't see them that often."

"Yes, if you happen to see them around. And Chet Murdock and the administrative assistant to Rutledge, the Johnson woman who visits your unit. She has an interesting background, too."

"Oh?"

"Yes, but we'll discuss that later. Nothing for you to worry about right now. Just keep an eye out for her."

"And what do *we* do? Stay in touch?"

"Yes, from time to time. More often, perhaps." He smiled and stood.

Hope got to her feet, too. She'd had enough for one day, and wondered if she could concentrate on her errands now. Probably not. Had he set a tail on her?

He rounded the corner of his desk, extended his hand, and smiled again.

Hope moved toward the office door, quite ready to leave. He escorted her down the hall. When they reached the reception room door, he assisted and said, "Maybe some time this week, we can touch base again. Especially with Noah elsewhere."

She pivoted. *What was he suggesting?* Not agreeing, but not refusing, she said, "We'll see."

With that, she turned and entered the empty waiting room – save for the colorful, energetic fish – gave Phyllis a brief wave and a thank you, and strode toward the main entrance. It was time to get out of there. No one would believe what she had just heard. And she had no one to tell, nor would she if the opportunity presented itself.

What other surprises, or shocks, are in store?

Chapter | 28

Wednesday

The day wore on. Spencer arrived home early, impatient to corner his wife again. She was still occupied in her home office with a zoom call when he walked in. He could hear her voice, and those of others droning on in the background. Madison was off with a friend, so they would have the house to themselves until mid-evening. They could duke it out verbally without their daughter overhearing, and worrying.

He had analyzed this proposed discussion, and the pressing need for it, from one angle and another, finally concluding that he could not wait, and this week was best before she took off on another business trip next Monday. All day he had worried that maybe he was jumping the gun. Should he put together more information before confronting her? That was his usual method. And admittedly, he had questioned his own motives and fears. How would this affect their financial situation? Was he looking for a reason to sack her? Disturbing thoughts, all of them.

Spencer went directly to their bedroom, changed into a tee shirt and shorts and, having shed the day, returned to the kitchen determined they would go for a walk. The trail behind their house, along the creek, was a good place to broach the subject. Even if other late-afternoon walkers or joggers came by, they would pass quickly. He didn't plan to raise his voice and make a scene. He wasn't so sure about Jacque, but perhaps that might constrain her tone a bit. He gulped down an energy drink while he waited.

"What are you asking, Spence?"

They huffed along the trail at a moderate pace, not quite breaking into a jog, but stepping along briskly. The thick summer air, and lack of breeze in the ravine, squelched any desire to run.

"I'm curious about the company's dealings, where is all the R and D money coming from?"

"We've talked about this before. We're positioning for an IPO, likely in the fall. You know that. The federal government, in the meantime, is supportive of our excellent progress. A private / public partnership. Nothing out of the ordinary these days."

"Not usually."

"What are you implying?" She warned him, "Don't play your cat and mouse games, Spence. If you have something to say, say it."

He stopped. Jacqueline covered a few more yards and halted. He closed the gap between them. Locking eyes with her, he got right to the point. "Jacque, I have some information that money flowing to your company has come from sources the federal government may wish to conceal."

She stared at him for several long moments, before saying. "Oh, Spencer, you've been involved in too much intrigue for too long."

"Maybe. But that doesn't change the fact that things may not be as they appear."

"Are you suggesting we are engaged in some sort of illegal activity, and on top of that, we're covering it up?"

"I'm not accusing you, personally, of knowing anything about such activities. I'm telling you now there may be evidence which comes forth to confirm that."

"That's crazy. Just because you all of a sudden don't like telemedicine, doesn't mean we are engaged in nefarious activities."

"You may be right. I simply want you to be aware that there are parties probing into the use of your technology, and that your company may come under scrutiny."

Jacqueline resumed walking. She said nothing. *Is she considering this news, or her options for dealing with me knowing this?*

He caught up, kept pace, and chose to remain silent as well. Maybe he had said too much already, had put her on alert? On the other hand, sometimes it's good, you know, if you lay something out there, some part of what you know, stir up some of the players, and see what happens.

"Are you one of those probing parties?" she asked.

"Not saying that."

"So, what do you expect me to do?"

"Be honest and be aware."

Oh, no, what's happened? Hope saw Mark's smiling face painting her screen. If she didn't answer immediately, he'd be sure to leave a message. By waiting she'd see what he had on his mind before calling back. She had wondered how long it would be that week before he contacted her about something. It was surprising it had taken until Wednesday for him to call.

The voice message binged only a few minutes later.

"Call me as soon as you get this message. It's about Noah."

Alarmed then, she hit redial. He picked up after one ring.

"Are you home?" he asked.

"No, not yet. On my way, why?"

"When Brandi picked Noah up today—"

Is that the sound of my teeth gnashing? "Mark, wait, let me get out of traffic."

Fortunately, she spied a familiar grocery store to her right. She veered into the outside lane, suffered a fellow driver's noisy warning, and whipped into the parking lot. She pulled into a near spot and slammed her car into park. "Okay, go on."

"—he told her something happened at Summer Season."

"Something... like what, Mark?"

"That there were men hanging around the playground watching them."

"What kind of men?"

"Two men who wore jackets and they stared at them through the fence."

"Jackets in this weather? That's a little strange."

"Yeah, I thought so, too."

"Did he say any more?"

"No, and I couldn't get him to talk about it again."

"Did he seem upset?"

"No, not when he got home."

"So, what do you have in mind?" she asked.

"Talk to the teachers first. See if they know anything. Maybe they've arranged for some kind of security."

"That's one thought. Maybe the jacket thing isn't quite true. Would you put Noah on?"

"I don't want you upsetting him, Hope."

"Any more than you and what's-her-name may have already, Mark?"

He ignored her question. She could hear noise suggesting Mark was walking through his house, then came faint television sounds in the background. Muffled, Mark asked Noah to come to the phone. "It's Mommy," she heard her ex say. Then more noises as the phone was being transferred to her son.

"Hi, Noey, it's Mommy."

"I know."

"How was your day?"

"Okay."

"That's good. I miss you and want to hear your voice. Did you do anything new today?"

"No."

This is like pulling teeth. "How do you like the new playground equipment they have?"

"Good." She could hear Noah breathing into the mouthpiece. "Jeremy jumped off the slide and hurt his leg."

"Really? That's not good."

"He went to the doctor. His mommy came."

"Is he okay?"

"Don't know." Noah paused again. "Teacher carried him in."

"I'm sorry to hear that. I hope he's—"

"—that's cause he was watching the men."

PAW Patrol! PAW Patrol!
We'll be there on the double...

Oh, oh, she had better hurry. Noah's attention was about to be stolen away. "So, Noah, hon, did you see the men, too?"

"At the fence."

"Did they say anything?"

"Don't know."

"Did your teacher see them?"

No answer. With his mouth obviously mashed against the phone's microphone, she heard heavy breathing and a muffled, "Have to go. Bye, Mommy." And her son clunked down the phone. Apparently, Ryder and his team of pups were more interesting than her or her questions.

A few moments later, Mark rescued his cell and said, "Did he tell you?"

"The same. Except that the other little boy fell off the slide, I guess because he noticed the men."

"Look, Hope, I think we should check with the school."

"Definitely. So, when will we go by?"

"I can't. The case. You'll have to go."

Of course. "Sure, Mark. I'll make time." *I'll just call a colleague tonight and plead to trade shifts.*

"And let me know what they say."

"You bet I will."

She hung up before he issued any more instructions, and planned her strategy in the next few moments. Texting an associate, she asked for a trade, days for evenings, even though it was short notice. She didn't wait long before he texted back with – 'Sure that'll work great. I can go to my son's baseball game. Thanks!'

That all set, she texted Mark. She would go by the school in the morning, no problem. But would he please plan to pick up Noah tomorrow afternoon instead of sending Brandi so he could hear for himself how Noah's day had gone? Thanks so much! She added a 'thumbs-up' emoji for positive encouragement, though a little frowning face would have felt much better.

Nerves on edge, and thoughts spinning, she rolled out of the safe parking spot and pulled into rush-hour traffic.

Chapter | 29

Thursday

Hope found a parking place, locked her car, and hurried toward the front door. There, she hit a buzzer for admittance. That, at least, was reassuring. Some security measures were in place to protect, or at least slow down, potential intruders, like unknown men in jackets. Which made no sense at all in the warm, muggy weather they were enjoying. It was only ten a.m., but she had already erupted in a 'glow' while hustling across the parking lot.

A voice answered, she stated hers and her child's name, and was buzzed in. The director's office was only a few steps down the hall on the right. The door stood open, and a friendly-faced stout woman sat behind the desk, a phone propped on her shoulder. The placard on her desk read, Rose Collins – Director. Miss Rose to the kids. Hope had made her acquaintance the year before when Noah first enrolled in Summer Season. She respected the capable woman and knew she intended to run a tight ship. Was that impression going to change after the discussion they were about to have? She remained at the door until Miss Rose waved her in, and pointed to a chair in front of her desk which Hope assumed without hesitation.

Moments later, Rose hung up, her conversation

completed with the mother of the injured boy. She smiled and warmly greeted Hope.

"What brings you in today, Dr. Nichols?"

"A matter perhaps related to the young boy's injuries."

Looking surprised, Rose said, "Oh?"

"Yes. Noah is staying with his father this week, and told him yesterday that two men outside the fence were watching them during recreation time. His father and I assume you know about that and wonder what you thought about the situation."

Miss Rose cleared her throat, sat back in her chair, and gazed at Hope. "I'm not sure which men you refer to. There were landscapers who came by yesterday to look at the area outside the fence. We're planning some improvements when the summer session is over. Could that have been them?"

"I don't know. Could it? Noah said they wore jackets which is odd this time of year."

"Jackets? That is odd."

"Yes, jackets."

"Perhaps he's mistaken. Children sometimes don't report things correctly, or they misinterpret a situation. The men who came by in the morning wore green short-sleeved polo shirts with a black insignia on the front. I spoke with them when they arrived. They were here about thirty minutes, looked around, took some pictures, then left. I'm not aware that they may have returned in the afternoon, during the children's playtime."

"Is that when the other child fell off the slide?"

"Yes, it was."

"Did the teacher outside with the kids report any such individuals to you after the afternoon recreation period?"

"No, she didn't. But she watches the kids very closely, and became preoccupied with the injured little boy. Perhaps, she just didn't notice. Or, perhaps whoever it was came and went quickly."

Hope nodded, considered what more she could do right then to press the point. It was not reasonable to assume Noah and the other boy were completely wrong or fabricating stories. Nor that a teacher would not notice two grown men standing near the fence watching the kids.

"You seem uncertain. What would you like us to do, Dr. Nichols?"

"I'm just having a hard time understanding how a teacher would not notice strangers at the fence."

"Yesterday, we were short. One of our teachers called in sick for the day, so there was only one available to go outside with the kids." She shrugged. "Maybe she thought it was the landscapers again."

"Perhaps." After a moment, Hope said, "I *would* like you to do one thing. Check with her, ask her what she saw, dig a little bit."

"Of course. Now that you've brought this to my attention, I will do just that. It is interesting, though, that not one of the children said anything to any of us after play time."

"Yes, that is interesting, I agree."

Hope shifted forward, signaling she would be on her way.

Rose asked, "Is there any other concern, Dr. Nichols?"

Hope stood and said, "No, not today. Thank you for your time this morning." Dissatisfied, she took a step toward the door and stopped. Turning to Ms. Collins, she added, "But, I think you should put two adults on the playground with the kids. I know we would all appreciate that. Perhaps, you could fill in if someone calls in sick?"

Rose Collins looked surprised, perhaps a bit taken aback, but recovered quickly. She nodded and said, "Of course. What an excellent idea."

The heavy traffic made her commute more annoying, not to mention calling Mark while en route. She'd left a message with his secretary well before lunch, but had not heard back. She was due in Urgent Care in thirty minutes, and would be there until closing at nine p.m., and after. She didn't have time to play phone tag with her ex. And if he was so concerned about Noah's safety, why didn't he make time to hear her report?

Hope wound through the congested lanes on the interstate, impatient to get to the clinic. Once there, she could remain in her vehicle and field his questions in private. She took the next off ramp. Her phone chimed just as she pulled to a stop. She hated to see people talking on their phones while driving, but she would have to violate her own policy for Mark.

"Hello, Mark."

"Hi. So, what happened?"

"I went there at ten. The director Rose Collins was in her office, so there was no delay. She and I talked, and basically she said no other adult, like a teacher, saw two men outside the fence. But only one teacher was with them at play time, and when the other kid fell off the slide, she focused on him. Rose did mention that two landscapers came by in the morning to look over the area outside the fence. And she also reminded me that children frequently don't get the story straight. Can't describe apparel accurately, or know the time of day when something happened."

"Makes sense."

"That may be the jacket thing. Did Noah say any more about the incident last night before bed?"

"No. And I didn't question him."

"And he didn't balk about going this morning?"

"No. And I took him."

Glad he hadn't handed their son off to Brandi the chauffeur, Hope pulled into the clinic parking lot, noted it was full, and shifted gears. "Look, I'm here now, and I need to go in. Looks like they're busy."

"You're working late tonight?"

"Yes. Remember, I had to trade with a colleague in order to go to Summer Season this morning."

"Oh, yeah."

"So, will you call me this evening after you pick him up, and see how he's doing?"

"Brandi or I will… get him."

Is that noise my teeth gnashing again? "Well, I'd like *you* to call and give me your observations, let me know if he says anything again about men at the fence or hanging around anywhere nearby. Can you do that, Mark?"

"Am I able? I don't need to answer that."

"G'bye, Mark. I'm late."

———————————

A pile of clinical notes and reports lay on her desk, waiting for her to return from seeing the last patient. They weren't going anywhere, and neither was she.

A young man with a fresh laceration had presented right at closing time. His wound required irrigation and suturing. He also required a tetanus booster. All in all, it was ten-fifteen when he left – thoroughly bandaged, boosted, and instructed in wound care – and the evening was shot. If she procrastinated, ran off, and delayed her paperwork, she would have to return earlier the next morning, and the leftover charts would still be waiting. Her other physician colleague and a nurse practitioner were already busy dictating, completing their work from the long afternoon and evening. Hope rounded the corner, ready to attack her charts. She would be the last to leave.

To make matters worse, there had been no call from Mark. That left her more than irritated, and she'd had no time to stop the patient flow in order to check in with him.

No time to wait with bated breath on his call. He knew she was occupied when there, and no doubt resented that. Resorting to his passive-aggressive games seemed to satisfy him no end. Considering all that, perhaps no call was a good sign. She decided to wait him out, and not ring him late... no telling what she might interrupt.

Hope entered the doctors' office, determined to finish something. After a few words to one colleague and the other, she then settled at her desk, exhausted but wired. She would dictate as fast as she could until she couldn't take any more, then finish the rest in the morning before things got too busy. Unfinished work piled up always bugged her, but occasionally it went that way. While she opened the next clinical chart, her cell chimed a text message.

Hope pulled it from her lab coat pocket, examined the screen, and saw Mark's smiling face.

"About done, Hope?" the other doctor asked.

"Soon, hopefully."

With a wave and a 'see ya,' he left.

She read Mark's message. "all went well. noah wouldn't talk about it again. denied any sightings when outside. went to bed without a hitch. still plan to bring him home saturday evening. leaving sunday around noon."

Well, there it was, all the essentials, no excess detail. She supposed she should feel relieved, but couldn't say she did. She turned her attention to the electronic chart before her, when a sudden thought intruded. *Maybe I should run this past Spencer Reeves.* Yes, that sounded like a very good idea. But when?

Hope tapped and clicked, finished a couple of dictations, then thought of Spencer again.

"I'm leaving now," the nurse practitioner interrupted. "Do you want me to wait?"

"Oh, no, you go on. I'll be a while."

"You sure?"

"Yeah, I'll be fine. I can get security to walk me out.

You go on."

Without further discussion, the young woman exited, leaving Hope alone with her thoughts.

She had left Reeves' office Tuesday shocked by his cred pack, doubting his story, and wondering whether that office was just a front for the FBI, or some other organization, clandestine or not. However, the past forty-eight hours had afforded her a chance to let the dust settle, and consider their future interactions.

Maybe it was time to push a button again. This situation with Noah was far from settled, and perhaps Reeves could help.

She pulled his card from her large leather bag, fed his number into her contacts list, and hit text messaging. She tapped in a brief, professional sounding message, hesitated for only a moment – would he forward it to someone? – and hit send.

The ball had just landed in his court.

CHAPTER | 30

Friday

H ope glanced at the wall clock in Urgent Care. It was nearly three o'clock and she had been there since seven a.m. Her early arrival had afforded her time to finish her charts from the previous evening before any colleagues stepped foot in the place. Several nurses had materialized around seven thirty to ready the department for opening at eight, but they left her alone when they saw her staring at her computer screen.

Eight hours had passed, and she only had three more charts to complete from the day. Her stomach reminded her she had missed lunch. A snack from her drawer stash would tide her over until dinner; she would grab that before she made her way to Spencer Reeves' office. That hastily-arranged appointment had not left her mind all day – between patients, conversing with colleagues, checking X-rays or labs – anything she engaged in. It remained ever-present. Perhaps because she had slept poorly after arriving home late the previous evening. Perhaps due to her discussion with Reeves three days before. He had texted her in return early that morning before she'd launched into seeing patients, asking her to stop by after her shift. He would wait for her, he'd said; it was important. Apparently, he had news for her too, not simply responding to her request to run something past him.

Was she turning into a paranoid delusional patient herself? Not a pleasant thought at all.

Hope finished her last dictation, took a few moments to straighten up, when Dr. Murdock entered, sank into his chair and turned to her.

"You about done?"

"Yeah."

"Whatever happened to that young man with the coarct?"

"He was worked up by cardiology, and referred to CTS for evaluation. He needed a repair, but they had to wait for his parents to get here from Norway for surgery on Monday. From what I heard, he did well. They had to put in a six-centimeter aortic graph, but he came through it like a champ. Good thing he was in such excellent shape."

Murdock nodded. "That was a great find. Glad he's doing well."

"Well, I haven't heard anything since Wednesday."

Chet looked thoughtful, spun around, and attended to his computer, obviously done talking. Ready to leave, Hope pulled a protein bar from her drawer. It was time to be on her way to Reeves' office.

As she walked past Murdock's desk, he muttered something unintelligible.

"Pardon?"

He glanced around at the empty room, and repeated his question. "I said, have you met that Kalisha Johnson woman, Rich Rutledge's assistant? She came by today."

————————

She stared at the humongous fish tank. It hypnotized, and she feared that might just happen to her if she sat there much longer. In such a condition, Spencer Reeves might be able to extract all kinds of information from her... if she had any to give up.

Perhaps she and Mark should consider going in together and getting Noah such a thing for Christmas? A tank full of colorful fish would keep him busy and would undoubtedly be a lot quieter than Bey Blades, or a dog. Immediately, she realized she'd then have another job – caring for the thing. And probably retrieving any fish unfortunate enough to hit the floor or float to the surface. She let her mind wander down that track a bit, until she heard the door open behind her, and a man clear his throat. Unlocking her eyes from the tank, she turned in her seat. Spencer stood there smiling.

"My fish have captivated you?"

"Thoroughly."

"Ready?"

"Yes."

They traveled down the hall to his office; he ushered her inside and closed the door. This time Phyllis did not appear to offer refreshments, but Spencer pulled two bottles of water from a small fridge under his bookcase and offered her one. *What else does he have in there?*

"So, you texted last night with a concern? One of your colleagues?"

"I'm not sure about them, but it involves Noah."

His face grew serious. "A threat?"

"Perhaps, of sorts."

He cocked his head, a question painting his face. "Please, do tell."

"I told you Mark, my ex, is keeping him this week." Spencer nodded. "When they picked him up at his summer program Wednesday, Noah told them a story about men hanging around, watching the kids on the playground."

"They? Them?"

Of course, be specific. No indefinite pronouns, please.

"They – Mark and Brandi. Them, the same."

"Brandi?"

"Mark's latest companion."

Spencer gave her a single, slow nod. He understood.

"Anyway, I spoke with Noah that evening, and he said that he and several of the kids noticed two men in jackets standing outside the playground fence watching them… the kids. In fact, one little boy lost his footing on the slide and fell because he was paying attention to the two guys."

Spencer said nothing, waited for her to continue.

"I had a hard time getting anything out of him, but that was the essence of the story. Then last night Mark sent me a text saying Noah wouldn't talk about it again. He didn't seem upset, slept well, had no complaints.

"I went by the school yesterday morning and spoke with the director. She's a very warm, capable woman. It seemed obvious she was surprised by the story, said two landscapers were there in the morning looking over the area outside the fence for a project they planned. But they weren't wearing jackets. Of course not, in this weather. The teacher outside later with the children when the kid fell from the slide didn't notice or report anything, either.

"And she reminded me that children often mis-tell stories about an incident, don't keep the facts straight, and so on. Of course, I know that. I think all the adults are focusing solely on whether men were wearing jackets as evidence of the truth to the story, not whether unknown men approached the fence and watched the children. And that episode was in the afternoon, not the morning when the supposed landscapers came by. Maybe those weren't the actual landscapers the director expected that day."

"Good point. The director's name?"

"Rose Collins. She goes by Miss Rose around there."

"Age?"

"I'd say… probably mid-fifties, maybe sixty."

"Other characteristics?"

Surprised, Hope asked, "Is that necessary?"

"It's helpful."

"Okay. She's stout, grandmotherly type. Short, curly blond hair, cheerful face. Ready smile."

"Thank you," he said as he scribbled notes on a legal pad.

"Very approachable."

"Right." He paused, then asked, "Did she offer to do anything? Investigate?"

"No. I asked her to do a little digging. Question the teacher again, see if she could remember anything."

"Is this summer program held at a church or school?"

"It's at a private school. They've had this summer program for about three years now. This is Noah's second year."

"Do they have security around the place?"

"Locked front doors. You have to be buzzed in. The playground's fenced. No obvious other security that I could see."

"Is the fence locked?"

"I don't know. And I failed to ask that."

"No problem. That's easy enough to find out."

"What are you suggesting?"

"That you hire me, I go by, chat with Miss Rose, and assess the situation there."

"I'm not sure…"

"What would *you* suggest, Hope?"

"I don't know. But I do know that Noah doesn't make up stuff. You saw for yourself… he's not big into imaginary play; he's frank, straightforward, even blunt at times."

"Children often are."

She added, "If he said he saw something, then I believe he did. I can't explain the jacket thing, but otherwise it sounds credible and makes me nervous."

"I trust your instincts, Hope. You're an excellent observer. If he were my son, I'd be nervous, too." Spencer softened his words with a small smile.

If he were my son. Hope's empty stomach clenched at his comment. Ignoring her unwelcome symptoms, she said, "So, I hire you. What exactly do you propose and what are your rates?"

"You pay me one dollar for now, sign an 'agreement for services form,' and we're set. Sound fair?" Before she could answer, he went on, "Let's do this. I'll drop by there Monday. Will Noah be back home by then?"

"Yeah. Mark's bringing him back Saturday evening. I'll have an opportunity then to try to pry more information out of him, if I can."

"Right, and I'm sure you'll do that gently. So, I'll go by, discuss your concerns with Miss Collins, tell her you've hired me as part of your security service – you know, your home system, etcetera – and see if I can find out more. Maybe by that time, she'll have talked with other teachers, and perhaps she'll have additional information for us."

"Okay. But I don't want her on alert about anything here at the clinic. Or about my failed marriage. Or who you are."

"Right. I know how to avoid certain issues."

"I'm sure you do." Hope took a big swig of water, suddenly needing to satisfy a parched mouth. What was she about to get involved in?

"And be careful that Noah doesn't see you. He might recognize you."

He smiled. "Good point. Now, all that taken into consideration, I have some news for you."

In a succinct manner he informed her of additional information he'd accumulated, or someone had unearthed for him, about Rich Rutledge's various connections. And he further informed her of the very interesting Ms. Kalisha Johnson, MBA.

Her parched mouth called again for 'Water!' Indeed, what *had* she involved herself in?

CHAPTER | 31

Saturday

It had been a long day in Urgent Care, in fact, a long week, and she was anxious to get home and relax. Hope negotiated the late-afternoon traffic, distracted by the memory of yesterday's meeting with Spencer Reeves.

Noah was due around seven, after one last supper with Mark. Surprisingly, he had offered to bring him home a little later that evening, so Hope could wind up her day at the clinic before Noah arrived. Those periodic bursts of consideration from her ex were appreciated, but threw her off-balance from time to time. Still, it squelched perpetual antagonistic feelings, which was at least beneficial, she reasoned.

She pulled into the driveway and garage, ready to shed her scrub clothes, and put together a quick dinner.

Two hours later, right on cue, the doorbell rang. Hope made her way to the front door, found Mark and Noah standing there, smiling, and welcomed them in. Noah hugged her legs, and explained he had to put his Bey Blades apparatus in the family room, and he'd be back. Still wearing his backpack he ran off in that direction, leaving Hope and Mark alone in the front hall. Mark handed over his suitcase, and waited while Hope placed it by the stairs.

He seemed anxious to converse. She opened with, "Thanks for giving me a little extra time today. Clinic was busy. How did the week go?"

"Fine. Do you have a minute?"

"Sure, what's up?"

"Why don't we step outside?"

"Just a minute." Hope called out to her son, "Why don't you take your suitcase upstairs, Noah, and pull out your clothes? We can get them washed."

He yelled back, "I don't want to."

Hope walked to the family room, and convinced her son that he would benefit from doing what she had asked. The youngster complied, gunching as he passed by them in the hall. When he reached the top of the stairs, he yelled out, "Don't mess up my Bey Blades!"

Hope and Mark shared a smile and stepped outside.

"So, what's on your mind?" she asked.

"What do you think? The issue at the school. It's not solved, Hope. Last night, Noah told me about one guy who hung around outside the building yesterday, watching them."

"Not a landscape guy?"

"How would I know, but it doesn't sound like it. And I think we need to do something. You should talk with the director again."

"I think you and I should go in together, don't you? Present a united front, use your legal clout?" Hope quickly mentally shuffled her options. Should she tell him about Spencer Reeves, the help he offered, and their plan for Monday? She instinctively decided against such a move. Her hiring a former FBI guy to intervene for a token one dollar would only raise his ire.

Mark gave her the expected response. "I can't do that next week, you know that. The big case."

"Of course. Okay, look, I have to work Monday, too, but I'll call Rose Collins and get an update on her observations and plans." *And I'll send in the feds behind your back.* "Then we can go from there."

"We should probably consider pulling him from the Summer Season program."

"Mark, we don't know if any person hanging around is there for nefarious purposes. And, if true, why do you think Noah's their target?"

He stared at her. "With what you told me several weeks ago about the issue at the clinic, I presume that could be the problem."

"Seriously? What about your big case in Chicago? Maybe your opponents are equally motivated to pull a stunt, lodge a threat. Huh? What about that?"

"Oh, come on. Opposing counsel isn't going to engage in threats against kids."

"Stranger things have happened, I'm sure, when so much is at stake."

He paused, then added, "I warned you, Hope, not to do anything to threaten Noah's well-being. If you're still on a tear, you better consider giving up your stupid mission. Or, it won't go well for you or our custody arrangement."

She glared at Mark, and said, "This discussion is over. Have a good trip, Mark, and call if you can spare the time or care to know what *I* find out. Good night."

Hope stepped inside, leaving him on the front porch, just as Noah tore down the stairs. Shelving her ex, she pivoted and asked, "Hey, kiddo, what about a movie tonight?"

His answer – Noah hopped and skipped through the hall to the family room, wasting no time getting started.

———————————

Kalisha stared at her computer screen and opened the folder. It was mid-evening. She couldn't believe she was spending a Saturday night this way. But seeing Rich was not an option – he had other plans – and she needed to get this work done. She opened the last unfinished document.

Dr. Rutledge had made his position clear to his colleagues – the entire clinic, actually – and to her. Telemedicine adoption could ensure the clinic's survivability and improve their bottom line. Sounded good, but there was more. His agenda might ease the older doctors out if they objected too strenuously to his initiative. Particularly the ones with hefty retirement accounts, interested more in reduced clinical hours than high productivity. Cut down their influence on the other doctors. Then hire only younger doctors excited about every technological advance, and bring on more extenders which would ultimately cost the clinic less. That was his argument, anyway, which he had shared with only a few, including her.

He had taken her into his confidence, and she understood the pressure he felt. As an internist with one kid in college and another close behind, he needed the financial end of this to work out. He needed the incentives and bonuses to come through, sooner rather than later. A portion of every virtual visit charge was credited to his ledger, if they met a threshold for total numbers of visits at the clinic each month. It had taken longer than he wanted, but over the past two months the uptick in numbers had pleased him. If he sustained that pace, or better, for at least three months, the first bonus would arrive. She was pleased it was moving along, at last. If the obstructers, like Hope Nichols didn't get in the way and slow things down. Kalisha was tired of the sluggish pace. She needed this project done, so she could move on.

She tapped in more figures. Once she finished the data entry, she could complete her narrative analysis, send off the two reports, and reclaim some of her evening. Had she forgotten anything?

"Ready for a story?" Hope asked.

Noah dawdled in the bathroom, brushing his teeth and humming, admiring himself in the mirror.

"Hurry up, Noey, so we can read." She had chosen a story which conveyed a theme of being careful, and watching one's surroundings like owls do. He loved the story and making owl noises while she read. She wouldn't press him about what he'd seen at the school, but if he wished to talk about it, then...

"Okay, Mommy, done." Noah jumped onto the lower bunkbed and grabbed Teddy, ready to snuggle in his covers, read the story with her, and drift off to sleep. His bleary eyes betrayed his fatigue. He'd probably sleep hard that night and clock more hours than his usual.

She opened the book and began, "The sun was setting. All the owls—"

"—Hooot!"

"—in the woods knew dusk would soon turn to night. Owen, the smallest owl, knew what to watch for – the deepening shadows, the bats who lived nearby swooping here and there—"

"—Taking flight, Mommy. That's what it says."

"Yes, taking flight. You're right."

"The insects singing their—"

"—Night songs," he added.

"Right again. Owen knew the other owls were waking up. It was time to go out, hunt, and keep watch—"

"Hooot, hoot..."

"With their—"

"—Keen eyes." He hugged his ragged teddy bear. "Mommy, what's keen eyes?"

"Sharp eyes, Noah, good eyes which help them see things clearly." She continued, "With their keen eyes, they could see clearly what was going on in the woods at night."

After a few more pages, Noah fell silent. Hope glanced at his cherubic face, noted his drooping eyelids, and doubted they would finish the story before sleep overtook him. She felt his grip on the book loosen. She lowered her voice and continued, knowing full well that hearing is the last sense to go. Maybe her soothing tone and the subliminal message would sink in.

She finished reading, set the book aside, and gently maneuvered her son into a more comfortable position before turning off the adjustable gooseneck lamp over his bed. He turned on his side, snugged his pillow and Teddy, and mumbled something unintelligible.

She crawled off his bed, ready to tiptoe from his room, when she heard him say, "Night, Mommy. Will Owen keep his keen eyes on the men at school?"

Hope halted in her tracks. She pivoted and returned to his bedside. Bending low, she stroked his head, and murmured near his ear, "Oh, my yes, Noah, I believe Owen will do just that."

A fleeting smile escaped, his eyelids fluttered shut, and he said nothing more.

CHAPTER | 32

Sunday

He had waited long enough. Jake should be up and around, awake and alert by then, even though it was Sunday. Time for an update, and he was anxious to hear more. Just before eleven, Jacque and Madison had left, planning to meet another mother – daughter duo for brunch. He had at least several hours to process new information, add that to what he already knew, and hatch a plan for the week. He would update Hope later, after his briefing with Jake. An uneasy feeling pestered him, no matter how he tried to push it away.

Spencer hit the recall button and rang Jacob Nelson. It took only two rings before Jake answered. His early morning voice let Spencer know it hadn't been long since he'd rolled out.

"Alone?"

"Yeah, unfortunately."

Jake had run off at least one wife, as well as several interval girlfriends that Spencer knew of. He certainly never let personal relationships interfere with work, his first love. The one thing his buddy did not understand, and which widened the gap between Jake and others, was how many agents maintained close relationships *and* effectively did their work. But the one thing he, Spencer, did understand was the spark of immediate attraction and faulted no one for running around. No one who was unattached.

"Right. What do you have?"

Jake cleared his throat, and said, "Interesting stuff. Starting with Dr. Rachel Baumann... she doesn't appear to be a factor in some questionable activity. She's not opposed to telemedicine, but always approaches everything in a very deliberate manner. Pragmatic, reasonable. Her background checks out and those we've spoken to through contacts in the medical community all say the same. We can watch, but I don't think we need to waste extra time on her."

"Okay." Spencer made notes as Jake talked. There was no need to worry about Jake recording him. They didn't do that to each other.

"Kalisha Johnson, the assistant, is in an interesting position. I told you she has the two degrees, including the MBA in health administration. That makes sense with the position she has with Rutledge. But one source reported that she had been a member of a healthcare watchdog group several years ago, right after she graduated from Columbia. Turns out, it was three years ago. Sounds reasonable for her field, but that group is known for keeping tabs on HHS and CMS, the whole issue of data collection by healthcare organizations and billing practices. Also, she has some friends at the state board, or at least several sources said she is acquainted with individuals who work for the state board."

Spencer, furiously scribbling as much as he could, asked a few clarification questions of Jake, then paused. "I sense you think there's something there."

"Oh, there's a there, there. Smells like it."

"So, you're still digging on her?"

"Right."

"The healthcare watchdog group has a name, I assume."

"Integrity in Medicine."

"Catchy. Now, how about Rutledge?"

"Okay, interesting guy. His political hob-knobbing has taken him to select places over the past several years. Seems he's attended a few prestigious events with various senators, from your state and others. Along the way, he's made the acquaintance of a couple of key people at HHS. That isn't all that unusual for ambitious doctors, but he keeps in touch with a few by email and phone calls; he's not too secretive."

"And?"

"We've uncovered a few things. There's been talk from time to time between parties about a bonus structure of some sort. What I've heard so far could be legitimate. Expansion of telemedicine seems to be at the root of it. The clinics that push it will receive incentives in return, apparently from HHS through CMS payments. But I'm not sure it's all above board, know what I mean?"

"I do."

"They're using taxpayer dollars."

"Got it."

"To collect and stockpile data on people, but then what do they do with all that, where does it go?"

"I hear you."

"We don't know yet. There are a few around here who seem to know something about it but won't talk."

"Do I know them?"

"No, they came on after you."

"What about Skipper G?"

"I haven't approached him yet."

"Maybe we shouldn't."

"Right." Jake paused, sounded like he slurped coffee, then said, "And, one more thing, Spence... the tech company which first developed the program is sharing in those bonuses, as well. And it doesn't look like just a public/private partnership arrangement."

The time couldn't pass fast enough that afternoon to suit him. Spencer retired to his cave where he wouldn't be bothered for hours. Even when Jacque and Madi returned, and he heard footsteps on the floor above, he did not emerge and greet them. He'd left a sticky note by the key basket in the mudroom, and they had left him alone.

He'd drilled down through every computer avenue he could find, which he still had access to, and basically confirmed most of what Jake had told him. Uncomfortable and restless, he felt he was just scratching around, and hadn't found the itch. There were more than a few moving parts to this scenario, and he was the one running this way and that, stopping no one. He glanced at his desk clock as the glaring red numbers silently announced three forty-five. Too soon to call Hope? And just how much should he disclose?

She had just tucked Noah in after reading *Forest Owls* again. He focused in on the 'keen eyes' phrase, and they had spent extra time trying to think of other words for 'keen.' That seemed to amuse him – learning about synonyms – as did practicing different 'hoots.' All in all, it took twice as long as usual to read, but she couldn't think of a better way to put a finish on her evening.

Hope's phone chimed, just as she closed the door to his room. She answered as she walked downstairs. "Hello?"

"Hi there. Is this too late?"

"Not at all. Just got Noah tucked in."

"So, I have additional information for you."

"Oh?"

"Yeah, and I called because it will probably change our game plan for the week."

"Our game plan."

"The approach we spoke about on Friday."

"Okay. Right." That idea had made her nervous enough. Now, what was he going to propose?

"I think you need another appointment with Dr. Rutledge."

Not the idea she wanted to hear. "And how will that make any difference? He's hell-bent on his approach. He won't change his mind, and I can't change it for him."

"Of course, and that's precisely why. We might pin him down on more specifics, and we'll get him on record."

"What are you suggesting?"

"That we outfit you to record your discussion."

Dizziness nearly overcame her as she entered her kitchen. Glad for a handy bar stool, she slid onto the first one she could reach, and lowered her head to her hand.

"Hope, are you still there? Are you okay?"

"I'm here, but I wouldn't say I'm okay. Just a minute." She reached across the counter and grabbed a partially empty bottle of water left standing near the sink. Readjusting herself and the stool, she said, "All right, I'm back. So, you want me to wire up?"

"That's the idea."

"So, why all of a sudden is this urgent? Obviously, something you found out?"

"Right. Let me go through this, and then you'll have a clearer understanding."

"I hope so." Partially recovered, she made her way to the family room sofa, sensing she might have at least some symptoms in the next few minutes, and wished to lie down if it got too bad. "Okay, what's going on?"

"Your colleague Dr. Rutledge is probably in a desperate situation. Backed into a corner, so to speak."

"Desperate? How so?"

"He's dancing with the devil."

Hope sat still, sipped water to quell the queasiness she

felt, and the bilious reflux which threatened to surface. References to the devil bothered her.

Spencer went on. "Money, money, money. From what we know, he's friendly with several notables in the Senate, and possibly partnered with an important bureaucrat or two at HHS. Which may have provided opportunities he couldn't refuse."

"So, you want me to get him to admit that?"

"We don't expect he will. But, he might lose his cool and admit more than he would have otherwise. With a recording of the conversation, we can analyze what he says. Usually, the objective analysis reveals more than you might think."

"And when do you propose I do this?"

"As soon as is feasible."

"Like yesterday, in other words." She gulped water, said, "Spencer, I don't know…" She paused again, considered his sudden proposal, and answered. "Look, the earliest I can call his office is tomorrow, and hope for some time on Tuesday." *Am I out of my mind?* "But what if he says no?"

"I doubt he will if you go in under the pretense of changing your mind."

"Oh, I don't know if I can carry that off."

"I have faith in you, Hope. Take the tack that you've seen the light, and you'd like to become an ally. You're very good on your feet, and you think fast. You don't have to have a lengthy conversation, just get him to admit some of the benefits of aligning with him. You might be surprised at what he offers you."

"Oh, you're good." She took a swig, and wished for something stronger in that bottle. The compliments were getting deep, and the feeling of manipulation building. "How many witnesses or snitches have you talked into something like this?"

"More than you wish to know."

"I thought so. Look, in all seriousness, what are the dangers in doing this?"

"Well, unless they scan you or pat you down, he won't expect you're wearing. With his ego, he probably won't hesitate to discuss this with you, and he'll hopefully offer to bring you into his inner circle. The more colleagues he can lasso, the more dependent they are on him and his scheme – if there is one – and the more he can hold over them."

"I see what you mean. And what's your role in this?"

"I get you fixed up. And I keep an eye on things."

"You mean, remotely?"

"Right. And don't forget tomorrow I'm going by the school, posing as your concerned security system representative, and engaging the charming Miss Rose."

"If she'll believe that story." More concerning for the moment – just how would he keep an eye on things? "Back to this other, you mean you'll be sitting outside in some unmarked van?"

"You don't need to know that. But I'll be handy."

"Like, to come rescue me if he suspects I'm up to something and threatens me?"

"Like that. And I may have help."

"I don't think I want to know." She paused, then thought better of turning him down. Such a ruse might blow this whole thing open, clear the air for her other colleagues sitting on the fence, prevent many older, experienced doctors from fleeing, and most of all, protect patients. But did she have it together enough to take such a risk? "Okay, here's my answer. I'll probably go along with you and do it. But I want to sleep on it, and give you my answer tomorrow. Can you wait that long?"

"Yes, I can. Why don't I call you when I'm finished with Rose Collins, and I've snooped around the grounds? Fair enough?"

"Fair enough. But I may change my mind."

"Understood. Look, it's late. I'll let you go. You sleep well."

"I doubt it."

"Talk tomorrow."

They hung up. Hope gathered herself and rose from the couch. She needed a small snack before bed to quell the pit in her stomach. And maybe she'd read Noah's *Forest Owls* book again, particularly about the 'keen eyes.' As she stared at the available snack selections, a small annoying voice intruded.

You better be clear about this, do not do anything which endangers our son, or compromises our joint custody. Or some such thing.

Fair warning, Mark, fair warning.

CHAPTER | 33

Monday

Hope hit the floor running that morning, saw six patients with minor concerns before nine a.m., and then returned to her desk, feeling distracted. What an understatement. She dreaded placing the call, speaking with his secretary then possibly his nurse, but knew she must do it. Like going for a dental procedure. You'll feel better on the other side. Yeah, right.

She had already texted Spencer early that morning and accepted his proposal. Having slept on it made little difference in her misgivings, but one concept emerged as the key point pushing her forward. If this situation needed a shove – someone to make a move, shake things up – then why not her? And him. Having backup was always a good idea. She would let him know when she had an appointment time.

Hope sat, preparing, reining in her paranoid thoughts, and psyching herself up for this little adventure. But, hey, neither his secretary nor his nurse needed to know what this was about. She could spin something about clinical issues – which it was – and avoid any further explanation. They would only be concerned with how much time she needed. *How long I need to entrap him.* Gathering her thoughts, planning her words, she picked up the phone.

Surprisingly, Rutledge's secretary was not in that morning, the recorded message said, so would she please ring his nurse's desk? It forwarded automatically, and without delay Darlene answered.

"This is Darlene, Dr. Rutledge's nurse, how may I help you?"

"Hello, Darlene, this is Dr. Nichols."

"Oh, hi, Dr. Nichols. Things treating you okay?"

"Oh, you know, this and that. Can't complain. Say, I need to speak with Dr. Rutledge fairly soon about several clinical issues, and wondered if he has some time tomorrow."

"Is this about the man with the bad leg?"

"No, not him, but I can catch Dr. Rutledge up on that, too. It's about several other issues in Urgent Care."

"How much time do you need?"

"Oh, I'd say twenty minutes, tops."

"Let's see…" Hope could hear her clacking around on her keyboard. "Let me put you on hold for a few minutes."

Classical music wafted over the air waves while Hope waited. Was Darlene checking with Rutledge? She would prefer to just spring herself on him tomorrow, no advance notice given. He might bring in reinforcements, like Ms. Kalisha Johnson. That woman was dangerous.

Darlene came back on the line. "Dr. Nichols?"

"Yes, I'm here."

"Okay, can you come in around four? He'll be done around then and can work you in."

"Sounds good. Thanks for your help."

"Welcome. Now, you let me know if you need to change that or if I can help in any way."

"I'll let you know."

What an interesting comment. Maybe Darlene could help. Maybe after ten years of putting up with him, she might be willing to confound his efforts. Just a thought, one she might share with Spencer Reeves later that day.

Spencer pulled into a parking slot, grabbed his navy sport coat, and took off for the front entrance. As Hope had indicated, he had to press the clearly marked buzzer to alert someone that he was there. After identifying himself, not as a parent, but a security person with an appointment, he was buzzed in. But not before the receptionist spent some considerable time either finding Miss Rose, or someone with authority to grant him admittance. Once inside, he thanked the receptionist, and asked where he should wait.

During the intervening ten minutes, he reviewed the text from Hope relaying her appointment time with Rutledge for Tuesday, four p.m. Excellent. But that appointment time caused a constraint. She further informed him she would return to Urgent Care after that for about another hour or two in order to finish up. One of her colleagues would stay until she had finished with Rutledge. He realized that would result in not as much time to review any recording they obtained, and discuss the atmosphere during the meeting. Oh, well. He couldn't complain, and wouldn't, about her medical hours. He knew she had unavoidable obligations.

A door across the hall opened and Rose Collins stood in the opening. "Mr. Reeves?" When he looked up, she offered a smile, and gestured toward her office.

He stood. "Yes."

Both inside, she closed the door and introduced herself. "Rose Collins, I'm the director of Summer Season. Please have a seat." She rounded her desk, and dropped into her own chair. Her cheeks pink with flush, she smoothed her loose, fluttery top, and asked, "What can I do to help?"

"I've come today for Dr. Nichols about an issue concerning her son Noah."

"You're with her security company, correct?"

"Yes. Security Solutions. She is a client of ours, and requested I discuss several concerns with you."

"And you've brought a permission slip from her giving me the okay to discuss her son with you?"

"Yes." Spencer handed over a hand-written note Hope had composed, granting permission to discuss any and all details of Noah's experience there. Rose scanned the note, asked if she could keep it, and secured it in her desk.

No problem, there are multiple copies at home.

All that taken care of, she smiled, and asked, "So, what are Dr. Nichols' concerns? Does this have to do with the men who came by, which several of the boys said were watching them?" She consulted a massive calendar serving as her desktop blotter, and added, "She came in just last Thursday, and this is Monday. We haven't had much time, yet, to address her concerns."

"Of course." He withdrew a pen from his jacket. "Would you mind going through that for me again?" Spencer scribbled notes as she talked. "Do you know who the men were?"

"As I told Dr. Nichols, we had scheduled a landscape company to give us an estimate for a proposed improvement, and very likely it was them. I don't know of any other men who dropped by that day." Again, she consulted her calendar and reminded him, "Which was last Wednesday."

"Were you here all day Wednesday?"

"Nearly all day. I had to leave for a short while early afternoon, then I returned. Part of that time was during the children's recreation period. As you probably know, there was a teacher outside with them, who assisted the boy with the injured leg."

"Yes, she told me of that. I presume you've had a chance by now to interview that teacher about what she may have seen?"

"I have. But she maintains she saw nothing."

Spencer scribbled, and Rose waited.

"Mister Reeves, do you have children of your own?"

"I do. One daughter, age sixteen."

"How nice. So, I'm sure you're well aware that young children may see things – not always clear to them – and fabricate stories about what they saw. Particularly rambunctious young boys are prone to construct scenarios, which at times bear no resemblance to reality. They watch too much TV, too much in my opinion, and are influenced by some pretty wild stories. Or, unfortunately, many watch terrible news reports, all of which stoke their imaginations and thinking." She smoothed her top again. "And increase their fear and dread."

"Right. I am aware."

Rose nodded.

Reeves redirected with, "Back to last Wednesday for a moment... Did you actually interact with any landscapers that day, scheduled or not?"

"Mr. Reeves, I did not. And I'll answer your next question. I have not called that company to ask whether they came out or not. Or returned that afternoon. That is on my list of 'To Do's' for today. Perhaps I can call you after I speak with them, to ease Dr. Nichols' worries."

"I would appreciate that. May I bother you with another question?"

She nodded.

"Have you had an opportunity to check the camera roll or videos recorded last week?"

That took her by surprise. When she noticed him jotting during her answer, she momentarily frowned, shook her head, and admitted, "No, no, I haven't. To be honest, I don't know who to call other than the police, and I don't wish to involve them if I don't have to. Looks bad, you know, and can excite the children." She regrouped and asked, "Now, would you mind telling me, if you know, whether young Noah has expressed fear since last week's incident – if we're going to call it that?"

"No, not serious fears that I know of. He was at his father's all last week, until Saturday night when he returned to Dr. Nichols'."

"Oh, yes." She cocked her head, and spoke in a resigned tone, obviously not a fan of divorced parents. "Well, I'm glad to hear he hasn't suffered. You know, divorce can be so hard on children."

Intending to show her a little humor and assure her he wasn't just all business, he said, "Apparently, though, he's quite focused on a certain book about owls, and their nighttime travels. Owls with 'keen eyes,' Dr. Nichols told me."

With a chuckle, she said, "Oh, my, well there you are… a young boy with quite an active imagination, full of ideas and questions. I can assure you we have not studied birds of prey this summer… though that is a great subject for boys. Ha, ha." She gestured toward her own eyes and added, "Keen eyes, of course… they all want keen eyes like eagles. Ha, ha."

"Yes, I suppose you're right. Ha, Ha." He had to get out of there before he reverted to his kindergarten days. *That playground was looking pretty good…* but, never mind, it was time to ask permission. "Miss Rose, would you mind too terribly much if I stroll around your grounds, check out the layout, and see if there is anything we might recommend to you?"

"Oh, by all means, be my guest. I would never turn down such an offer. Be aware, the eight to ten-year-olds will be outside soon, but I'm sure you can stay out of their way, and they yours. And please, let me know if you see anything which we should address. We do want the school, including the Summer Season, to be as safe as possible for our children."

He smiled, and said, "Well, you might consider having

those video clips looked at."

"Excellent idea," she said with a forced smile.

She exuded so much grandmotherly love, he wondered if she would give him a hug as he departed. Maybe he could use one.

Spencer stood, said his thanks for her time, allowed her to see him to the door, and accepted her detailed directions for leaving the building and finding the play yard. Where to re-enter if he needed to, and where to find a bathroom while he was at it. She didn't have to say, 'No going on the playground or against some tree at the back of the property.' All in all, exactly what he had expected from Miss Rose.

———————————

Jacqueline had departed on a one p.m. flight for Seattle, pursuing yet another week immersed in the tech world. Spencer hated to admit he actually felt very relieved. They had not settled any dispute between them, but had pursued a quiet truce the rest of the weekend. No yelling or hollering in front of Madi, no sarcastic remarks exchanged, but nothing warm between them, either, to recall as the long week wore on. He would have time to focus on his new 'case' and Hope Nichols. He would deal with Jacque's end of the whole deal when she returned. It could not be avoided. He would delay, though, telling Jacob just how his wife was entangled in the situation. He didn't need Jacob's advice on that right now. Or did he?

Madi sequestered in her room, he remained in the kitchen in case she came looking for him, and called Hope.

"So, hello," she answered.

"Is Noah down?"

"Yes. Just a few minutes ago."

"Okay. I got your text. You're still on for four tomorrow?"

"Right. How did it go at Summer Season?"

"That Rose Collins is quite the director. We had a good chat, but I didn't get much out of her."

"Has she looked into the kids' story?"

"Not really. Says the other teacher didn't see anything. Talked about the landscape company again, and kept reminding me it's only been a few days since it happened."

"Oh, Lord. She is a nice woman, but doesn't seem to understand that this could be a serious situation. Seems to want to brush it under the rug."

"I agree. She made sure I understood how imaginative children can be, especially boys, and attributed their comments and reports to that. She doesn't like how much TV they watch, and assigns their fears or concerns to bad television – I got the impression bad parents who don't monitor TV watching – and to bad news stories which breed wild tales."

"Of course, but I don't let Noah sit here watching such stuff. I make a point of that."

"And she's impressed with Noah's interest in owls and keen eyes."

Hope chuckled. "So am I. We had to figure out synonyms for 'keen' the other night."

"Smart kid."

"Thank you. I think so, but hey, I'm biased."

"One more thing, she allowed me to tour the grounds, and other than a densely wooded area behind the school, the playground is contained with that high fence which is locked. There's no other way in and it looks secure. Of course, it could be scaled; there's no razor wire."

"Perish that thought."

"As you know, the sides of the building are well-exposed. Anyone walking around can be easily observed. There are cameras on the four corners, which I noticed when I arrived, and large lights around the perimeter and on the parking lot. I did get her to admit there's video camera monitoring and suggested she have the tapes checked. She claims she doesn't know who to call."

"Maybe you could help her with that."

"We could, if my identity didn't freak her out. Right now, Hope, I'm not too worried about what the boys saw. Maybe it was nothing."

"But you don't know that for sure."

"I admit that. We're not done there, but you and I need to move on to the next step."

"I know. How are we going to do this?"

"I have a plan for tomorrow, and it'll be easier than you think."

"That's not very reassuring."

"Mind if I come over?"

CHAPTER | 34

Tuesday

As the day wore on, a parade of annoying symptoms plagued her. First, an early morning headache – finally relieved by her migraine medicine – followed by dyspepsia, for which she downed a handy Pepcid, then by afternoon, the queasiness set in. All of that helped her ignore her achy shoulders, which she attributed to excessive computer time. But, obviously, she would have felt a whole lot better if not for the anticipated appointment with Rutledge.

Spencer made short work of his visit the previous evening, got right down to business concerning the wire she would wear. He advised her to clip it to the inside of her bra, under her scrub top, but thankfully didn't ask her to don it in his presence. He presented several options, but both agreed that was the best spot. He instructed her to put it on about fifteen minutes before she left Urgent Care, and certainly after seeing her last patient, and he would make sure the thing was transmitting properly before she went upstairs to Rutledge's office. He would text her to let her know she was good to go. And she asked that he give her a reassuring pat on the shoulder, figuratively speaking, of course. He had chuckled, said sure and departed, leaving her alone with her anxious thoughts. Good night, sleep tight, and all that. Yeah, right. Perhaps that's why she tossed and turned, and awoke that morning completely lacking enthusiasm for the day.

Three-thirty p.m. came, she entered the last patient's data on their chart, and headed for the restroom, the tiny device burning a hole in her lab coat pocket, or so it seemed. Was she really going to do this?

One very compliant colleague believed she was dropping in on Rachel Baumann for a brief chat about Family Medicine department policies, or some such issue. Had she given him that impression or fabricated such a lie? She couldn't remember exactly how she put it, but he smiled, said sure, and she was set to depart. Perhaps from the clinic, period.

Hope shut herself in the private bathroom and locked the door. She removed her lab coat and set about attaching the device to the inside of her sturdy bra, which she had selected that morning just for the occasion. No going without that day, or wearing some flimsy, shifting elastic job. The candidate for the mission had to have some heft, underwires and all, to hold itself, her and the wire in place. As she was adjusting the piece, someone knocked on the door and rattled the knob. Her heart skipped a beat... several beats. She sucked in a sharp breath, then managed in an even tone, "Just a minute."

Without vocalizing, the person stopped knocking and, hopefully, moved on. She wasn't sure she could maintain any kind of normal expression when she left the restroom if someone were loitering there.

Her last thought as she pulled open the door... *this is crazy, just plain crazy.* No one waited outside for their turn in the restroom. Within a minute or two, Spencer sent a confirmatory text, reassuring her the device was working and encouraging her to relax, things would go well. *Fine and dandy, easy for you to say, wherever you are.*

Practicing slow deep breathing, she made her way down the back hall to the elevator. She didn't wish to climb four flights of stairs and present to Rutledge's office visibly short of breath. Not a good thing. So, she waited for the slow-moving lift to arrive.

————————

As she approached Rutledge's office, she kept a sharp eye out for Darlene, supposedly her new ally. Distracted, Hope rounded the corner in the Internal Medicine wing, and nearly ran over an electrician crouched on the floor, working on an outlet. He wore an impressive tool belt outfitted with too many implements, and a hat emblazoned with the name *Heartland Electric.*

He looked up, made eye contact and smiled. Nodding his head, he greeted her, "Ma'am." Hope noticed his very new shirt bore a matching logo. Returning his friendly greeting, she took a few steps toward Darlene's station and the armchair waiting for her. Suddenly struck with realization, she turned. He smiled again and touched the bill of his hat. *Is this Spencer's 'help'?*

She pivoted and walked toward the end of the hall, at once calm and confident she could carry this off. Well, almost. She greeted Darlene, and took the armchair, glad for a moment to compose herself. A couple of deep breaths later, she felt her pulse slow and the pressure in her neck ease. This was it. She was ready.

Five minutes later, Darlene slid off her stool, and covered the short distance to Dr. Rutledge's office. Hope watched as she stuck her head in the door. She could hear her speaking in a low tone, and Rutledge's voice in the background. Darlene stepped back, left the door cracked open, and gestured for Hope to come forward.

As Hope made her way to the door, she glanced at the electrician, who made eye contact and nodded. *That's my man.* She entered the office, ready to tangle. This would be over soon, she reminded herself, one way or another. Just like the dentist's drill. But not soon enough.

CHAPTER | 35

"**D**r. Nichols, come in. Sit." Rutledge seemed entirely too jovial for this late-in-the-day meeting.

Hope took two steps inside and stopped. There in a chair, initially concealed by the door, sat Dr. Chet Murdock. Shocked, Hope schooled her expression, quickly regained her composure, and greeted both colleagues. Murdock was off that day, and obviously this was the last place she expected to see him. Rutledge indicated a matching side chair which she took without hesitation, glad to sit before her legs gave out. She felt Murdock's gaze settle upon her.

Rutledge began. "I admit I was surprised at your request for a meeting today, Dr. Nichols. So, I decided to ask Dr. Murdock to join us, given you work together, and you mentioned this was about urgent care issues."

Hope nodded and said, "Yes, that's right. And I appreciate you accommodating me on such short notice."

"Of course. So, let's get started. Why don't you tell us what *is* the issue?"

Addressing Rutledge, she said, "Our last meeting just two weeks ago did not end on a friendly note—"

"—I'm afraid I missed that one," Murdock interjected.

Rutledge shot him a look. "No, it did not."

"And I regret that. The issue of telemedicine hangs over this clinic, and all our practices. It has caused dissension, I'm afraid, which we need to address."

"I absolutely agree," Rich said with a smile. "So, have you changed your position? Am I to be so rewarded?"

She returned his smile, and let him know, "I have spent time considering the pluses and minuses of the technology, and how we might integrate it without worrying we're causing harm. And I agree it's here to stay. My question is, how do we do so smoothly."

"Splendid! I'm glad you've seen the light, Hope." He paused. "Chet?"

Murdock sat forward in his chair, and added, "Yes, that's excellent." His quizzical expression, though, alerted Hope that he might not believe her new attitude. He knew the steadfast position she had taken, knew it better than most. He had watched her in action, and he also knew the cases which had spun her into orbit. And he didn't altogether disagree with her. This is why he was there – perspective.

I better proceed with caution. "At any rate, what can we do from here to ease our colleagues' reservations? I would hate to see people leave over this. We need to retain the experienced doctors, don't you think?" she asked both men. Of course, both she and Chet realized he was in the group of doctors who were 'aging out.'

That last question did not please Rutledge who frowned at the phrase, 'experienced doctors.' She waited. How would he respond, especially with one such physician sitting in their presence?

Rutledge said, "Let me ask you something first. You brought forward certain cases several weeks ago. Have you resolved your concerns over how they were handled?"

"For the most part. I admit I'm concerned about which patients are referred by our offices for virtual visits. There needs to be better triaging, for sure. But, I believe we can develop that."

"I will say, I appreciate you seeing my man with the peripheral vascular disease last week. He seems to have done well, from what I've heard. You were right that he needed to be seen, and I've checked on how he got shuttled to the virtual thing in the first place."

"You're welcome. I'm glad he's done well. Perhaps his wife has also seen the light and will stop smoking for everyone's sake, including their dog's."

Rich and Chet couldn't restrain their laughs, asked what she meant by "their dog's sake," and enjoyed another chuckle or two at her description of the canine's intolerance for cigarette smoking, his sneezing and wheezing. And their veterinarian's smoking cessation advice.

Back to business then, Rich looked at Chet, who took the cue, glanced at his watch, and begged off from further discussion. He and his wife had plans for the evening, he explained, and he must run. Excusing himself, he left. She and Rich Rutledge were at once alone. At least, Kalisha wasn't there to spy on them. *Where was she, anyway?*

Rutledge stared at her, and asked, "So, what do you really want, Hope?"

She held his gaze. "Just what I've explained. I still worry about patient harm, but I've come to realize that we can't stop this from being utilized. We just need to make sure we've built in protections for patients as we expand its use. Don't you agree?"

He hesitated. How could he disagree with protecting patients? "I do, and I'm impressed with your show of judgment. You're a smart lady, Hope. I'd like to have someone like you on board, encouraging others to set aside their worries, and join this movement."

Movement?

He explained, "By movement, I refer to a coalition of professionals who believe this is the way to go. So much so that they've developed an inner circle of like-minded individuals to drive this thing forward, faster than would be expected otherwise. You get what I mean?" He didn't wait for her affirmation, and charged ahead. "We believe that's the only way to build momentum, get this thing established. Then, there's no turning back." Apparently satisfied with his speech, he sat back and threw her a smile.

At that moment, Hope knew she had scratched the surface of something big. Something Spencer already knew about, at least in part, and she was there precisely to get Rich to reveal the real deal. What to say next?

"That sounds fascinating. I had no idea. Can you tell me more about this coalition?"

He leaned forward, and said, "Professionals from around the country, and including some politicians, who are committed to seeing this implemented widely. To be frank, there are financial incentives to be had by clinics who are early adopters, who help kickstart this."

Politicians, huh? "Incentives? You mean payments other than those we would receive just for the virtual visits alone?"

"Something like that. We are paid for the visits already; that's established. But, additional incentives are in the works, sort of like the production bonuses we receive now."

"And who provides those? CMS or the insurance companies?"

"Not the insurance companies, yet. The federal government is so interested in expanding telehealth, they are willing to incentivize doctors eager to use it. You could participate also, if you're now willing to get on board and promote."

Bingo.

"I'm not sure what to say. That seems a little... How does that work, exactly?"

He appeared suddenly more cautious, less willing to

gush about his arrangement. Had he just realized he'd said too much, revealed too much, flown too close to the flame? She smiled, hoping he would relax and continue, not raise his guard. Going into the enemy's camp, exuding charm is not so hard, after all!

"There are more details I'll share with you if you decide to help promote." He leaned back in his chair, assumed a much less enthusiastic posture. "I'm sure you want to consider what I've said. You'll probably have more questions. And we can talk again. How does that sound?"

"Yes, of course. Sounds very interesting. I'd like to give it some thought. I didn't realize telemedicine had gained such traction, enjoyed such widespread enthusiasm." It was time to bring this conversation to an end, before she raised his suspicions, if she hadn't already.

She glanced at her watch and made moves toward leaving. He took the cue and sat forward. "I won't keep you any longer today," she said.

He stood and rounded his desk. As she moved toward the door, he said, "I'm glad you came in and we had this opportunity to discuss, to iron out our differences. Seems we might be able to help each other, after all. You would be a real asset, Hope."

At the door then, she smiled and said, "Thank you. Perhaps this will work out." He opened the door and stepped aside for her to pass. Once in the hall, she turned and prepared to thank him again. *Best to leave on a high note.*

Before she could speak, he smiled and asked, "So, how's that little boy of yours? Noah, is it? I trust he's having a safe summer."

What? How does he know about Noah? Rich's patronizing expression and comment both nauseated and alarmed her. Instead of slapping his smart face, she hurried down the hall, sure he was watching her retreat.

And just where is that friendly electrician, now?

"I thought I would throw up."

Spencer wore a frown as Hope described the encounter. He had arrived late, after she tucked Noah snug in bed. Thankfully, the child was completely oblivious to his mother's dilemma and fear, and Reeves' visit.

The intervening hours could not have passed fast enough. There was no way she was going to confide in Mark. He would go ballistic and attempt to take Noah away. And what was Chet Murdock up to? God only knows. What a nightmare! Spencer was the only person she could trust now. And hopefully, that was true.

"Hope, we need to listen to the tape, and then I'll have it analyzed. You have to admit you may be overreacting to what he said about Noah."

"No, Spencer, I'm not. He's never paid any attention to me or my family before now. He had to get that information, find out Noah's name from someone. But who?"

"How about Murdock? He was sitting right there. Maybe they were just chatting before you arrived."

"Oh, come on. My son's summer program? Murdock knows very little about it. And that information isn't anything they would care to chat about." She couldn't contain her irritation. Maybe Spencer was used to having his family threatened, but she wasn't, and now wished she'd never agreed to go along with this. He had resources and could have found out anything he wanted about Rich Rutledge without drawing her into this scheme. She leaned back in her kitchen chair. How could she extricate herself from this?

"Okay, okay. I agree—"

She interrupted, "—I will not have Noah threatened. Or myself. I have to take care of my child, and am not willing to risk losing him to his father and whoever he chooses to have mother him – or worse – due to some scheme about telemedicine. That's just nuts!"

Spencer had assumed his well-practiced bland expression during her tirade, which irritated her no end.

He said, "Let's listen to the tape and see what you hear now, okay?"

She glared at him. What choice did she have? She had already galloped down the road to perdition, hadn't she? There was no turning back. "Okay, all right."

He looked at her, then smiled. "Have anything to drink around here?"

Surprised, she squinted at him. "Are you asking for strong drink?"

"I am."

She got up and informed him, "You can have one pour of my good whiskey, that's it. We need to keep our wits about us."

"Yes, ma'am, one pour."

Chapter | 36

Wednesday

Spencer hunkered down in his cave, prepared to work remotely with Jacob. He could press ahead without interruption, had purposely avoided the office for just that reason.

His daughter would not vie for attention all day. Madison had departed for her job at the neighborhood pool, lifeguarding and teaching swim lessons, which now kept her busy and off the streets most days. It had taken a few weeks for the opportunity to firm up, but soon fell into place when another girl left for a higher paying job at a local mall. Madi moved quickly and secured the position through August, a few weeks after school would resume.

He dialed up the secure line and waited. Within minutes, Jake answered, sounding enthused, not like he had just rolled out. He had reviewed the tape Spencer transmitted to him the night before, and felt they could go forward, not wait and wait investigating this thing into oblivion. Jake filled in where he'd left off on Sunday, expanding Spencer's understanding of the tech company's involvement, which only increased his anxiety. He had to keep a cool head through this process, or the whole thing could go sideways. There was no way, he realized, he could now avoid an all-out confrontation with Jacque. No way.

"Who do we have lined up for this?"

"We're limited here. How many do you think we need?"

Spencer answered, "I'd say four here, and four or five in Washington."

Jake let a few minutes pass. "I said we're limited here. Not sure there's enough available, or that I can get this past one of the AD's."

This was it. He had to put pressure on, considerable pressure; Jacob expected it. Both of them knew too much. It was precisely why he'd left the Bureau. He dove in.

"Look, buddy, we've known for a long time this was coming. What's been going on violates federal law, and the Bureau has looked the other way, ignoring reports while money poured in from selling patient data. You all are complicit. I can yell all I want from the outside, but you've got to hang in there with me, point the finger from inside. But, if I have to go it alone…"

"No, no, you don't. I just want to make sure we have some help, some cover lined up."

"So, let's get it in order. I shouldn't have to remind you that selling citizens' personal data to overseas entities, corporations set up as covers, is illegal. The CCP and those pesky eastern European organizations all up to no good." Spencer paused to let that sink in. Jacob understood exactly what he had just said and didn't need reminders. He gulped coffee and went on, "And more than a few agents on the take—"

"I didn't say that for sure."

"Okay, but you have data indicating that the problem exists. Specific data, details, remember?"

Jacob cleared his throat.

"Don't bail on me, buddy. Don't be one of the ignorers, or it may not go well for you either."

"Are you threatening me?"

"Take it however you want." He paused; Jacob said

nothing. Spencer continued, "I know enough to make life miserable. Don't hang out in the wrong corner, Jake. We can do this."

"All right, Reeves."

"So, go to your favorite assistant director privately, tell them what you know. Convince them it won't go well if they continue to sit by and just watch. We'll put together our teams and move. Surprise is our best asset." He added, "And they'll eventually be glad we did."

"This is Wednesday... you still stuck on Friday?"

"Yes. Why wait? Descend on the federal HHS office, and I'll swoop down on the local clinic here."

"That's a bodacious plan, Spence."

"The bigger, the better. You find good people on your end, and put me in touch with the SAC in the Kansas City office. I'll talk to him, get the three others I need. I'll brief them here, and briefer is better. They don't need days and days to prepare. We both know more than enough. You do the same, and we'll go for it Friday morning."

"The other clinics scattered around may hunker down, destroy evidence in the meantime."

"They'll get the message. And it's a little hard for them to erase all electronic evidence of payments and transactions. You know that. And it'll send them scurrying, which is usually evidence enough."

"You may have lost your mind."

"Maybe, but a lot is at stake here and we need to make a move. I bet I have more to lose than you do."

"You may be right about that. If this flames out, and I'm booted, is there a spot for me in K.C.?"

"You bet."

"I'll get going. Be back in touch."

"Thanks, buddy."

CHAPTER | 37

"Listen to me, Reeves. I don't want someone trailing me or Noah around."

With her speaker phone on, Hope stood at the kitchen sink, ready to eat lunch, and prepare for her later shift in Urgent Care. She had traded again with another colleague and would work three to nine p.m. that evening. Noah would be ferried from Summer Season to a friend's house for dinner and the evening, until she could fetch him later. Having his friends' parents who understood her schedule predicament had saved the day more than once. She'd need to invite the whole gang over soon to repay their kindness. If she could get this situation out of her hair.

"Look, Hope, I agree, but this situation is giving off threatening vibes. You said so yourself Tuesday evening."

"I know, and I'm not changing my tune. I just don't want a tail. And when are you going to tell me what you've found out about the men at the playground? Who were they, Spencer?"

"We're still running that down. Hang on a bit longer, and we'll have it. In the meantime, please accept the security I've put into place. Don't run them off. I wouldn't do it if I didn't think it was for the best."

"Okay, but Rose Collins is getting suspicious. She pulled me aside when I took Noah inside this morning, quizzed me about you, and tried to quash any concerns we have. She doesn't want other parents to get word of this and pull their kids. She's on alert, Spencer."

"I'm aware. We're discreet."

"In fact, in a roundabout way, she asked me if I would consider withdrawing Noah for the rest of the summer, if his attendance was attracting an 'unsavory element'."

"I'm not surprised. I want you to be reassured that things will resolve in a very short time. This won't drag on, Hope."

"How soon?"

"I can't say."

"Can't, as in not able, or won't?"

"Okay, won't."

Hope glanced out her kitchen window, scanning the street. "There they go again, rolling on down the avenue. The neighbors will eventually wonder what's going on and complain, or call the police. Are you prepared to deal with that… will you come running, flashing your credentials in their faces, explaining why I need protection? This is just ridiculous." She took another look, noted they had disappeared, and added, "Why don't you have them do something, like yard work? I could use some trimming around here."

"That's not a bad idea."

"Well, why don't you arrange that? Maybe they can be useful while they're watching." As she turned to prepare lemon water, a thought struck her. Why hadn't this occurred to her before? "These guys aren't the ones who hung around the playground, are they? Were they your guys, Spencer?"

There was no answer on the other end, and too long a pause. Her empty stomach clenched. "Spencer?"

"Don't overthink this, Hope. Just please cooperate, and

things will fall into place very soon."

"You've already said that." She gazed out her window once more. The grey SUV came into view, rolled around the curve, clearly going under twenty miles an hour. "Okay, they're here again." Still annoyed, she said, "Why don't you switch them out to a van, and set them to work on my landscape?"

He chuckled, which didn't cure her irritation. "I'm on it. Just let them know how much you want trimmed."

"You bet I will. And weeded. I need weeding." She turned off the kitchen faucet. "And they better do a good job, Reeves. Goodbye."

––––––––––––––

Hope glanced in her rearview mirror. No landscape van behind her. Good. It was two-fifteen, and she was well on her way to the clinic. She had planned to arrive a few minutes early, check emails, and patient records before taking over for the evening. She took a deep breath, sighed it away, and pressed on.

At the next light, things changed. Her newly developed habit of checking all the mirrors fed her newly developed paranoia, as well. Behind her sat a grey SUV with two men occupying the front seat. That she could see. It looked like the same one cruising incessantly through her neighborhood not four hours ago; she couldn't believe it. Had the landscapers suddenly shed their work clothes, left their van at her curb, and hopped in their SUV, ready to follow her around? Apparently so. And they better not plan to come to Urgent Care as patients, which would be preposterous. There was no way this would work. She would not tolerate them hanging around the clinic even in the waiting room, keeping watch. The receptionists would immediately get suspicious, call security, and all hell would break loose. There was no way she was going to tell the front desk she now had a security detail. No way. She would just have to repel them if they trailed her into the staff parking lot. Enough is enough! She turned in.

She hit her key fob, and checking in all directions, saw the SUV round the corner and prepare to turn into the lot. Rather than flee indoors, she stood by the side of her car in the shimmering heat and waited. Best to take care of this promptly, and send them back to... wherever. They cruised along a row and pulled to a stop behind her vehicle. Two clean-cut younger men alighted, lean and fit, appearing quite well. They could never pull off a visit to Urgent Care, unless they came for... *never mind that.*

She turned to them and said, "Hi, I'm Dr. Nichols, and you might be?"

Kalisha exited the building, ready to get on with several errands she intended to complete that afternoon. The black asphalt covering the parking lot radiated waves of heat. She donned her sunglasses, which cut the glare somewhat, and strode toward her BMW 530i, anticipating the black interior would be hotter than hell for a good bit of her journey. Rutledge was very busy seeing a load of patients in his office, and had no time to consult with her, which was just as well. As she rounded the end of her row, she pulled up short.

There, partially blocking the row, stood a large gray Yukon, one man standing in the open driver's door, the other talking with none other than Dr. Hope Nichols. *Now, this is interesting.* Kalisha slowed her pace a bit and considered. *Should I greet her, get the gist of their conversation? Or move along like I'm oblivious or blind?* After only a few seconds, she chose her approach.

As she neared the scene, she affected a disinterested air, threw Hope a brief wave and smile. The doctor did not return her greeting, looked very irritated, and continued in heated conversation with the men. Kalisha moved along – as if this were nothing out of the ordinary – and circumvented their obstructing vehicle, hoping she'd grab a word or two in passing. No such luck.

Suddenly, a motorcycle roared into the lot and finally found a narrow slot near the building wall. The rider, gunning his engine repeatedly, announced his arrival to all. *Damn.* As the deafening noise continued, she passed by the small, tight group, noting that Hope had moved closer to one man. Frowning and obviously upset, the doctor's lips moved, but nothing could be heard. Abruptly, the roaring stopped, as did the heated discussion. Kalisha glanced back and recognized the young radiologist who jumped off the cycle, removed his helmet, and sauntered toward the back entrance.

Her opportunity to eavesdrop lost, Kalisha stepped it up and hurried to her car. Opening her door, she turned and snapped two pictures with her cell, hoping one of them proved useful enough to ID the curious visitors. Perhaps she had underestimated the nice Dr. Nichols, after all.

Chapter | 38

Thursday

Rich Rutledge gazed at Kalisha over the rim of his coffee cup. Their usual Thursday morning meeting underway, he now wondered how much Kalisha actually knew. Why had Hope Nichols suddenly changed course, insisted on a meeting, and made like she was jumping on board with telemedicine. Or, at least she put forth that she wouldn't stand in the way, and wouldn't rally fellow doctors against him. He sipped the steaming brew. Darlene knew what he liked. He glanced over at his credenza, bathed in morning light.

"Croissant?" he asked.

Kalisha turned and assessed the assortment. "Perhaps a little later."

"Suit yourself. They're delicious. Darlene picks them up for me several times a week since I mentioned that new place not too far from here."

"She *is* such a good nurse."

He regarded her, not appreciating her tone, tinged with sarcasm. "Yes, she is. Quite."

She seemed preoccupied, sipping her coffee and tapping on her tablet. "So, you had an interesting meeting with Dr. Hope Nichols. I have some news regarding her, as well."

"Oh?"

"It'll keep," she said. "You, first."

"All right. You knew she had called on Monday, requested some time to meet as soon as Tuesday. I thought that was curious, so I took the appointment. Had Chet Murdock here to begin with. We had agreed he'd hit the road during the meeting, not hang around, after he'd seen what she wanted."

"Right."

"We got right down to business. She said she was ready to put aside her resistance, and join us in our efforts to expand virtual visits. Of course, she remains concerned about patient harm, and correct triage – that's selection – of patients who would best benefit from such visits."

"I'm familiar with the word triage."

Her retort irritated him. Where had her compliant attitude gone? Had he misread her? She was not just self-assured, but becoming damn arrogant. Beautiful, yes, but edgy. Maybe too edgy. "Of course. At any rate, she brought up her concern that various of the older doctors might leave, you know hang it up, if we don't address the dissension within our ranks."

"And you don't agree?"

"No, not entirely. Many of them should retire. For one thing, they're set with their fat retirement accounts, and their health insurance claims are higher than younger docs'. They're all developing symptoms now, needing cardiac testing, urology procedures, you name it. Too many colons, call back mamms and breast biopsies, you get the picture. Except for the younger gals having babies, the aging docs are the biggest insurance expense we have every year, driving up our group premiums. And so on."

He noted Kalisha cringe at his choice of terms – gals, in particular – but he didn't care. "And they don't use extenders as much as the younger docs do, either. So, we can't save money there, having extenders see more of their patients."

Kalisha nodded. "So, did the bonus structure come up?"

He paused before answering. He considered how much to say, although this woman already knew of the arrangement. What did she think of it? He admitted to himself he did not know. "It did. Just the basics. She came back with a question about whether it was in addition to the virtual visit charges."

"And you told her what?"

"That it was sort of like the production bonuses we now receive. That there are financial incentives for clinics who are early adopters of the technology."

"You're frowning. Is there something about the meeting you regret?"

He directed his frown at Kalisha. *What's this probing?* "She asked if CMS or the insurance companies were paying the incentives. I denied the insurance companies were paying. But when I mentioned the feds were interested in expanding telemedicine – which is no secret – I over-stepped and said something like she could participate if she is now willing to get on board."

He couldn't ignore Kalisha's face; her brows shot up. *She does not like hearing that.* He forged ahead with, "At any rate, I may have said too much. She asked exactly how that works."

"And you said…"

"I think I regrouped by telling her there were more details I'd share if she decides to help promote. I advised her to give it some consideration."

"Did she commit?"

"Not yet. She did agree to give it more thought." He paused, sipped his coffee, and said, "I'm not convinced she's for real. I got an uncomfortable feeling toward the end of our meeting. I wonder what she's up to?"

"I agree. And I have something I think will interest

you."

He appreciated her warm smile directed his way, recalled her warm touch. "You said."

He watched as she pulled her cell from her pocket, swiped until she came to the item she would show him. "Two pictures I took just yesterday afternoon." She handed over her phone.

Surprised, he stared at the very clear pictures of Hope, obviously standing in the parking lot, arguing with two men. He enlarged the photos and examined both images. "Who are those guys?"

———————————

It was the remains of the day, as they say, and Kalisha enjoyed a glass of crisp, white wine. Refreshing and relaxing. She sat on her balcony, the evening breeze cooler than expected, easing the heat of the day. She was glad she had turned Rich Rutledge down for an early evening encounter. Wise decision. At the time, she wasn't sure she could carry it off. And she wasn't sure she liked his rather suspicious attitude. The pictures probably eased his fears a bit. She suspected he would study them no end, and perhaps ignore his misgivings about her. Hopefully.

She stood and lowered a bamboo shade at the side of her balcony. The evening sun had dropped below her roof line, adding heat to her space. While standing there, she noted the traffic flowing through the Plaza streets. It was a beautiful setting. Thursday night, but the weekend was not quite underway. After the wine, she would make the call. Two calls, actually.

CHAPTER | 39

T here was no question he had to contact her that evening. Still, it was not the type of thing one usually broached over the phone, but he couldn't wait for her return. By then, it would be too late. Spencer glanced at his watch and decided to give it another thirty minutes before he rang Jacque. In the meantime, he sat down for one more review.

Madi had gone to a friend's for the evening. She would not overhear any of what was said, which was a good thing. But she would be directly affected by what happened next, and he couldn't shield her from the fallout. That bothered him. Alot.

All the arrangements were in place. Everyone directly involved had been briefed. He looked at his flowchart, the type he always constructed, satisfied that the when, where, and how were covered. Only he and Jake, the deputy director, and the SAC in the Kansas City office knew the whole story, the why. They approved the operation, though both higher-ups expressed some reservations concerning the apparent suddenness of the plan until reminded of the five-year-long intentional ignoring and procrastination the Bureau had engaged in. That realization sped up their decision-making considerably. It was set.

Closing out that screen, Spencer picked up his cell and dialed her number.

Jacque answered after three rings. "Hi, Spence, you're calling a little late."

"I wanted to wait until you were done with dinner, so it *is* two hours later here."

"Sure. So, how's your week been going?"

Why did she have to ask that question? "Fine, good." *You can't imagine.* "Yours?"

"Busy, as always. I think we're working out some of the kinks, finally." She sounded upbeat, not worn down as she usually did come Thursday evening. "How's Madi?"

"She's busy with her new job at the pool. Seems to like it, especially teaching the little kids' lessons. It keeps her occupied, less time to zip around in the car."

"That's probably just as well. Is she there now? I'd like to say 'hi'."

"No, she's over at Gwen's."

"Oh? Well, I'll have to catch up with her tomorrow when I get back."

"She's at the pool tomorrow 'til closing at nine."

"Those are long hours she's putting in."

"She doesn't go in until noon tomorrow." *Right in the middle of my surprise raid.* "What time are you due in?"

"Around nine there. My flight doesn't leave until four-thirty."

And, you may not make that flight.

They were running out of chit chat, both avoiding talk of her work, telemedicine, and his newfound resistance. It was time to shift gears. He could not keep the tension bottled up any longer.

"Jacque, we need to talk."

"About?"

"Come on, you know. Your work, my concerns, and the tech issues we've discussed."

"Look, Spence, can't this wait until I get home? We've

been over and over that, and frankly, I don't know what more there is to say."

"We certainly haven't come to any agreement, have we? When you left Monday, we left *it* hanging... once again." *And with what I'm about to do, I can't stay tangled up with your company and your money.* "It's time we cleared the air and with that, one of us will have to change our position."

"Spence, what are you talking about?"

"Jacque, I've become aware of the bonuses your company has enjoyed. Money provided by several federal agencies for developing and marketing telemedicine. Taxpayer's money."

He could hear her expel a long sigh, but she said nothing. He went on, "Money that is not running through the usual public/private channels as described. Under the table money directed only at specific parties."

"Oh, Spence, stop. You don't know what you're talking about."

"I'm afraid I do, Jacque. And you are one of those particular parties. Maybe you have nothing more to say, but I do."

Her tone weary and irritated, she said, "Spence, you're tired, you've been there all week by yourself, thinking too much and conjuring up all sorts of wild theories. You're good at that."

"Maybe you're right, but this once my analysis has proven right. Bottom line, Jacque, I can't keep going on like this. It's time things change."

"What on earth are you saying?"

"I'm saying, I think we should separate. Take time apart. Reappraise our situation, our marriage."

"You can't be serious."

"I am, very."

"That's just crazy! Because of telemedicine?"

"No. Because of the divide which has steadily grown

between us over a very long time. The technology deal is the last straw, I'd say."

"I'm shocked, and not one bit okay with this idea of yours." Her voice rising, she added, "And the fact that you brought it up tonight right before I come home. You're being a jerk, Spence."

"Maybe. And you can cut the histrionics, Jacque. You're gone ninety percent of the time. I don't call that a happy arrangement, and you refuse to listen to my concerns over your career and how it affects our lives, our outcome."

"And what about the career you threw over? Have you conveniently forgotten about the strain that put on me?"

"My business is not just a hobby you know."

She ignored that and asked, "So, how does our daughter fit into your plans?"

"Madi is a resilient girl. She's strong and she'll cope, perhaps not well at first, but she'll be okay. She only has two years before leaving for college."

"How little you know of teenage girls, Spence. At her age, they are profoundly affected by parents breaking up. I don't know if it will work for her to stay there with you. We'll have to see about that."

"Don't start talking about taking Madi away, Jacque. Fact is, your schedule doesn't provide a stable environment in which to rear any age child. Talk about disruptive. She can't just sit out there on the West coast by herself while you fly all over the country. Would you really tear her away from her school and all her friends?"

"We'll see about that."

"Jacque, you need to calm down, consider our whole situation, and wait before you jump to conclusions."

"I'm not the one who's jumped to conclusions, Spencer!"

"No, maybe you're not. But I have finally come to terms with the truth. Fact is, very soon things are going to change in a profound way, and I've tried to warn you,

Jacque."

She huffed her indignation, said, "Goodbye, Spence," and hung up.

He stared at the phone. Had he really done that? Started the process of ending his sad marriage, without giving his wife of nearly twenty years a truthful heads up? How her life was going to be turned upside down in a few short days?

Yes, as a matter of fact, he had.

———————

She had sent the files, had done exactly what they'd asked. Now, she wanted to touch base, make sure everything was in order. Kalisha left her balcony, lest any nosy neighbors might overhear her end of the conversations, went inside and closed her sliding door. She rinsed her wineglass and settled onto her large, semicircular sofa.

She dialed the first number and waited. After five rings, she left no message, as instructed, and tried to control her impatience. Where were they? Things were coming together; this was not the time to avoid talking. Within moments, her head felt full, her heartbeat erratic. This anxiety she'd recently developed was more than annoying, and she hated it. Deep breaths, in and out, would bring relief. She set aside her cell, practicing the exercises she'd been taught. Eventually calming herself, she reasoned they might have family constraints at that moment. Yes, they would return her call as soon as they could, when they saw the special cell number. After a few moments, she felt calmer, more centered, and rang the other party.

"Yes?"

Kalisha answered, "Yes." After a pause, she added, "I sent the report."

"We received it."

"Are there any questions?"

"No. Anything else you want us to know?"

"I believe he's getting suspicious. Or at least watchful. When Dr. Nichols went in to talk, he began wondering if she was up to something. I think he's wondering about everyone now, including me."

"There's no way he can trace you to us."

"No, I don't think so, either."

"Has he offered you more money or position?"

"Not since four weeks ago. He drops hints now and then, but nothing substantive."

"Well, keep recording your conversations. We have the earlier ones."

"Right."

"Anything else?"

"How soon will I be done here?"

"Soon."

"I'm ready now."

"There's scuttlebutt… something may be going down."

"When will I know?"

"You won't until it happens."

CHAPTER | 40

Friday

S pencer Reeves sat in the front seat of the Yukon and watched. He glanced at his watch – seven forty-five. The parking lot gradually filled, a steady stream of nurses, doctors, lab and X-ray technologists making their way to the clinic's back entrance, apparently unaware they were being observed. A rookie agent occupied the driver's seat, and two other veterans sat in the back, keeping an eye on all who arrived. Avoiding conversation, they sipped iced drinks – Coke, Mt. Dew, anything heavy with caffeine for starters. Spencer wedged his iced coffee in his lap, while he swiped his cell screen, waiting for word from D.C. It was muggy and warm that morning, and the vehicle's A/C labored to keep the interior cool until they made their move. It wouldn't be long.

Washington, D.C.

Jacob Nelson, and his band of three brothers, walked calmly into the low-rise building – known for its post-WWII Brutalist style – scanned the lobby with one look, and removed their shades. It was a warm day in D.C., and they wore only sport coats and slacks – no labeled jackets – and open neck shirts. All dressed similarly, they immediately caught the eye of a tall, thickly-built security guard, who could have been a defensive lineman in a former life. The guard correctly assessed that they were not a group of employees traveling in a pack, nor curious visitors. He stood behind a semicircular desk located smack dab in the center of the lobby, watching their every move. In turn, Jake watched him as the guard pressed a button on his desk phone.

Without hesitation, Jake approached the desk and withdrew his cred pack from an inside pocket. The guard's eyes widened. Several employees stopped in their tracks, apparently having observed the foursome's arrival.

"How can I help?" the guard asked.

"By being aware we're here, manning your station, and providing us with a security escort to the fifth floor."

"Yes, sir. That's an HHS office."

"We know." A moment later, Jake added, "And don't call ahead. We won't require an introduction."

"Yes, sir." The guard nodded, and pressed another button on his phone.

Jake and his associates pocketed their credentials for the time being and waited. They continued scanning the lobby, while those passing through scurried to the elevators, obviously ready to get upstairs without delay and spread the word. Presently, another security guard materialized from a back office, and they were on their way.

While in the elevator, Jake texted Spencer with a, 'We're in,' message. Their efforts would be coordinated, minimizing someone potentially alerting others or fleeing with evidence. Hopefully. Bank records on both ends of the deal had been secured days ago, although leaks always occurred, and neither could be sure that hadn't already happened. They'd soon see.

The elevator door opened on the fifth floor. They approached a reception desk. Jake smiled at the woman manning that desk and presented his credentials. His associates maintained impassive, unamused expressions as they scanned the space, not that it mattered. Two of them had been there the day before, posing as tech repairmen, checking out the office they now intended to invade.

Obviously, the receptionist was not expecting them, judging by her expression, and sat mute behind the curved counter. She gathered herself. "What should I do?"

Still friendly, Jake spoke. "You should show us to this person's office right away." He presented a business card with a particular manager's name scribbled on the back.

"Yes, sir." She rose, took a few wobbly steps, and gestured for them to follow. She now had a story to tell, and likely there would never be another day like this during her remaining time at that agency, or any other for that matter. They had that effect on people.

The group reached the end of the hall and a closed office door. Jake gave her a hand signal to knock, prior to showing them in. This was to be a civilized raid, no blazing invasion. Without hesitating, she did as told.

Through a partially open door, Jake heard the exchange. "Yes, what is it? We're not done with our meeting yet."

"Pardon, sir, but there are several people here to see you."

"Do they have an appointment?"

"Uh… no sir… I don't believe they need one."

"What?"

Jake had heard enough. He nodded to the receptionist, who stepped aside and hustled back to her post. Leading the way, he entered, one agent with him, two remaining in the hall.

"What is the meaning of this?" the irate bureaucrat asked.

Credentials on full display, Jake answered, "Jacob Nelson, FBI. We're here to pay an overdue visit."

The woman occupying a side chair, sat forward, ready to flee. Jake instructed, "Ma'am, just keep your seat. You will leave when we tell you to do so." Her look of shock and dismay was bested only by the HHS manager's sour expression.

"How dare you barge in here, unannounced. You could have made an appointment for whatever is on your mind."

"We don't operate on an appointment basis in situations such as this."

"Then state your business, so I can make a phone call."

"No, sir, you're not making any phone calls right now. Just sit tight."

Thoroughly indignant, he shouted, "How absurd! Why are you here? I have a right to know."

Jake presented a proper search warrant, slapped it on his desk. "That is correct. Taxpayers' money, telehealth, selling patient data. Ring a bell?"

The man's face fell.

As Jake recited the litany, he signaled another agent to enter and begin gathering material from the office. The incensed manager rose slowly, backed away from his desk, and for support leaned against the bookshelves which lined one entire office wall. He glared at the agent who rifled through his desk, took jump drives, and piles of paper. The terrified woman slumped in her chair, no doubt planning how to extricate herself from the mess her boss had created, if she didn't faint first.

"I've done nothing wrong," the man protested.

"Someone else will decide that."

"I demand to call our legal counsel."

"You'll have that opportunity, and I suggest you say nothing more in the meantime."

Kansas City

Spencer saw the text and smiled. It was go time. Just minutes before, at eight-fifteen, he and the other agents had zeroed in on Dr. Rich Rutledge as he left his car and walked slowly toward the building entrance. He certainly did not appear in a hurry. Just another day unfolding. He was likely considering the patients he would see, or the duties he had scheduled as Chief Medical Officer. Or, the money he would line his pockets with.

Before they exited the Yukon, they spied Kalisha Johnson slinking toward the back entrance, ready for her day. The woman was stunning, dressed in a floral summer dress, coordinated spike heels, her long hair flowing in the breeze. One agent let out a low whistle, which the others tried to ignore. They were not there to admire this woman, whom they might need to haul away in a few short hours. Focus is what they must maintain.

That small distraction over, they waited, and Spencer watched as she disappeared inside. If they could catch the two of them together, that would ice the cake, but that might be too much to hope for. The pair had been very careful and discreet about their meetings and rendezvous, especially while at the clinic. Not too often, not too private, always appearing above board. Spencer knew all that.

They left the SUV in unison, armed with a card key Hope Nichols had provided. There would be no stopping them at the back entrance. No metal detector stood in their way, and the sole security guard casually manning the clinic's front door had no clue.

CHAPTER | 41

Hope gripped the exam room doorknob, ready to address a patient with shortness of breath. Urgent Care had opened at eight, and already there were ten individuals waiting to be seen. A very busy morning was unfolding. *Would this be the day?* Her attention and focus were divided, to say the least.

Pushing that thought aside, she closed the door, introduced herself and verified the patient's chief complaint. The worried woman began her story.

Deciding fifteen minutes later that several tests were in order, she emerged intent on finding a nurse to perform the ambulatory oxygen saturation before sending the woman to radiology. Instead, she met Chet Murdock in the hall, looking perturbed and anxious to speak with her.

"Can you hold on for a moment?" she asked, scurrying down the hall toward the nurses' desk.

He didn't answer, turned on his heel, and headed for the next room. When she returned to that spot, he was gone. Checking the doctors' room, she found no one there. And she was not going to loiter about waiting for him to finish with a patient. Instead, she moved onto the next room. They would cross paths again, soon enough.

Spencer's group approached the back hall elevator. Ahead, two nurses waited for the slow car to arrive. He watched as they alerted and returned his stare. They stopped chatting, and backed up against the wall opposite the elevator door. Clearly, the duo sensed a threat, and were silently considering what they might do next. Flee? With a jerk of the head, his foursome ducked into the stairwell adjacent to the elevator and nearly sprinted up the four flights.

There, they emerged into a hall, stopped, and caught their breath. Now, where exactly was Dr. Rutledge's office? That was the one small detail Spencer had minimized. Hope had given him the location of internal medicine and general directions through the labyrinthine halls, but the door numbers he was staring at made no sense. In the next moment, he determined they would start in one direction, to their left, and ask along the way. No harm in acting friendly.

But, it did not take long to know which way to go. Within moments, a wail arose, "Ahhh…," and grew louder. At once, a nurse sprinted past, nearly colliding with them as she turned from an interior hall. She sped away, covering the entire back hall in only a few minutes, and disappeared around a far corner. The tight cabal of agents exchanged glances and pivoted into that same hall lined with closed doors. Near the end, a young woman stood in a doorway, hand over mouth, staring into the interior. She recoiled and took off, oblivious to the pack approaching, and ran to the nurses' desk. Moments later, the Code Blue announcement boomed through the clinic's PA system.

Spencer and his crew jogged to that particular door and took up positions. In the distance he could hear doors slamming, feet pounding the stairs. The Code team was on their way. He drew his weapon, pushed the door open wide, and stopped. There, his head in a pool of blood on his desk, rested Dr. Rich Rutledge. The surrounding area – more than a mess.

A slack-armed woman stared back.

"Kalisha, drop the gun."

She returned his stare and whispered, "I didn't do it."

"Kalisha, drop the gun. Back away."

She blinked several times, drew herself up tall, and gingerly laid the weapon, obviously equipped with a suppressor, on the desk. Taking two steps backward, she explained, "I found him like this… picked it up." She pointed to the floor adjacent to his chair.

Loud voices and heavy footfalls drew near. There was no question the Code team was not needed. The approaching commotion ceased. In the next moment, one doctor – the tall cardiologist – pressed into Spencer's shoulder from behind and commanded, "Step back, step back."

In the background, Kalisha chanted, "Found him like this… like this." Suddenly, she fell mute, turned and, giving them her back, gazed out the large office window.

Spencer took one long stride into the office, pivoted, and flashed his cred pack at the doctor. "No need to shout. He doesn't need CPR."

Eyes wide, the cardiologist retorted, "I'll be the judge," and pushed his way inside. The remainder of the code team, with cart, crowded the door, staring at the ungodly scene. Several gasped. Others muttered expletives and turned away.

Immediately understanding Rutledge's condition, the doctor locked eyes with Spencer and mumbled, "I'll pronounce him."

"Be my guest."

"What?"

"I said there's been a shooting... upstairs!" Murdock repeated.

"I heard the Code. Where?"

"Internal medicine."

"Oh, my God!"

As Hope took off running down the back hall, she heard Murdock yell after her, "Don't go up there! We're not needed!"

Ignoring his warning, she took the stairs two at a time. Breathless when she reached the fourth floor, she trotted to the Internal Medicine corridors, rounded the corner and abruptly stopped. At least eight people crowded around Rich Rutledge's door. One individual stood balanced on the familiar armchair, surveying the entire scene. Sensing she would only be in the way, Hope stood down the hall and waited. Spencer was nowhere in sight. *Where had he gone?*

The whole scene swam in slow motion. Queasy, and fearing she might faint, she backed up against a wall, and pressed herself into its firm support. A moment later, she felt a hand on her shoulder and turned to see Rachel Baumann standing at her side.

"Come sit down, Hope. You look pale. Here... here's a chair." Baumann pointed to two chairs in the hall. She propelled Hope along slowly, and gently pushed her onto the nearest seat. "We'll have a sit," the kindly woman said. She wrapped her arm around Hope's shoulder.

Hope gazed at Rachel and said, "I didn't think this would happen."

"You've had a shock. We all have. Just wait."

Hope nodded. A few minutes passed, as both women sat mute, staring toward the CMO's office, or at the floor. The crowd there shuffled. The cardiologist emerged wearing a fierce look. Stricken, the Code team silently followed him. As he passed – cell phone to his ear – he merely gave Hope and Rachel a crisp nod, and proceeded toward the back hall. It was the clinic CEO he spoke to; Hope heard him mention their names as he passed by. The wail of approaching sirens in the distance then broke through her thoughts. The police were on their way.

A few moments later, several nurses entered the hall and hurried toward two exam rooms. Looking distraught, they ignored Hope and Rachel and slipped inside, dealt with the patients within, and presently, escorted those individuals to the back hall and toward the elevator, apparently thinking there was no reason for the patients to wait. Although as witnesses of a sort, their interviews with authorities would come, sooner than perhaps they or the nurses expected.

Presently, two men bearing stern expressions emerged from Rutledge's office escorting Kalisha Johnson away. As the threesome approached, Kalisha freed herself of one agent's grasp, stopped, and said, "I tried to warn you, Dr. Nichols... tried to warn you." She said nothing more, turned and headed to the back hall, presumably to be handed over to the local police. She also would have her chance to say more soon, very soon.

Scrambled thoughts crowded for attention. *What on earth is she referring to?* Hope considered scene after scene, desperately trying to recall such a moment. The last six short weeks felt more like six months. Time expansion, for sure, worked her memories. *Is this over?*

One person would know, and he was walking toward her. They locked eyes as he approached.

Spencer put a hand on Hope's shoulder, as Rachel Baumann's arm slipped away.

"What on earth happened here?" Hope asked.

He paused, divided a look between them, and said, "Looks like he finished what he'd started." He withdrew a white envelope bearing the clinic logo. "We found this."

Hope nodded. "Is that all?"

"We're not done. We'll know more details soon, I'm sure."

She held his gaze and dared to ask, "Is Noah safe?"

"Yes, very. We have him in tow."

Hope lowered her head and wept.

CHAPTER | 42

Jacqueline refused eye contact. She sipped white wine and gazed into the distance. Their large deck was the perfect place to spend a Friday evening, three seasons of the year, but not that night. The smell of freshly-cut grass filled his nostrils. He listened as cicadas buzzed their crescendo, decrescendo racket and watched fireflies flit around, but she said nothing. Spencer sipped his own whiskey, waiting for her to cut through the summer sounds. He wasn't going to interrupt her silence. Dusk had overtaken the landscape, and he wasn't so sure she would say anything. Maybe they had said enough. Jacque had arrived home earlier than he expected, having changed her flight. She was there waiting when he made an appearance around seven, and she was not in a good mood.

By late afternoon, the Kansas City field office had relieved him of his assumed temporary duties, 'but thank you for all your help, by the way, and calling this situation to our attention.' Their attention? The federal agency had known a good deal of this way before he got hold of the situation. He and Jacob had exchanged much of that information over just the past two weeks. Question was – would they pursue this to the fullest extent, or brush it under the carpet with their other untidy bits of trash?

Probably not this time, unless they wanted whistles blowing from both inside and outside the Bureau. It was time to shut this down, and he sensed they knew it. Knew full well about the selling of citizens' personal data to adversaries, and the quid pro quo arranged between big tech and the several government agencies. What a mess. And if they dealt Jacob a bad hand, well, there was a place waiting for him in the heartland. Now, only time would tell.

He reined in his musings and looked at his wife. "Jacque, we need to talk."

Her gaze swung to him. "What for? You've made up your mind."

"Yes, I have, but there are still things to work out. Your involvement, for one."

She sipped her wine, and said, "I'm fully aware you sold me down the river."

"You wouldn't listen, and I didn't."

"How could you do that?"

"Jacque, you ignored my warnings, a long string of cautions I gave you."

She said nothing, pulled her knees to her chest, and looked away.

"Big issues with people's safety emerged which we couldn't ignore. We couldn't wait."

"Always harping on telehealth."

"No, actual local people were under threat. It wasn't just some exaggerated worry about potential harm to patients."

She turned and stared at him. "What are you saying? Us?"

"No, not us directly. Others here who some considered adversaries."

"I don't know what you're talking about, but I'm sure you'll be glad, even excited, to explain it to me over the next few days. But I am so tired right now, and sick of all this, I'm going to bed." She rose, took a few steps toward the back door and stopped. "And I'd appreciate it if you would sleep in your *cave* tonight." Saying no more, she left him sitting alone.

He sipped and listened to the night, absorbed the present, and knew he'd made the right decision. He picked up his cell and sent the text.

———————

Hope hugged Noah an extra time or two that night, then snugly tucked him into bed. She resisted an urge to just lay there with her son until both fell asleep. He had noticed her yawns, told her she was too tired to stay up, and advised her to get more sleep. She worked too hard, he had added. There was more truth in that statement than she wished to admit.

Their nightly ritual had changed over the past week, and that evening she urged Noah to read a different book to her, avoiding *Forest Owls* with keen eyes. She couldn't take any more talk of watching, spying, or surveillance of any kind from any source. He had agreed, and they read *The Little Engine That Could*. Both were satisfied with the choice. When he nodded off, she rose from his bed and left the room, a blanket of heavy exhaustion weighing her down.

As Hope retired to her back deck, she welcomed the deepening dusk. Soon, she would be sitting alone in the dark. Literally and figuratively. Other than her cell, she carried only a tall glass of ice water and too many thoughts to dismiss. Avoiding any liquor – which she reasoned would only depress her more and disrupt her sleep – she longed to erase the day and wake up the next morning with a clear head. The weekend lay ahead, unfettered by urgent care shifts. She knew no matter what she attempted to do, though, the drama of the past weeks and this day would consume her thoughts. The dreaded long process she could not escape.

Mark's trial in Chicago had concluded sooner than expected; he was winging his way back to town. He planned to pick up Noah the next day around noon for the remainder of the weekend. She needed to think through what she would tell him, before Noah had a chance to spin some tall tale, although he knew next to nothing of what had happened, and she intended to keep it that way. Mark, on the other hand, would get wind of it shortly after landing and would react. She was sure of that. Best to start with a summary statement, add a few key points, and quit explaining while she was ahead. Undoubtedly, his further questions would flesh out the whole story, or what she knew of it. She would allow him to conduct his interrogation and would bear up under it.

Her key concern – were she and Noah safe now? Was this truly over? Could she reassure Mark of that... without referring him to Spencer? Probably not.

She sipped the icy cold water, savored the tang of lemon, and stretched her legs on the chaise lounge. Evening cicadas sang their tune, and lightning bugs flitted across her back yard. Did she deserve such a peaceful setting, expected for a late June evening? Such a contrast to the mayhem of a few short hours ago. Could she have done more? She knew that question would plague her for many months, if not years. Her cell interrupted, chiming a text.

Would seven o'clock tomorrow evening work, Union Station?

She gazed into the dark distance and considered. After a time, she texted back.

CHAPTER | 43

Saturday

Hope wasn't sure why she had agreed to this. Not enough time had passed – definitely not enough time – to recall the events of yesterday with any clarity, much less recover from the shock. But something had compelled her to accept his invitation, despite any rational warnings to the contrary. Maybe she just wanted to get out of the house, not sit alone with her jumbled feelings. Maybe she wished to take advantage of the time while Noah was safely tucked in at Mark's until tomorrow. Maybe she wished to share the shock with someone. She glanced up at the huge Union Station clock and confirmed she was five minutes early. Hope pivoted, surveyed people strolling here and there and, glancing at the mezzanine bar above, saw a man rise from a chair and wave. It was him.

As she approached the corner table, Spencer got to his feet again, and extended his hand. *No hugs, please.* Reserved greetings completed, she took a seat across from him and locked eyes with the man. He had chosen the spot well, which obviously afforded him the opportunity to keep the entire bar under watch. He hadn't asked nor gestured for her to sit beside him, which was just as well. He could pretend to engage with her while surveilling the surrounding area, but she could also take in the area beyond the bar – the humongous open lobby below. And inform him of threats? Situational awareness, right? How good she had become at this game... or how ridiculous a thought.

And where is your wife this Saturday evening?

"Did you bring friends with you this evening?" she asked, scanning the immediate area. *Like that single male over there – waiting on a date, trolling, or watching over them?* Her mind had since blurred his fellow agents' faces from her immediate recall as they had escorted various people from yesterday's shocking scene. She wouldn't recognize any of them on the street if she had to. And, admittedly, that surprised and bothered her; she prided herself on such strong visual memory. Well, obviously, that gift could be compromised given the right circumstances.

A smile spread across his face. "Why would you think that?"

"Because this game never stops, does it?"

He dropped the smile, said, "You've become a cynic so soon."

"I suppose so, yes."

Without further discussion, he suggested, "Care to order?"

She picked up the small menu and quickly saw nothing which appealed. She had eaten what she cared to consume, and which her stomach would tolerate, several hours before. Deciding on a small glass of white wine, she tabled the menu and waited. Spencer seemed far more interested in the offered selections, taking minutes more to make his choice. She stared at him until he looked up and met her gaze.

Before either could speak, a waiter appeared, took their orders, and left.

He resumed. "So, how have you felt since yesterday?"

How absurd a question. What does he expect me to say? Fine and dandy? She said, "How should I feel?"

He didn't respond immediately, and she went on.

"Let's see… shocked, horrified, disgusted, angry, afraid? Pick one." Clearly, she was venting and abruptly stopped. She must work to curtail her irritation. Having an outburst right there was a very bad idea.

Still wearing that well-practiced impassive face he adopted so easily, he only nodded.

Thoroughly annoyed by his calm demeanor, she spoke in a low tone. "Well? How does one feel after a scene like that? Couldn't something have been done to avert such a tragedy?"

"I understand, and in a word, no."

"Well, I don't believe this outcome was inevitable."

"If you'll permit me to explain some things, I believe you'll see why this happened—"

Their waiter appeared, interrupting Spencer, and presented their orders. He inquired of other possible needs and quickly retreated when Spencer shot him a sharp look.

"—in this way."

Hope took a sip of her chilled wine. "I'm listening."

Spencer took a few bites of the generous appetizer he'd ordered, sipped his whiskey, and looked at her. "I admit this whole thing took shape and moved along faster than most investigations the Bureau launches. But much of what went on at the several agencies was already known, at least in part. For a few years, an FBI task force had targeted the ones pushing telehealth, and were keeping their eye on several big tech firms working on it. Watching the flow back and forth. Gathering data."

"You mean harvesting data? Can they legally do that?"

"Harvesting is a good term. And, yes, they can do that, if something rings their bell. When it's part of an investigation or something seems out of order."

"So, who rang the bell?"

"Several entities, but primarily a watchdog group."

"So, did you know about this emerging concern while you were still at the Bureau?"

"No, not then."

"So, when did you learn of it?"

"After we met, when I contacted a friend still there."

"So, very recently." She sipped and considered. When was he going to tell her why he quit? "Spencer, why *did* you quit?"

He put down his fork, took another swig of whiskey, and leaned back in his chair. He allowed some time to elapse. It was obvious he was choosing his words carefully. Glancing about, his gaze finally swung back to her.

"Over time, I became aware of certain positions the Bureau took on ongoing investigations. Several, in particular, were troublesome. Evidence of serious issues being swept under the carpet. That sort of thing."

"Those are pretty broad statements. So, it wasn't this deal?"

"Not exactly. But obviously, I can't go into details. Suffice it to say, serious situations." He ate and drank, and she waited. He added, "It's not uncommon for agents to disagree with how something is handled, but we understand we must do our job and let Justice handle the case once we turn over evidence. The behaviors I saw ran counter to that principle."

"And you were expected to keep quiet and go along."

"Right. And finally, I concluded I couldn't. So, after fifteen years I hung it up. Figured it would be better to say something from the outside, if I were to say anything at all."

"But, you still had friends on the inside."

"Right. And they knew what I knew, and vice versa, which kept all of us in line until this situation came to a head."

"You mean my little situation. And Madison's condition? Seems small when you're talking about the feds."

He threw her a sharp look. "Not small at all,

considering the growing use of telehealth, the harvesting of patient identification and personal data, and the damage that could do. Likely already has done. And yes, I'll admit my daughter's case woke me up, made me pivot."

He took time to eat and drink. Arresting the tense moment, she did the same and played with her wine. In her peripheral vision, she saw movement, glanced over and watched as the young man she had noticed earlier stood from his chair, cast them a look, and left.

She refocused on Spencer who resumed with, "And so you'll know, an impressive number of clinics around the country have suspended their use of virtual medicine with the news of this operation. HHS had no choice but to interrupt further expansion at least until the dust settles."

"Well, that may help in the short run. I'm sure they'll find a way to resume as soon as they can, and deny any problem existed in the first place."

"But, hopefully, with more protections in place. As we dug deeper, we found a far-reaching network of connections suspicious for a quid pro quo scheme which would enrich the parties involved. Had already enriched the parties involved. Something analogous to a river with dozens of tributaries snaking through the landscape, but in this case, money flowed upstream, and robust cooperation flowed downstream. And a well-oiled propaganda machine churned out disinformation to the public, engaging them with the glitzy new tech."

Hope sipped her wine. He seemed geared up to say more, and she wisely chose to be still.

"And my wife sits at the headwaters of one large tributary." He completed his statement and held her gaze.

Stunned, Hope landed her wineglass with a bit more force than warranted. She stared at Spencer. *What?*

Apparently reading her expression correctly, he said, "That's right. She is smack dab in the middle of it all. She's a key VP at the major tech company involved in the development of the software which made all this possible. I now know she participated in the bonus scheme, innocently or not, which the feds used to lure these companies and, in turn, the clinics. Obviously, that being so, I have enjoyed the benefits of those spoils, as well."

Hope couldn't find an appropriate word, and realizing the import of his statement, which bordered on a confession, she sat mute.

He prompted her, "Well?"

"I don't know what to say. So, you didn't suspect even before you and Madison came to Urgent Care?"

"As I said, this situation wasn't on my radar screen until after my daughter's visit. I've had concern for at least five years about other long-standing investigations and evidence involving selling citizens personal data to foreign entities. Investigations which were being slow-walked or ignored by the feds. But no, I wasn't tuned into telehealth and some related coverup before then. Didn't like the idea of e-visits, but I hadn't paid much attention."

He added, "When you brought up your situation at the clinic, it struck a chord with me. After you gave me names and the further we dug, we realized your Dr. Rutledge had developed a working relationship with a key bureaucrat which benefited them both financially. That was the link we needed to push deeper."

Financial gain here, there, and everywhere. Processing his revelations, she said, "My God. You believe that was enough for him to commit suicide?"

"Apparently so. You know, not everyone can fight such charges. He became desperate, I would wager. Rutledge was a proud, arrogant man, who figured he couldn't stand the shame."

"What about the Johnson woman? She was there, too."

"The investigation has only gotten underway. It looks like suicide, but we'll see. I will say this, which will become common knowledge fairly soon… it does appear she walked in after he shot himself. And she's in an interesting position. I'll explain more later, but it was not just by chance that she got that job."

More convolutions, more intrigue. Having regained her composure, Hope asked, "And what about your wife?"

Spencer didn't rush to answer. Finally, he said, "Jacque and I have talked… quite a bit. She is *not* happy, not with me or the recent revelations, which are one and the same in her mind. If I hadn't bird-dogged this, it wouldn't have happened, which is false thinking, of course. She's convinced I'm throwing her under the bus, all that."

He sipped the remains of his whiskey. Hope felt his unrelenting gaze. An uncomfortable warmth spread through her. *What is he about to say?* She abandoned her wine, and reached for a handy ice water.

"I've asked her for a separation."

Stunned, she sat silent. This was not a moment to jump in with additional questions. This man was in distress, far more than she had experienced during this saga.

"No questions, then?" he asked.

"Can't say that any come to mind."

He managed a tight smile. "I'm sure you'll have a few, sooner or later."

"Perhaps so. No, I'm sure I will. This whole thing's a real mess." She drank water, then added, "What an understatement."

He pushed away his plate as their waiter approached. The young man gathered their food and drink remains, and handed Spencer the check.

Hope watched as Spencer glanced about the small bar and gave a quick nod to someone across the way. This time she turned and checked out the subject of his attention. A lone man rose from the table he occupied, made his way to the nearby curved staircase, and disappeared below. They had been chaperoned, as it were, or protected. Relief, tinged with a bit of dread, welled up. Not a very reassuring way to live one's life, is it?

The bill settled, he looked at her. "So, shall we stay in touch?"

"Yes, I think I'd like that, considering."

They stood. He escorted her from the bar, and together they descended the staircase to the marble-floored lobby below. The time approached eight-thirty, and the crowd had thinned. Off to other Saturday evening entertainments.

Turning to her, he said, "I'll see you home."

"I'll be fine, I'm sure. You shouldn't leave your car here."

"No, I mean I'll follow you home, make sure all is well."

Considering the alternative – driving home alone, distracted and worried – his offer sounded good, quite comforting, in fact. "All right. I'm parked out front."

As they left the cavernous lobby and stepped into the warm summer evening, she relaxed for the first time in days. At least this time she knew the character of the man who would follow her home – or did she?

Chapter | 44

July 2022

Although it wasn't quite ten a.m., waves of heat radiated from the parking lot pavement. As Spencer stepped from his car, he scanned the lot and saw only one other car he recognized. Reaching in, he grabbed his sport coat and slung it over his shoulder for the short trek to the building. The thick, humid air gloved him as he made his way to the front entrance.

He stepped inside, glad for the over-air-conditioned lobby. There stood Kalisha Johnson, outfitted that morning in a conservative summer suit, her hair pulled up into a restrained French twist, all business but still stunning, as always. Two other men stood alongside. Spencer had only recently made their acquaintance. Greetings exchanged, one gentleman gestured toward a hall, indicating it was time to move and get underway.

Midway down the passage, they arrived at an open door, which welcomed them to an empty conference room. Moments later, one man – Carter Lloyd, the SAC from the Kansas City FBI office – entered through a far door and greeted them. Obviously, he was in charge and would moderate this meeting. He gestured toward the table, and those gathered carefully chose their seats. As if it would matter once this meeting got underway.

Although introductions seemed unnecessary, they engaged in reminding each other who they were, where they came from, and why they were in attendance. That day they were joined by a Mr. Purdue, chairman of the watchdog group Integrity in Medicine, and the state medical board's chief counsel, Jack Latrell. Two other individuals had yet to put in an appearance.

Preliminaries accomplished, Agent Lloyd said, "We all know why we're here today and what we hope to accomplish. I believe we will satisfy our goal. While we wait for the other party, I would like Ms. Johnson and Mr. Purdue to give us an overview of the plan which they initiated and launched last spring."

And so it began. Spencer now knew much of the scheme which the medical watchdog group had formulated to monitor the subject federal agencies and the individuals involved, not only at South Metro Medical Associates, but elsewhere. At least a dozen clinics around the country had come under scrutiny. But as Kalisha and Purdue outlined more operational details, Spencer had to admit he was surprised at their methods and perseverance. This had required at least a year of dogged work, and devoid of leaks, had produced the outcome they sought. Lloyd was also obviously impressed.

Twenty minutes later they concluded their presentation, and fielded the few questions thrown their way. That completed, lawyer Jack Latrell picked up the ball. As legal counsel for the state board, Latrell had worked closely with Kalisha throughout the operation; had, in fact, been involved from the git-go. From a legal perspective, he authorized Integrity in Medicine sending in Ms. Johnson as an applicant for the administrative assistant position. Of course, there had been no guarantee Dr. Rutledge would accept her as the new hire, but Latrell and others considered it a reasonably safe bet. But just to tip the scales, Latrell and Purdue made sure the other two applicants bowed out at the last minute. Made it worth their while to do so.

Compiling the data Kalisha amassed, as well as recording Rutledge in the process of making deals, was key to taking him down. She certainly had met and exceeded their high expectations. The same type of operation ran in various states against other doctors and clinic administrators convinced they could benefit from scheming with the feds. Catching such individuals in the act and making conspicuous examples of them was their intent, and secondarily scaring and intimidating others who might be tempted to follow the same course. However, death and destruction was not the desired outcome. Dr. Rutledge had apparently beaten them to the finish line. Or, had he?

What Spencer saw and heard next admittedly surprised even him. Up to that point, he had expected Agent Lloyd to ask him to summarize the role of his wife's tech company in telehealth's software development, the bonus structure she had enjoyed, which had in fact financially benefitted him, and how he uncovered those details – a mea culpa opportunity of sorts. But, he was not called upon. Instead, Lloyd stood from his chair and walked to a door at the far end of the room. Opening it, he spoke quietly to someone in an adjoining space. In the next moment, in walked a woman wearing a solemn expression. She did not look particularly happy to be there. The men present got to their feet. Kalisha remained seated and only offered Darlene a fleeting smile.

"Please have a seat," Lloyd said to her. No one spoke as she took a chair next to him, with their backs to the far door. "We've scheduled this meeting today, Darlene, to clarify details about Dr. Rutledge's involvement in the telehealth initiative at the clinic. You understand that, correct?"

"Yes."

"And to explore further details regarding his death."

Darlene nodded and stared, in turn, at those assembled.

Spencer divided his attention between Kalisha and Darlene. It was obvious that the two of them held the key to this whole debacle. His recollection of Darlene sprinting from the hall where Rich Rutledge occupied an office, and the horrifying scene – Kalisha standing within that office behind the doomed doctor, gun in hand – flashed through his mind.

"So, would you like to tell us what you know?"

Darlene straightened in her chair, glanced around the table, her eyes resting on Kalisha, and said, "I would."

"And I have given you the opportunity to have legal counsel here today and you have declined, correct?"

"Yes. I don't need a lawyer here today."

Several present exchanged quick looks, which apparently did not phase Darlene or cause her to think twice.

"You may proceed, then, and I am recording your comments for accuracy. Do you agree?"

"Yes."

Agent Lloyd dictated the date, time, and place, recited the witnesses present, and said to Darlene, "Please state your name, birth date, and your present address."

Without hesitation, Darlene complied with his request, and with gusto launched into her description of that fateful day. Rather than interrupt her with specific questions, he allowed her to tell her story. And told it, she did, while the others sat spellbound and silent.

Spencer listened intently, fascinated with her enthusiastic recounting of how she assisted Kalisha to bug the doctor's office, how she pretended, for effect, to dislike Kalisha, how she grew to despise her employer and his arrogant ways, how she pitied his wife – the wonderful Dana Rutledge who had put up with that man for so many years – who never seemed to complain, and so on. Oh, and she had overheard Dr. Rutledge threaten Dr. Nichols, and in a sense, her young son. That was the final straw, in her mind.

The woman had excellent memory for all the wrongs, from her perspective, which she had witnessed and catalogued. Only once did she make eye contact with Kalisha, seeming to seek affirmation for their combined efforts. After fifteen minutes or so of laying out the timeline and describing her observations in detail, Darlene stopped. Was she done or waiting for further prompting? Spencer couldn't tell. She looked as if she had said her all.

Agent Lloyd looked around the table, then asked, "Do any of you have any questions for Darlene?"

No one spoke up. After the tedious silence had endured long enough, Lloyd swiveled his seat, faced Darlene and said, "I do have one question."

She stared at him, appearing completely unruffled.

He withdrew a white envelope from his inside suit pocket and slid it to her. Darlene only stared at the envelope embellished with the clinic's logo. A slight frown creased her brow. She cocked her head as if thoroughly puzzled by his gesture.

"Do you recognize this envelope, Darlene?"

"Yes, it's from the clinic."

"Let's have a look, shall we?" Not waiting for her answer, he opened the unsealed envelope and withdrew a tri-fold paper from within.

"There's no need," she suddenly said, expelling a long sigh.

"Did you write this letter, Darlene?"

She nodded.

He said, "Could you state that?"

"Yes, I wrote that letter."

"And what is in the letter?"

"It's Dr. Rutledge's suicide note."

Lloyd let several moments pass, then asked, "Dr. Rutledge didn't commit suicide, after all, did he?"

With firmness, Darlene said, "No, he did not."

Her pronouncement done, silence hung over the room. No one moved. In the background, the air conditioning cycled on, offering a low hum of white noise to the tense setting. Suddenly, the perspiration moistening Spencer's brow and back initiated an unwelcome chill. He dared not move and suppressed an impending shiver. Was she about to finger someone there? He glanced at Kalisha, who remained calm, cool, and collected, a neutral expression painting her face.

"Do you know who killed him, Darlene?"

"I do."

"Will you tell us?" Lloyd prompted.

"Later." After a brief pause, she added, "But I will say this... he deserved to die. Someone had to put him out of our misery. He'd taken a wrong turn and refused to see that, to turn back, to do the right thing. He'd changed in a bad way, and I'm not sorry in the least that he's dead."

That said, she fell silent.

Several in the room released long-held breaths, while others took the opportunity to squirm or improve their posture. Spencer watched as Lloyd rose, took two steps to the far door, and welcomed another man into the room. Darlene glanced up at the Sheriff and nodded. She waved off Carter Lloyd's offered hand, and under her own power got to her feet. Before the Sheriff could escort her from the room, she turned to the group and said, "He had to go. Someone had to do it."

That said, she marched from the room, head held high.

CHAPTER | 45

Spencer stood on her porch and pressed the bell. He heard nothing from within, no footsteps, no music, no TV – nothing. Was she home yet? He was sure she'd said she was scheduled for the early shift that day. He glanced at his watch – five p.m. – and pressed the doorbell again.

After only a few moments, the sound of an approaching car caught his attention. He pivoted as Hope turned into the driveway. She threw him a wave. Wasting no time, she got out of her vehicle and hurried toward the front porch.

"Hi, what are you doing here?"

"Thought I'd drop by and update you."

"Update me?"

"Yeah. There was a meeting today and out of that came important news."

"It's hot out here, let's go inside," she said, manipulating her front door lock. The door swung open, and the cool air welcomed them inside.

Hope deposited her shoulder bag on a nearby bench and gestured for him to follow her into the kitchen.

"How about something to drink? I've got tea and lemonade made."

"You know, lemonade sounds good."

"Any addition to that?"

"No, thanks."

Hope busied herself pouring two tall glasses of iced lemonade, and indicated they would take seats at her countertop.

Spencer straddled a bar stool and leveled a look at the tired doctor. Hopefully, his news would not add to her obvious weariness.

She returned his gaze. "So, what's up?"

"I met with a small group today at the invitation of Carter Lloyd, Special Agent in Charge at the Kansas City field office."

"That's a mouthful."

He smiled, then added, "We heard an update from the Integrity in Medicine group, and the state medical board's legal counsel. Kalisha Johnson also attended."

"Oh, really?"

"Yes." Spencer sipped lemonade, aware he'd captured her attention. "As a matter of fact, she was a key player in the operation which the watchdog group launched, and the state board facilitated."

"You'd mentioned some of that last month. So, it's known for sure now that she was a 'plant'?"

"Right. But, there's more...background." He gulped lemonade and continued, "Ms. Johnson's a widow."

"A widow?"

"Yeah. Her husband died in an auto accident about five years ago. Interestingly, she was pregnant at the time."

"Really? I didn't know she had kids."

"Well, just listen. She finished her MBA that semester, graduated, and delivered a healthy baby boy. According to the story, when that child was six months old, he suddenly became ill. She was told he didn't sound sick enough to go to the ER. Instead, a virtual visit was recommended. A couple of days later he died. Basically, a year after his father's death."

Hope clapped a hand over her mouth. Silence settled over the room. She finally muttered, "How tragic." After a long pause, she added, "And probably preventable. So, her motivation for getting involved."

"You bet. In spades."

"And you knew this before?"

"I knew about the husband, but not about the baby until our detailed debriefing. Quite a shock. And there's more."

"More?"

"Yes. Also in attendance was Dr. Rutledge's nurse Darlene." Hope looked surprised, said nothing, and he went on. "Lloyd asked her to tell what she knew of the shooting incident, and she did. But then, he confronted her with the suicide letter."

"Confronted her?"

"That's right."

Looking stunned, Hope shook her head. "No, Spencer, no... you're not telling me..."

"Yes, I'm afraid I am."

"She wrote the letter?"

"She did."

"Did she confess?"

"Not quite, but essentially, yes."

Hope looked away. Finally, she asked, "But, why?"

"We're not entirely sure, but basically, she got fed up with him and his ways, thought he'd changed for the worse, had caused harm and was not repentant. When Kalisha came along, she was ripe for the picking, and formed an alliance of sorts with Ms. Johnson. Apparently, she also thought by helping Kalisha she could secure a better position elsewhere. We don't know if Kalisha actually offered that, or if Darlene just presumed. She resented her own situation, felt trapped, and had misinterpreted Kalisha's statements. But, in the end, she took matters into her own hands. And was glad for it."

"Oh, my God." Hope closed her eyes, lost in thought. After an interval, she observed, "She was always helpful and nice to me. I sensed she might become an ally of sorts. Maybe she thought she was."

"It appears so."

"So, how is Kalisha doing?"

"Okay, from what she said. It takes some time to get over being part of an important sting operation. She's a survivor, though. I'm confident she'll eventually be all right."

Hope sipped lemonade, then added, "It'll take me a good while to get my head around all this."

"I'm sure." Spencer glanced around. "Where's Noah?"

"Oh, I just dropped him off at his dad's for the weekend. That's why I was a little late getting home." Her stomach let out a loud growl as she finished her drink.

An opportunity had just presented. "Sounds like you're in need of some food."

She mustered a faint smile. "You're very observant. Yes, I missed lunch today; we were swamped."

"So, why don't we grab a bite to eat somewhere, and I'll fill you in on more details."

"More details? I don't think I can stand any more details right now, but I'll benefit from some food for sure." She slid off her barstool.

Without thinking, he reached out and wound her in a hug… more than a fleeting embrace.

She pulled away, and gave him a direct look. "Let me change out of these scrubs so we can be on our way." As she turned and meandered down the hall, he heard her add, "Wow!"

Was it me? Or the story I just told? He called out, "Take your time. I'm in no rush." In no rush, indeed. He would give her all the time she needed to move in his direction.

He could be a very patient man.

EPILOGUE

August 2022

Hope waited at the Classic Cup for Kalisha to appear. She had snagged a corner table at the cozy Plaza restaurant and ordered her first coffee. *Was this a good idea? Would the woman even show up?* Kalisha's answer seemed rather tentative when they had spoken by phone. When the waiter returned, she glanced at her watch and realized it was fifteen minutes past the appointed time. Hopefully, this wouldn't be a total waste of a good morning.

After weeks had passed, Hope felt compelled to reach out and engage the woman who had sacrificed so much for 'the cause.' Although she would not have chosen such a path herself, she gave Kalisha credit for her courage and perseverance. Hope scanned the small, narrow restaurant as she sipped steaming coffee. She'd wait another fifteen minutes, maybe order a tasty croissant, then leave if Kalisha didn't show.

While staring at the windows and lost in thought, a figure approached. Startled, her gaze swung to the statuesque woman who stood before her. Always outfitted perfectly for the occasion, Kalisha smiled and waited for an invitation to sit. Hope gestured to an opposite chair.

Settled, Hope spoke first. "I'm so glad you've come."

"I considered not. But, your invitation intrigued me. I

decided it might prove beneficial for both of us."

The solicitous waiter returned and took their orders. Giving Kalisha a smile, he retreated.

The two women locked eyes. After several long moments, Hope broke the uncomfortable silence. "I felt a need to reach out to you. It didn't seem right to leave such unfinished business. And I admit I was overcome with curiosity. Perhaps I shouldn't have bothered you."

"You're not bothering me." The server interrupted at that moment, and delivered their small orders and fresh coffee. After the pause, Kalisha continued, "I don't know if I'd call it unfinished. It seems the local investigation is winding down, and I'm done with my role in the operation. Done until the trial, of course."

"I've heard." Hope sipped coffee, and pivoted to the main point. "Kalisha, are you comfortable telling me what happened, why you got involved, particularly in that way?"

"I am. And I assume you already know most of this, and your interest is sincere."

"Yes."

A faint smile softened Kalisha's face. She began. "You're aware I was married, and that my husband died in an auto accident about five years ago."

Hope nodded.

"It was a crushing blow. I was pregnant at the time with our first child. Frankly, I didn't know if I could go on. Somehow, I completed my MBA at Columbia, and that summer I delivered our son. A healthy, happy baby to a sad, depressed mother. I didn't know what to do, so I threw myself into my new role with the help of my own mother, and somehow got through those first three months. Later that fall, I took a position with a large health administration company. Frankly, looking back, I don't know how I did it."

Kalisha took a bite and sipped coffee before continuing. Her face darkened. "That winter little Trevor, who was six months old by then, became ill one day. He was at home with the nanny who also had a mild cold. No big deal, right? Well, he ran a high fever that night, sounded very congested, and seemed too sluggish, so I contacted our pediatrician's office and spoke with the on-call provider. After listening to my story she told me he didn't sound that ill, probably had a virus – 'it's going around, you know' – and to call in for a virtual visit the next morning. They were very busy and probably couldn't work us in, she'd said. Oh, and I could give him some infant Tylenol for the fever and discomforts."

Hope agreed with a nod. "Sounds typical, right?"

"Right. What did I know? New mother, first baby, first time he'd been ill. I was told little kids always run a high fever when they're sick, and we had time to see how he would do. No need to run to the ER. So, I didn't. But, I was up all night with him, impressed with how sick a baby could look and act.

"By morning, Trevor was no better. I was exhausted, and stayed home. The thought of dragging him in was too much, so I got online and did the virtual visit as recommended. That didn't add much to the plan, but they encouraged me to continue as we were and see how he did over the next several days. The nanny, who then offered to stay the nights, seemed skeptical but kept quiet, and we forged ahead." Kalisha paused to sip her cooling coffee, locked eyes with Hope and said, "That night baby Trevor died in his sleep." After a pause, she added, "It was one year after my husband's death. I nearly lost it."

Hope's heart skipped a beat; pressure spread through her chest, filled her neck. Although, she knew the crux of the story, hearing it from Kalisha, the grieving, guilt-ridden mother, overwhelmed her. She laid a hand on Kalisha's arm, and sustained eye contact as tears welled. There was nothing to say.

Hope finally exhaled, broke eye contact and closed her

eyes. Kalisha looked aside, pushed away her coffee, and savored a sip of cold water. After a time, she said, "So, you probably want to know how I got involved."

"Only if you want to tell. You've explained the why."

Kalisha dove in. "After about a year, I regained my energy. During that time, a smoldering resolve had taken shape. I felt I had to make a difference for other people facing similar situations. It was clear telemedicine was getting a foothold, and I could barely maintain any objectivity about it. Admittedly, vengeance played a role.

"I became aware of the Integrity in Medicine group and joined the organization. They addressed all sorts of issues, but virtual medicine caught their interest, too, particularly when the pandemic hit and more people utilized it. Then the scheme promulgated by the feds and several clinics around the country came to light. Through covert investigations, all that. I knew my involvement was 'meant to be,' so I volunteered to help with further observations and data gathering." She paused and sipped. "And that's how I ended up interviewing and snagging the admin assistant position with Dr. Rutledge."

"Your courage and commitment are admirable."

"Admirable, maybe, up to a point. I admit I became obsessed with achieving our desired outcome – curtailing telemedicine. So much so, I didn't avoid plunging into an affair with him when the opportunity arose. It was a foolish, wild ride."

"I can imagine."

"You don't know the half of it, and I'm not going to go into the sordid details. Suffice it to say, it got out of hand, went off the rails, and ended tragically. Obviously, that was not our intended endgame. I definitely misjudged Darlene, to say the least."

"No one had a clue."

"To be sure. But I regret if I implied an advancement, or encouraged her deranged thinking in any way."

"You couldn't have known."

Both women stopped talking, lost in thought.

Hope broke the silence. "So, what happens next for you?"

Kalisha shifted and smiled. "I've had a good offer back home in Chicago."

"Oh?"

"Yes, but no more sleuthing. It feels like a good fit with a well-established health research company. My mother still lives there and needs more of my time. My father passed some years ago. And I have a sister and her family close by."

"Sounds like a positive move. When do you start?"

"After Labor Day. I'm nearly packed and will be on my way in a week. I want to get settled before the holiday weekend. It's exciting and I'm ready. So, your timing was perfect to get together."

"Kalisha, I am so pleased you agreed to meet and share your thoughts. I hope I didn't cause you pain asking you to recount your experiences."

"Oh, there's pain. It won't go away any time soon, if ever. But you didn't aggravate it."

"It may lessen with time."

"It has. I admit that going through the last year working to entrap conspirators and seeking vengeance didn't bring the relief or closure I expected. It was a hard lesson – putting my integrity on the line – but a necessary one for me, I guess. I'll get past it someday. It's time I move on, you know?"

"You are so right. It's done. That chapter is over."

"Thankfully."

Both women sensed it was time to go. They'd said enough for now. Both knew they would have to tell their own version of this saga to a judge and jury before too many months passed.

They stood and wove their way through the tables, as

the early lunch crowd arrived.

Outside, they turned to say their goodbyes. Instead, they fell into a warm hug. Parting, they smiled, gripped hands, and said, "See you again, soon."

"Yes. Be well."

"Take care."

"Thank you. You, as well."

And turned, each to their own way.

Author's Note

Changes in medical practice are upon us. I wager there is little disagreement with that. For nine years, I've chosen to navigate those choppy waters, developing and exploiting characters and their conflicts to magnify recognized shifts in medicine. Hopefully, those characters are engaging or entertaining enough to dispel any depressed feelings which threaten to push in. Take heart; there's more! As you've discovered, SEEN & UNSEEN is a shorter novel, the first of a three-book set, each exploring different issues in medical and nursing practice. Keep an eye out for the other two in coming months.

Remember, it's all fiction. These characters – doctors, nurses, and patients – are no one in particular I've known during my practice years. The clinical cases presented here illustrate conditions people may bring to Urgent Care or other practice settings, and are certainly not uncommon.

Now to the scenes featuring FBI characters – hopefully, they are realistic enough to be believable. If not, I assume all responsibility for any errors in those depictions.

Again, I thank my editor Laura Taylor who offers her insights and advice in such an encouraging manner. I am fortunate to have met her a few years ago at the *Southern California Writers' Conference*. She took on my first bulky manuscript, and has persevered with me since. That manuscript, waiting its turn for publication next year, will launch a new series.

Thank you also to Sharon Kizziah-Holmes for manuscript formatting, and her frank opinions, sense of humor, and good advice. And to Jaycee DeLorenzo for cover design, patiently working back and forth with my ideas, sharing her wisdom and design expertise.

I enjoyed bringing these characters to the page and wrestling with their conflicts. Hopefully, you found SEEN & UNSEEN to be a good read, and I appreciate you sharing your time.

JJ Renek

September 2024

If you're enthralled or appalled, or somewhere in between, feel free to leave a review at Amazon.com. Writers do appreciate hearing readers' opinions.

And check out my website from time to time for updates and news: www.jjrenek.com

While there, consider joining my quarterly newsletter group and stay in the loop.

Thanks!